SEASON

CW01508873

SEASON
OF
HATE

Michael Costello

Michael Costello.
17 - 9 - 15

SHORT
STOP
PRESS.™

SHORT STOP PRESS
AN IMPRINT OF
A&A BOOK PUBLISHING
admin@aampersanda.com
www.aampersanda.com
www.shortstoppress.com

ISBN 978-0-9943294-0-0
First published 2015
Text © Michael Costello 2015

Cover illustration and design, text design and typesetting by
David Andor / Wave Source Design
www.wavesourcedesign.com

National Library of Australia Cataloguing-in-Publication entry:

Creator:	Costello, Michael, 1952- author.
Title:	Season of hate / Michael Costello.
ISBN:	9780994329400 (paperback)
Subjects:	Australian fiction.
Dewey Number:	A823.4

For Johnny, Harry, Kitty and Biddy

CHAPTER ONE

1985.

As I wandered through the house with Dad's shoebox of memories, those lifelong questions buried in the subconscious, resurfaced.

'Who am I? What *is* my purpose for being?'

For me everything had changed and yet looking around, very little had. I'd revisited my little sunbaked town many times since leaving twenty years ago in 1965 for university. My last stay was with my wife and kids for Dad's funeral. This time I was reluctant to come back, for my wife and I were here by ourselves to settle Dad's affairs and put 'Kilkenny' up for sale. In every room and in the branches of the giant jacaranda were snapshots of my childhood that I wanted to remain forever. Here every languid summer blended into another, filled with games and boyhood fantasies.

Those first two formative years here and meeting Johnny helped shape Doug and my lives. His friendship toward us and his treatment at the hands of others changed the very way we viewed the world. There was also that one night in particular that jolted us out of our small-town lethargy like an electric cattle prod. That night where one wanton act placed the town's very livelihood in jeopardy. The night that ended in tragedy. But I am ahead of myself.

❖

Doug and I were eight when we left Sydney permanently with Dad in 1955. We went to live at Kilkenny with Nan after Poppie died of a massive heart attack. He was only sixty-three. Doug and I were twins. And when I say twins, everyone thinks identical, 'cept we weren't. We were fraternal twins and didn't look anything alike, 'cept only in the shape of our faces. He was black Irish with an olive complexion and dark brown eyes like Dad, while I'm pale, freckly and blue-eyed. My hair was curly light brown and Doug's was dark almost black and dead straight. He was also two inches taller and athletic.

Born an hour after him with iron deficiency anaemia, I was always referred to as being 'a bit on the weedy side' by the women of the Country Women's Association at Nan's afternoon tea fundraisers.

Invariably my health would somehow come up in conversation with her baking rival at the CWA, Gwen Grady. Gwen had won third place years ago at the Sydney Royal Easter Show for her fruit cake; and never let anyone forget it. She'd usually pin me to the wall under the pressure of her considerable bosom and proceed with the full examination of pulling down my lower eyelids, scrutinising the amount of blood flow in the area, and then telling me in her whiney voice to poke out my tongue, before continuing with the same line of questioning of my Nan as always.

"You're feedin' him enough red meat Maureen?"

"Yes Gwen."

"And the fish emulsion? He's very pasty."

"Yes Gwen."

"He's not caught a wog?"

"No Gwen," Nan would reply, with a roll of her eyes at me and the other ladies of the CWA, behind Mrs Grady's back.

"Mmm. Well I s'pose there's bound to be a runt, when you give birth to a litter. Hopefully he'll get a bit of colour once he's filled out."

The unspoken inference being, that no matter how well you cook Maureen, you've got the sickly grandkid while mine are as fit as mallee bulls. You could see Nan struggle to keep her congenial demeanour in front of all her CWA sisters. What she really wanted to do to 'old horse face', as most called her behind her back, was to give her a serve.

It was usually at this point I'd disappear into the bedroom to read, or take a couple of scones and join my brother in the giant jacaranda tree out front. Here we'd dream away another frying-hot summer's day under its frilly canopy. We'd lie there looking out over the town and the creek and the distant wheat fields that stretched beyond the horizon.

Since I can remember, Doug and I had spent all of our Christmas school holidays at Poppie and Nan's house. Dad would drop us off along with our 'not to be opened until Christmas' presents. He'd come back to pick us up, but in between go off on a short holiday by himself to recharge. As twin boys, I suspect we were a handful for a single father.

❖

Ours was like any other 1950's small to medium size town west of the Great Dividing Range, in New South Wales – just a flyspeck on the map. The Shire was primarily a wheat growing district but there were smaller tracts of land for cattle farming and a few sheep. The district was so dependent on its wheat crop, that its destruction by fire from a lightning strike or someone's careless actions was always a constant fear.

Poppie and Nan had moved off their wheat farm at the start of the Great Depression to the town proper, after one too many unfulfilled promises of rain; and before mounting financial debt left them flat broke. They were the lucky ones. Seeing the hard times coming, Poppie also withdrew all their money from the bank before they closed their doors. He never returned it fully to them, maintaining a healthy mistrust. He wasn't on his own in that thinking.

Kilkenny, was on Main Street, south of the Railway Street train intersection. It was one of the largest weatherboard houses in town and the only one with a jacaranda tree. As big as the house was, it was dwarfed by this thirty foot high tree. Its branches stretched around the side of the house, one close enough to Doug and my bedroom window that we often used it as our secret entrance and exit to our room. Nan was born in Grafton, and when they moved into the house Poppie had the tree transported especially from there as a reminder of her childhood town.

The house itself was of the Queenslander style but rather than the usual three sided version, it had a verandah all the way around. It was mounted on sump oil painted tree stumps with metal capping on the top of each to stop the termites. The stumps were ten feet high, designed to save a house by letting flood waters pass underneath and to aid ventilation in the hotter months.

We were susceptible to the westerly dust storms that blew in from the Centre and blanketed the town, getting into every crack and crevice. When the rare cool breeze hit late on a hot afternoon after a stretch of white bright days and suffocating nights, windows and doors would be flung open to let it race around and through the house to cool it down. Where our town was located, when it was cold it was freezing, and when it was hot, it was *bloody* hot. Rather than the house being updated over the years, Poppie and Nan maintained and restored its interior and exterior as a museum to the 1920's.

North of the Main and Railway train intersection was the city business area. It was relatively small in comparison to the larger centres. Though during the post war economic boom of the 50's under the Menzies government, it grew large enough to contain at various times, a baker, a grocer, a small post office, two butcher shops, Green's Mixed Business, two milk bars, a stock and station agent, a barber shop and separate hairdressing salon. There was also a hardware store, tea rooms, both a Chinese and an Italian restaurant and eventually a chicken and hamburger takeaway, a chemist, a haberdasher, funeral parlour, police station, bank, a combined men's and womenswear shop, a district newspaper called *The Echo*, a plumber, a blacksmith, an electrician, Poppie's motor shop and even a boot maker. We had two hotels, the

Railway and the rougher Exchange, diagonally opposite at the Main and Railway intersection. There was a Golden Fleece service station, fire station and the Sacred Heart Church and Primary School.

We even had a School of Arts where dances and wedding receptions were held. Films, or 'pictures' as we called them then, were shown there every month or so – occasionally first releases. However public primary and high schools, hospitals, doctors, dentists, solicitors and any other shop or profession, were two and a half hours walking or three quarters of an hour of steady driving, away. There wasn't any school bus for the district until the early sixties. But what we didn't have, we never really missed. As Poppie might say, 'No use complainin', 'cause that's yer bleedin' lot.'

Thirty miles south of the town was the old Aboriginal Reserve. It was termed an 'unmanaged' Reserve. Unmanaged Reserves differed from 'managed' Reserves in that managed Reserves or stations were usually staffed by a teacher-manager and education, rations, and housing were provided. The 'unmanaged' ones like ours, provided the very basic of rations but no proper housing or education and were under the control of the town police. In our case, that was Sergeant Farrar.

❖

Doug and I didn't attend Poppie's funeral for as Dad said, at eight years of age, we were too young. We stayed in Sydney with Mrs Crofter, our housekeeper. All we knew was what Dad had told us, holding back his own emotions as best he could.

"Poppie has died and gone to Heaven, boys." Doug and I both looked up to the sky.

"Can he see us?" asked Doug.

"I'm sure he can," Dad faltered then continued, "but now we must think of Nan and pray for her to get over losing Poppie, as she's very upset."

"We can still visit her for the Christmas holidays, can't we?" Doug pleaded.

"Sure, mate."

"If we were with her now, I'd give her a hug and make her a cup of tea with four sugars, just as she likes," I offered. Dad smiled and ruffled my curls with his hands before pulling us to him in a tight embrace. He instructed us to be on our best behaviour for Mrs Crofter while he was away helping Nan tidy up Poppie's affairs. This included putting his motor shop up for sale.

Poppie left us with heaps of memories and invaluable advice only he could come up with, like how to catch a pigeon. All you had to do was put salt on its tail to stop it flying away. Doug and I once spent a whole afternoon crouching in the bushes, both armed with a bag of salt, waiting for an unsuspecting pigeon to stand still long enough so that we could tip the salt on its tail. Only when we caught Poppie laughing himself silly on the verandah, did we realise it was impossible.

Doug and I talked about our loss as we put on our pyjamas.

"I'll miss Poppie taking us fishing," Doug sighed.

"You think he really can see us?"

"Sure, that's what they say. All the dead people are up there behind the clouds, seeing everything we do and guiding us to do the right thing."

"Poppie, I miss you," I blubbered.

"You're such a girl."

"Am not! You take that back or ... or –" I threatened hollowly. He placed a gentle arm around my shoulders and I stopped crying. Leading me to the side of my bed, we both knelt and said our prayers.

"And please look after Poppie. Amen," I added. We jumped into bed and Dad's hand came around the door to turn out the light, as if he had been in the hallway all the time. He cleared his throat.

"Goodnight, boys."

"Goodnight, Dad." We spoke as one, as we often did when our thoughts and tongues aligned.

After some time, I thought I could hear the muffled sound of Doug crying. I got out of bed with my pillow and pushed my way under his covers. There was no objection as he moved over to let me in. Nothing was said as I put my arm around him and we both fell asleep.

The two weeks until Dad's return went quickly. One morning as Mrs Crofter got our breakfast, Dad made an announcement.

"Boys, how would you like to go to Nan's?"

"It's not Christmas," Doug pointed out, for Easter had just passed.

"Not just for holidays, I mean for always." I looked over to Mrs Crofter who nodded in agreement. Doug and I looked at each other.

"Yes please!" we sang out together, excited at the prospect of the carefree existence at Kilkenny. The later sad realisation that we would have to leave our friends behind soon sunk in, but couldn't dampen the prospect of embarking on this new adventure.

"Who knows Dr McNally, you might even meet a nice new mother for the boys," Mrs Crofter offered to an unresponsive Dad.

With teary waves through the back window of Dad's Holden at Mrs Crofter, we said goodbye to our old home at 222 William Street, Kingsgrove in Sydney, for good. After many hours driving we would soon be in the welcoming arms of Nan at Kilkenny. Mrs Crofter would stay on to oversee the removalists and forward our belongings. Before we left, she had packed us sandwiches, marble cake and a thermos of soup for our trip. She also gave us a present each of books with lots of colourful pictures to read on the journey. Doug's was about pirates and treasure and mine was about the adventures of a young English boy, who grows up and joins the army to fight against the bloodthirsty Zulus in Africa.

We read them one at a time. Both of us lingered over and discussed each picture, taking in all the detail, and saying the words together. When we came across a difficult word, we spelt it out. Dad taught us how to say it properly and what it meant. I could see he wasn't too impressed with Archie from my book, as he fired his rifle, 'the bullet smashing the jaw of the six foot savage' or 'stuck his bayonet into the evil chief's chest', but he did explain 'bayonet' to us and let us continue. I guess from his point of view, it stopped us from getting bored or feeling sad about leaving Sydney as we drove by town after town.

We pulled into several petrol stations on the way and stopped many times on the side of the road to prevent the car from overheating or to stretch our legs. Also I suspect, to give Dad a break from our repeated singing of *Ten Green Bottles* and games of 'I Spy'. His only full relief from us came when Doug and I dozed off to the rhythm of the wheels spinning over the endless stretches of hot bitumen, through the middle of the day, or fell asleep in the backseat at night.

By the time we reached Nan's place on the second day, close to bedtime, Dad was exhausted. He'd driven day and night. Nan hugged us so tightly on arrival, I thought my bones would break. Later, under our barrage of pestering, "Oh please, please, please ...", that every child knows will get positive results if it's whiney and prolonged enough, Dad finally relented and let us stay up another two hours. He took one of the spare rooms and Doug and I remained in our normal holiday bedroom. While he unloaded the other suitcases and boxes from the boot, Doug and I lugged our smaller suitcases crammed with the most vital of our toys that we couldn't be parted from, up the front steps. We arranged them on the two bookcases Poppie had made for us. They were wide enough to fit our larger planes and cars and toy soldiers as well as my growing library of books.

After a cat's wash and a glass of warm milk, Doug and I gave up all resistance to going to bed. Dad hung up our clothes as we changed into our pyjamas. Tonight we were allowed to say our prayers in bed. Dad gave us both a goodnight kiss before leaving the door slightly ajar.

"Goodnight boys. Sleep tight. And don't let the bed bugs bite."

Lying in bed, I felt warm and secure to be with Dad and Nan, even if Poppie wasn't there. 'Cept he was. He just wasn't there to be seen. Unable to settle, I got up and went to the window. I brushed aside the lace curtains before pushing open the window and climbing out to sit on the thick jacaranda branch, as Doug and I would do during our holidays. Tucking my knees up tightly under my chin I breathed deeply, savouring the fresh country air. My eyes wandered up and down the moonlit street of what was to become our town, our home. A strange round of sounds louder than a bunger, more like gunshots came from far away in the distance from the direction of the Reserve, but too far away to be of concern. Shortly after, an old truck with three men in the cabin passed our place coming from the direction of the Reserve. They let Mr Wood off at his place. I took several more deep breaths as I looked up at the stars, twinkling between the leaves of the jacaranda's canopy.

"I wonder what the school is like. Do you think it'll be as good as Our Lady of Lourdes? Doug? Doug?" I too was asleep within minutes of my head hitting the pillow.

CHAPTER TWO

"Doug. Doug wake up! Look!"

"What?"

I pointed towards the window at the sun disappearing from the front of the house.

"We've slept in!"

On holidays we were always up at dawn, helping Poppie collect the eggs for breakfast. Jumping out of bed, we headed barefoot to the kitchen.

"Sit up, almost ready." Nan's plump sausage fingers gripped a wooden spoon as she stirred away over a saucepan. "Yer dad's gone into town to wait delivery of his old furniture for the surgery. You two villains are to stay in the yard 'til he gets back." We both let out a disappointed,

"Oh, Nan."

I watched as her generous backside, like an over-stuffed armchair, moved around the stove. The skin of her underarms wobbled as she reached up for plates.

"But we want to go and play with Raymond and Barry," Doug tried to argue.

"Not today. He wants ya here where he can find ya. He's taking ya to the Sacred Heart to get enrolled. That's where all yer friends are anyway. It's not school holid'ys 'round here now." The penny dropped. "Yer scrambled eggs are ready." She served up before sitting down between us with a cup of tea.

"Boys, now that Poppie ... Now that Poppie is, well ..." We both reached out and squeezed her hands. She leaned over and in turn, kissed us both on the head.

"You miss him Nan?" I asked.

"Every day, darlin'. Every blessed day. He's in God's hands now. Prob'ly makin' Our Lord a nice set of shelves as we speak." Nan blew her nose. I pinched myself hard on the leg under the table, for asking such a hurtful question. I just wanted to know whether she missed Poppie as much as we did.

"Did Poppie die peacefully?" Doug asked softly. I kicked him under the table.

"Owwh."

"Come on you two. Yes, he did, love. In his sleep, mercifully. No pain. Ya know, I'm so fortunate for the rich and full life I've had with yer Poppie that, well I wouldn't say 'bum' for sixpence." We looked at her in shock. "It's an old sayin'. Don't dob me in to yer Dad for sayin' 'bum'. It just slipped out. So, now you're both here, and I haven't got Poppie to help me, I'll need ya to do some chores – besides makin' yer beds, puttin' yer toys away and keepin' yer room tidy. Will ya do that for me?"

"Anything," I gushed, trying to redeem myself as we both wolfed down our breakfast.

"Bags chopping the wood!" Doug cried.

"No, I think we'll leave that for yer dad. What I do need a hand with, is waterin' the front and back gardens and the veggie patch, feedin' the chooks and collectin' the eggs. Oh, and cuttin' up the newspaper into squares and puttin' it on the nail in the toilet. Ya think you can manage all that between ya?" We nodded in agreement. I waited a few moments.

"Can Doug and I go outside now?" I asked. We were both itching to re-explore our territory.

"Not in them pyjamas."

We nearly knocked each other over as we dashed up the hall, trying to beat the other to be the first dressed and out the door. A few minutes later and we were belting past the kitchen, now fully clothed. With her back to us Nan called out,

"Now go back and put some shoes on. What if ya tread on a snake or a red-back bites ya on the toes?"

"I told you, she *has* got eyes in the back of her head, like Dad says," I whispered, or so I thought.

"You two'd have to get up pretty early to put one over on me. Shoes on and I'll call ya when lunch is ready. Remember, stay inside the yard."

Fully shod, we were out through the front screen door and up the jacaranda tree in seconds, straddling its branches. From there we could see up and down the street. The further up you went, you could see over the roofs of the houses across the road, and beyond. Mr Symonds lived directly opposite. He was sitting on his wraparound verandah with the timber blinds pulled up.

"G'day Mister Symonds!" Doug yelled.

"Mister Symonds!" I echoed.

Mr Symonds and his wife were the owners of the town's tearooms and were about Dad's age but childless. I overheard Nan and Gwen Grady talking about their situation once.

"I'm not one to gossip, but he looks to me like he'd probably only have one or two trout in the stream, if ya know what I mean. And they're obviously doing the backstroke," was Mrs Grady's charitable observation.

"Gwen! All I know is they've been tryin', but the Good Lord doesn't hear their prayers."

Mrs Symonds would still be inside baking the scones for the Devonshire teas that day. Everyone knew the exact time they were due home from the tearooms and sometimes, if there were any leftover cakes or scones, she'd bring them home. And then all we kids would swamp her before she even got to the front gate. With begging hands outstretched, we'd wait for her to remove a tea towel over the tray to reveal our booty. Then we'd cheer and take a piece each. If it was lamingtons, sometimes we'd get two, gorging a mouthful in turn out of each of our hands.

Mr Symonds looked around to see where the voice was coming from.

"Up here Mister Symonds. It's Doug."

"An' me, Pat."

He stood and moved to the top of his steps, followed by his old blind dog Honey, a dingo blue heeler cross. We both slid down the tree and continued our conversation hanging over our picket fence.

"Nan needs us to water the plants and collect eggs now that Poppie has gone to Heaven," I informed him.

"Dad's going to do his doctoring from town and we're going to go to Sacred Heart," followed Doug.

"So ya dad said. Well, won't that be good?"

"Is Mrs Symonds doing some baking?" I asked, hoping that it might include some vanilla slices or cream buns as well.

"She sure is." Mr Symonds smiled, picked Honey up and headed for inside. "Ready Esme?" he called, as the screen door banged shut behind him and we climbed back up the tree.

Over beyond the Symonds house and the wide paddock with its long grass, that ran behind his and all the other houses on his side of the street, was the creek. It snaked around most of the township, serving as a natural barrier during the mice plagues. Now it was flowing way below normal levels, but still deep enough for swimming and fishing.

Beyond the creek were the wheat silos, dotted over the harvest landscape and jutting into the sky. We turned over onto our backs on the thick, almost horizontal centre branches. I watched the leaves quiver as the smallest puffs of warm wind feathered through the tree top. And all around you could hear the she-oaks in the paddocks and especially along the creek bank in whirring conversation with each other.

Minutes passed in silence. Then more minutes, as I turned back over onto my stomach and looked further up the road to the Elliott's mulberry tree in the front yard. Like our jacaranda, theirs was the only mulberry tree in town. We'd had Nan's mulberry jam made from them on holidays, but we longed to taste the fruit straight from the tree. There wasn't any yet.

I looked over my left shoulder. Raymond's house, next to Nan and Poppie's on the southern side, wasn't like ours; it was still wooden, but not mounted on big stumps. It only had a few steps to their lattice enclosed verandah. It was painted white as well, like most of the weatherboard houses in town, 'cept Raymond's had blue trimmings as opposed to our green. From our side verandah you could look down into their backyard and also his parents' bedroom.

One summer night when we were on the verandah sleep-out, we saw Mr Smith's bare backside as he got changed for bed. We turned the torch off and put our hands over our mouths so that he couldn't hear us laughing in the stillness of the night.

That nocturnal secret we kept to ourselves because Doug and I were supposed to be asleep, 'cept we weren't. We'd taken Poppie's torch out of the kitchen and were reading comics by its light instead. Raymond was a year older than us with wavy golden hair that always looked liked it needed a good comb and tortoiseshell framed glasses that were forever slipping down to the tip of his nose.

He had the respect of all of our gang because he was the only one of us who could suck in enough air to say their whole name, in his case Raymond Archibald Charles Barrington Smith, on the one released burp. Best I could do was Patrick Michael of my name and up to 'H' of the alphabet. He was also part of the street cricket team along with Barry and some other kids nearby. Over the Christmas/New Year break we'd join them and have our own Test match, which went for days. Raymond's sister Sandra was in sixth class but a hopeless catcher. She was even more hopeless than I was which made me feel better. As we lay in the tree, I reminded Doug of the sight through Mr Smith's window.

"Boomp ba boomp ba boomp ba boomp," I laughed, imitating with my hands how Mr Smith's bum wobbled when he walked.

"Boomp ba boomp ba boomp ba boomp," Doug repeated then we both went into a fit of the giggles. As the humour died away, we sighed and rested there with nothing to do again 'cept listen to the faint sound of a piano coming from the Walshe house next door. The occasional passing vehicle or horse stirred up small clouds of reddish brown dust that had settled in a film on the old bitumen road. They hung in the air for a second then drifted back down onto the road.

These periods of being in the doldrums we would grow to accept as part of the everyday. Just as surely as holidays turned into school days, we would begin to fall into the slower rhythms of country life and the dictates of the seasons, but it would take time.

"Let's check out the chooks!" Doug suggested. We raced down the tree then around the side past the shed to the large chook run. With his longer legs, Doug came first, as usual.

Poppie kept half a dozen layers at a time in the twenty by thirty foot pen. It was made of strong double thickness chicken wire secured on iron posts to keep the foxes out. As well as benches, there were boxes filled with straw for sleeping and laying. He said he felt funny giving the chooks names.

"But everyone's got to have a name," I once insisted. With some misgivings he gave in, naming the chooks after movie stars of the day. There were only five chooks that day; Shirley, Rita, Lana, Betty and Lauren. We lost Greta last Christmas. Poppie told us he had to mend a hole at the edge of the wire fence where she either got out and ran away, or one of the foxes got in and carried her off to eat. It made Doug and me sad whenever this happened, but Poppie always got a new one before we came the next year.

❖

There was one problem for us in agreeing to help Nan with the chooks. The feeding was okay. We could stand at the gate and just throw the chook pellets in on the ground and aim the hose at the water trough. Collecting the eggs was another thing. I was packing it.

"I'll feed them if you like and you collect the eggs," I offered.

"You collect the eggs and I'll do the feeding," Doug countered.

"Toss you," and I dragged out my lucky 1936 halfpenny that I always kept on me.

"Heads I collect 'em, tails you do," directed Doug. I tossed it high into the air with a little flick of my thumb.

Tails.

"Best out of three?" I pleaded, but Doug wouldn't be in it.

I loosened the catch on the pen gate. Lauren came running over so I shooed her away and made my way to the benches – easy. I waved my hands about and made as much noise as possible and Shirley, Lana and Rita took flight. I moved slowly toward the boxes. Doug was encouraging me to go faster.

"You're scared," he taunted.

"Am not." So I acted like I wasn't. I peered inside the first box; no Betty, no eggs. The second box was empty as well. I edged my way to the third box, my heart beating in my ears. I turned my head away and stuck my hand in. Betty pecked me hard and I ran screaming to the safety of the gate then outside as chooks squawked and took to the air in all directions. Doug was on the ground laughing as I slammed and bolted the gate shut. I was fuming.

"You're supposed to throw some feed on the ground to distract them, like Poppie showed us!"

"I forgot," he smirked. I was rubbing my finger where she had attacked me, when Nan stuck her head out of the kitchen window.

"You two, leave them chooks alone. I got today's eggs and fed 'em." This only made Doug laugh more, so I punched him on the arm then ran to the safety of the house steps before he could get to his feet.

"Whippy taken one, two, three, safe," I declared. It was a lesson learnt. From then on we'd feed them *before* we even entered the pen. Eventually the chooks were ready and waiting for us and egg gathering would soon become second nature – the hens our pets.

❖

"Stand still or I'll nail yer bleedin' feet to the floor," Nan threatened as we wriggled about while she tried to hold us in turn with one hand while dragging a wet comb through our hair with the other. We were that eager, we were up and dressed for our first day at our new school even before breakfast. "Never seen anyone as keen to get some schoolin' as you two," she added. Dad was already at the table fully dressed in his suit and tie for the surgery as we took our seats in our old school uniforms, complete with freshly polished shoes. Nan had declared the uniforms would have to do until she could get into town later that week to buy new ones in the school's colours.

"Well boys, excited?" Dad asked. We nodded enthusiastically. Not about the schooling, though I liked it better than Doug, but because all our holiday mates were there.

Nan waved goodbye from the top of the front steps as we strode on either side of Dad up Main Street, with our brown leather satchels on our backs.

Next door, Miss Bridget, one of the Walshe sisters, was cutting back a lantana bush that was strangling her roses. Her younger sister Miss Kitty had rarely been seen only talked about, or heard playing the piano when her sister was out working. They were both spinsters in their sixties. Barry had told us that his dad told him that no one ever saw Miss Kitty, especially of a day, because she was a vampire. She only came out at night to suck the blood of cats, after sticking her long fangs in their necks. That's why cats slept all day.

"'Cause they're too weak to do anything else," Barry maintained. And the ones that disappeared altogether, Miss Kitty sold to the new Chinese restaurant, "but only after she's sucked 'em dry of every last drop of blood and skinned 'em alive," he concluded.

"Good morning Miss Bridget," Dad greeted, tipping his hat. We hid behind his back, our heads peering out from either side.

"Mornin', Harry. Off to your new school, boys?" We froze, supposing she was a vampire as well. After all, she was Miss Kitty's sister.

"What, cat got your tongue?" she cooed, leaning over her fence to get a better look. We both recoiled, handfuls of Dad's pants twisting in our fingers. Dad slapped our hands to loosen our grip.

"No, just bad mannered is all. I apologise for their behaviour. What's gotten into you two today?" Dad asked. We had no words to explain. A smile came over Miss Bridget's face.

"They look so cute with those satchels on their backs, I could just eat them all up," she gushed. Doug and I shielded our faces completely behind Dad's back, fearful she might follow through with her menu selection.

"Say hello to Miss Kitty for us," Dad concluded, before giving us one of his disappointed looks, as we continued up the street.

"Bye boys," she called out as she waved, with a pair of sharp secateurs in her hand. I swallowed and exchanged a knowing glance with Doug, who was just as afraid. Barry was right, I thought.

Other neighbours were going to their gates and saying goodbye to their children before letting them walk to school. We felt like babies accompanied by Dad, when all the other kids our age and younger were allowed to go to school by themselves. Mrs Figgins was saying goodbye to Barry as we passed. Doug and I ran up to him and slapped him on the back. He was shorter than us with black spiky hair and large full lips that looked like someone had hit him in the mouth with a hot frypan. He'd lost a front tooth since we saw him last. We were all so pleased to be together again.

While Mrs Figgins told Dad how thrilled she was at having a doctor in the town again, in breathless whispers we filled Barry in on our brush with death at the hands of Miss Bridget. Then the three of us raced through questions and answers, catching up on everything we'd done since we saw each other last Christmas holidays.

Once Dad finished passing the time of day with Barry's mum, we bombarded him with relentless arguments as to why we couldn't walk to school together, just the three of us boys, as Barry's mum lets him walk to school alone, and Barry could show us around and after all, it was just up the road, and he could get to his practice earlier. He finally gave in to our whining pleas by the time he'd shown us across the Casuarina Street crossing. We were already on our way as he called out.

"And watch yourselves crossing the tracks. Look *both* ways. And come home together, all of you, straight after school. Alright?" Doug and I waved back as Dad turned toward home to get the car and drive to the surgery. It was only a ten minute walk from home, but Dad needed the car in case he had a home visit or got an urgent call-out.

We went past Poppie's motor shop on the opposite side of the road, now owned by the Girotti family from Sydney, but originally from Calabria. They were at the start of a younger wave of residents moving into our town and its surrounds. Usually immigrants, but also some city folk, or people from other nearby smaller towns who could see the post war growth potential.

CHAPTER THREE

Inside the school gates, we stood out with our navy shorts and blue shirts against their grey uniforms. The children gathered around us like thirsty dogs around a summer puddle – all yapping at once, saying "g'day" and wanting to know all about us.

"What are youse doin' here?" one of the older boys from fifth class demanded. He was tall and solid for his age, the size of a small man, with Brylcreemed hair and a split lip.

"That's Steve Wood," Barry mumbled through the corner of his mouth.

"I've seen him 'round on holidays," Doug whispered back.

"You know Doug and his brother Pat, from Sydney."

"We don't like city people," Steve declared, pushing his finger into Doug's chest. "Y've got tickets on yerselves. Think yer smarter."

We didn't have a chance of a reply, before he pushed Doug backwards. A mate of Steve's had got down behind Doug on all fours and Doug went crashing over him. Laughter broke out everywhere. I was trying to help him up, when he pulled his arm away and launched himself at Steve. Even though he was physically outmatched, that didn't stop Doug. He kicked him in the shins. It soon progressed into an all-out wrestle on the ground between the two of them.

"Fight, fight, fight," was chanted around the crowd of eager onlookers. I was trying to pull Doug away, while he was fully intent on finishing his opponent off. Punches were flying but few finding their mark. Steve managed to land one on the right side of Doug's nose, after Doug had ripped the pocket from Steve's shirt.

At this stage, the girls had joined ringside and there were cheers of encouragement from the rest of the boys. A good few were on Doug's side, I might add. I yelled at Barry to help me pull them apart. Raymond arrived at school at that precise moment and raced to grab Steve's arm. As we were scrambling about, the crowd mysteriously went quiet and parted as swiftly as Moses had parted the Red Sea. Storming toward us was this tall, slender nun, with strange rimless, blue-lensed spectacles. She went straight over to Steve.

"Get my cane and wait for me outside the classroom. And wash that grease out of your hair while you're at it," she directed with cool control.

"He started it," Steve spat out. She gave him an icy stare. He sauntered off, but only after giving Doug a hateful sideways glance. She then focused her attention on Doug and me. I swallowed hard and felt sure she must've heard me it was so loud.

"You two must be the McNally boys."

"Yes Sister," we said together, and in the confusion of the

moment I also crossed myself. This gesture seemed to save both our necks. She gave a perfunctory smile.

"My name is Sister Mary Placid. Welcome to Sacred Heart Primary School. As this is your first day, I will forget your participation in this brawl – this once. I know Master Wood well, and have every belief he was the instigator. Do not let me catch you engaging in fisticuffs ever again. Not unless you want to join him in his punishment. Understand?"

We both nodded.

"Good." She squeezed Doug's cheeks firmly between the palms of her hands as she examined his face.

"No blood. Barry, take him to the wash shed and get him cleaned up; once Master Wood has finished getting that muck out of his hair." She then turned, faced the crowd and roared,

"You have one minute to line up for assembly!" Everyone scattered and faced the main weatherboard building in formation. A pretty curly-headed girl pulled me into my spot as Barry led Doug away.

By the time Doug and Barry joined the assembly, we'd finished the Morning Prayer, allegiance to the Queen, our free bottle of milk and were now marching off in pairs to the classrooms. There were a number of weatherboard buildings in the grounds, as well as a small brick office. Our line headed towards one wooden building that housed three classrooms. Outside the end classroom stood Steve with his hair dripping wet, holding the cane. As we filed past him he threatened Doug in a clenched-teeth whisper.

"I'll get you later."

❖

27

We emptied our satchels then placed them on the pegs outside the second classroom before filing in. Barry led us to two empty desks up the back. Because of the size of the school, our third class was combined with second class.

The clatter of opening our desks and filling them with our belongings then dropping their tops shut, soon stopped as everyone waited in silence, listening for the number of strokes of the cane Steve would receive. One, two, three, four, five, six. He started it, but he didn't deserve that much, I thought. On hearing the clomp of heels coming along the wooden verandah, everyone stood to attention beside their desk. Doug and I couldn't see the door from where we were, but by deduction knew whoever it was must be our teacher.

"Good morning class," a female voice sang brightly on entering. It was Sister Mary Placid. She moved to the desk at the front of the room, tapping the cane gently against her leg. Doug looked at me. We mirrored the same doomed expression to the other realising that she was to be *our* teacher. She placed the cane on the desk.

"Good morning Sister Mary Placid," we all rejoined.

"Eyes front Dougal McNally." After a singsong of more prayers led by Sister, we were allowed to sit. "The two new boys, out the front and tell us a bit about yourselves."

Doug and I moved in front of her large desk and faced the class, while Sister made her way to the back of the room.

"My name's Dougal McNally. My friends call me Doug." As he hesitated and nervously pulled at the front of his pants to adjust himself, I jumped in.

"And I'm his brother, Pat, short for Patrick. We're twins, but not identical." Some of the class laughed at my obvious, nervous joke 'cept Sister.

"Please tell the class how it is that you've come to join our school." I took the lead, as Doug was always shy about answering questions, especially about himself.

"We used to come visit Nan and Poppie –" I began before she interrupted.

"You mean you used to come *and* visit your *grandmother* and *grandfather*. Go on."

"Well we used to visit them."

"Who did you visit?"

"Our Nan –" I caught her piercing stare and proceeded with more caution. "Our grandmother and grandfather," I corrected.

"Good, we don't use baby talk in this class. Proceed." I quickly gathered my thoughts.

"We used to visit our grandparents each Christmas school holidays. Then when our grandfather died, we moved here for good – to help Nan." As soon as the word 'Nan' left my lips I froze and went red. I could feel even my ears were burning. Sister squinted at me through her blue lenses. She was not amused. Doug came quickly to the rescue.

"Our Dad is a doctor and he's opening a ..." he pulled at his pants again as he looked at me to rescue him, but I hesitated for just a split second too long. Sister pounced in with the answer and now we both felt small and silly.

"He's opening what we call a 'practice', class. We also call it a 'doctor's surgery'. Isn't that good, class? We'll have our own doctor, rather than having to travel miles when we're sick." Of course it was a surgery. It was only our nerves that blocked our brains.

"You didn't mention your mother."

"Our mother's gone to Heaven," I added softly. Her face softened as she remained looking at us for a second before making her way back to the front of the room.

"Thank you boys. You may take your seats. And Doug ..." she added in an aside, "the next time I see you rearranging your boy's bits, I'll cut them off."

"Yes Sister."

"Thank Doug and Pat, class." The class gave a little clap. With great relief, we took our seats.

"Second class, take out your writing books, and third class, prepare for a spelling test."

Doug looked at me and crossed his eyes, signalling his fear of imminent disaster, while we all opened up our desks and took out books and pencils. I was a better speller than him, only because I studied. Even so, I felt that this was going to be a long, long day for the both of us. And it was. The text books were the same but they had different ways of setting out work to the way we did it at Our Lady of Lourdes.

At lunchtime we kept our eyes open for Steve and his mates. Several of our classmates joined us in the shade on the seats around the big rubber tree. We checked out each other's lunches and swapped them around. When the old nun who was doing playground duty fell asleep while sitting under a tree, Steve and his gang came over our way. Just as they got about six feet away, they diverted their attention to the only Chinese boy in the school. He was sitting by himself.

"Ching chong Chinaman," they all repeated menacingly over and over as they pulled on the corners of their eyes to make them appear Asian. The boy was sacred and looking for a way to escape. Steve looked over in our direction.

"Ching chong Chinaman," I joined in and encouraged Doug to do the same with a sly whisper and a jab to his ribs with my elbow. "Say it. Otherwise he's gonna come over here and pick on us again."

"Ching chong Chinaman," all of us on the seat chorused.

Steve smirked at us then turned his attentions back to the Chinese boy. Just as he did, the old nun woke up, checked her watch then started to ring the handbell laying beside her for the resumption of school work. As we scurried back to class I couldn't help but feel relieved at how lucky we were to have escaped Steve and his gang's attention.

Keeping the news of the fight to ourselves and away from Dad wasn't likely to happen. By the end of the day, a small but noticeable bruise near the inside corner of Doug's right eye had formed. We thought our best course of action was to tell Dad ourselves and get it over with. He'd told us repeatedly not to get into fights, even with each other, and that "it was the better man who chose to walk away." We reckoned the only way Dad could say this was because he never had someone pick a fight with him. He said a lot of smart things, but not saying it was okay to fight if someone else started it, to us seemed like you were scared. Walking away only made it worse. They'd end up calling you a 'yeller belly'.

We decided we'd walk into town to the old dentist's, now Dad's new surgery. It was good to see on the way all the old familiar shops again. As we passed, some of the owners would smile and wave and we'd wave back. I ran my fingers over the letters of his brass doctor's sign, DR. H. McNALLY GENERAL PRACTITIONER, that he'd attached to the wall beside the surgery doorway.

We heard him unpacking tea chests in the back room. Doug just went in and owned up straight away like we'd practised, trying to emphasise we had no choice.

"What have I told you two about fighting?" We both shrugged our shoulders.

"Walk away," Doug mumbled, his chin nearly touching his chest as he tugged at the front of his shorts.

"You know how many men I've had to patch up because they've been fighting? Look at me when I'm talking to you. So bashed up and swollen, even their own mothers couldn't recognise them. Is that how you want to end up?"

"No sir. It's just that he start –" Doug began to explain.

"It doesn't matter who started it or what they said, you walk away and be the better man. Now if this ever happens again, God forbid, what are you two going to do?"

"Walk away," we both mumbled begrudgingly.

"You want to lift your heads and say that so I can hear you?"

"Walk away," we called out together.

Dad parted Doug's hair falling over his forehead then got out his little torch and pointed it straight into his eyes, one at a time. As he did, I remember seeing a sort of funny look on Dad's face. His eyes were practically grinning, while a small smile played across the rest of his face for the briefest of moments.

"No damage, but that's gonna be one hell of a shiner. Now

let's go and see about getting you both new uniforms." Dad locked up and led us up the street – an arm around each of our shoulders, to Renshaw's Menswear.

My uniform was one size smaller than Doug's. We got pullovers as well in the school colours, as the cooler autumn weather was nearly on us. Mr Renshaw was pleased to see Dad, stating that he remembered selling him his first uniform.

"You know your dad used to be the smartest boy in school. Dux, if I remember. Always studying. No wonder you ended up a GP."

I felt our chances of Dad just letting us spend our spare time catching tadpoles, or mucking around with Barry and Raymond or even him taking us swimming or fishing like Poppie did, fading fast; replaced with long weekends taken up with extra schoolwork.

"How's Mrs Renshaw, Sid?"

"Oh, as well as can be expected. Since you were here last, she's developed a touchy vagina." Within an instant, Mr Renshaw's face went the colour of an overripe tomato as he quickly corrected himself. "I mean a t-touch of *angina*." he stuttered. This always happened when he got flustered. Dad fought a smile.

"I'll be opening Monday if she needs to see me about her heart – or anything else. What else is news, Sid?"

This is what everybody asked of everyone in town – the quickest way the entire district's news got passed on. Little could happen without everyone finding out. Nan used to say there were times she felt she couldn't even sneeze 'without the whole blessed town knowing.' Though there were other times she concluded, 'when I was glad there were people who cared.'

The favourite spots for picking up all the gossip were at the barber's or the hairdresser's. Most of the news came via Pearl Binslow, who ran the local telephone exchange. She'd pass it on to the redoubtable Gwen Grady. After that, the whole town would know within hours.

Doug and I wandered around the store, both a little down. I know I was still thinking about our mother a bit and certain he was as well. Not having a mother singled us out from all our other friends who did. It made us different when we wanted desperately to fit in. We couldn't even remember what she looked like. Unlike Poppie and Nan whose wedding photo was on Nan's dresser, Dad didn't have one photo of himself and our mother anywhere, although he still wore his wedding ring.

Bored, Doug and I looked around the rest of the store. I held up a big pair of men's 'Y' fronts, stuck my finger through the fly and wiggled it about like a penis. Doug smiled and we both giggled behind our hands. We overheard Mr Renshaw telling about someone getting married and someone having their fourth grandchild, someone leaving and a new publican at the Exchange and that the Aboriginal Reserve was closing down shortly, before we wandered back to Dad. I pulled on the leg of his pants, to get his attention.

"Thanks for all the news, I best get these boys home. Seems they've got some homework they're busting to do." It was my turn to cross my eyes at Dad's comment – for Doug's eyes only.

"See you Sid. Thanks for everything," Dad added as we each took our brown paper wrapped uniforms from the counter.

"My pleasure, Harry. It's good to see you and the boys. Give my regards to Maureen."

The trip back to pick up the car in the laneway behind the

surgery was interrupted at intervals. People, who had known Dad over the years, were reintroducing themselves and passing on their best wishes for his new practice. Everyone knew everyone in town.

Driving home we stopped at Green's Mixed Business on the corner of Casuarina and Main. Dad was welcomed into the store like he was royalty by an effusive Mr Green, greeting us with handshakes all around. He was bald on top and had little sunken piggy eyes peering out from under overgrown eyebrows, and when he spoke his lips barely parted. Dad purchased cheese, a loaf of bread and a jar of vegemite for our school sandwiches. Apart from the same sort of gossip as Mr Renshaw, he added as we walked out the door,

"I s'pose you heard about the Reserve closing, Doctor?"

"Harry's still my name."

"Yes, well Doctor, um Mister, Master Harry, I mean Harry …" He drew a deep breath. "… we were happy for it to stay open, but Sergeant Farrar's been instructed to turn off the water and close it down. Says he's just following Gov'ment's orders. The Aboriginal Welfare Board's bought the old Hudson place, you know, on the far end of Railway Street near the bush and's doing it up for a mob of them. Not ones from the Reserve but from out west. Movin' 'em right into the middle of town, if you don't mind. There's a meeting at the School of Arts about how we're gonna cope. This Frid'y at eight." His last words he had to call out from his shop verandah as Dad had already got in the car without bothering to answer him.

"You going?" Doug asked as we drove off.

"No Dougal."

Now it needs to be explained that when Dad called us by our

full names, it was usually because he was mad at us and we were just about a second away from his threatened whack on the bum or a lecture, or else he had something on his mind. I elbowed Doug to keep him quiet, but nothing happened anyway. Dad remained deep in thought. And we left it at that. Occasionally he'd look past me in the middle of the front seat to Doug near the window, who was just staring at nothing in particular through the windscreen. It was a very quiet trip home.

School continued fairly uneventfully. Except Doug and I no longer sat together. After a monthly test, you were moved up or down in seating order depending on your overall marks. The second class had three rows of seats and we had three for third class. I was at the front of the second row for third class, next to Penny, the pretty curly-headed girl I met at that first assembly.

"My dad'th Thargeant Farrar," she lisped through two prominent buckteeth. She had a lovely smile.

Doug was halfway down the last row. Third class boys who got to the top seats of the first row, as a reward, were allowed to assist Father Prittenden as altar boys at Friday Benediction. The school taught all the kids in the area from all denominations and to serve at Benediction was the biggest honour anyone in the third class could win. But only if you were baptised Catholic.

Sometimes at home I did my best to help Doug with his school work, but he just didn't seem to be able to concentrate. Everything else though, social studies and geometry and sport – especially sport – he was good at. He was the fastest runner in our class and a good batsman at cricket. I was usually one of the last ones a captain would pick for his team and always, they'd send me way out where no balls ever seemed to go, which suited me fine.

However, when the side was desperate, when there was no one else left to bat, I'd get a go. Bradman I wasn't, but I usually managed a few runs. Once they were in a desperate situation against a side with Steve and his mates in it and needing the seven runs I scored for our side to win. It was the one and only time I was carried aloft from the field as a champion sportsman. Still, I liked reading better – about places and people, wars and the ancient civilisations like Greece and Rome and Egypt.

The hardest part for both of us was when the school reports came home. Dad regularly said 'just always do your best' and would never say one of us was better than the other. The things that got him mad though, were comments like 'bit of a daydreamer' or 'can be disruptive' or 'can do better', that seemed to always conclude Doug's reports. My reports, besides the scores for each subject out of one hundred, luckily ended with 'continues to show improvement' or 'excellent effort.' I felt a bit self-conscious about my school reports in the face of Doug's, but knew I only achieved them not through being smarter, but by the fact I worked harder. Doug was smart, just as smart as me. He could have achieved similar results, but for him the view outside the classroom window was always more enticing than the work on the blackboard. That was Doug.

CHAPTER FOUR

May was the month of Mary, as Sister Mary Placid kept on telling us. All religious readings and stories at school and church on Sundays were about Mary. She was the mother of Jesus and not Mary Magdalene who, as Sister pronounced when asked by a classmate, "was not related in *any* way whatsoever" to the Virgin Mary.

It seemed like the longest month ever. The 24th of May was Mary's Feast Day, known as Mary Help of Christians. Sister maintained that this was the real reason why we were celebrating it. Some adults said it was because it was Empire Day, initially in honour of Queen Victoria. None of that mattered to us. It was Cracker Night – our first Cracker Night in town.

For the whole month, every kid at school was on their best behaviour, with the promise of crackers as the reward from their parents. We'd all seen them on display at Green's the grocer and also the service station.

For Doug and me it meant besides the collecting of the eggs

and watering of the gardens, we'd do extra things like sweeping the verandah, gathering the vegies for Nan, getting home early enough to set the table and keeping quiet when the news was on the wireless. We also declared a truce on kicking each other under the table. By the time the 24th came around, I swear, if there was anything more we could have possibly done, they'd be renaming it the Holy Day of Doug and Pat.

Cracker Night was weeks in the planning. Several bonfires were prepared around town, for it was also the chance for everyone to get rid of all that year's rubbish in one fell swoop. Our bonfire was for everyone in Main Street south of the Casuarina cross-street. Doug, Barry, Raymond, myself and some of the other boys dragged old palings, broken pieces of furniture, old tyres and any fallen branches we could find or that neighbours gave us, to a large clearing about fifteen yards in diameter. The men had made it a few weeks before in the long grass in the paddock behind Mr Symonds place. Mr Wood, Mr Symonds and other parents helped us build the bonfire on the weekends. Mr Green even gave us some old fruit crates.

Old mattresses, the furniture and tyres were stacked into a big pile. These were then surrounded with the palings to form an overall conical shape. Branches, twigs, old newspapers, smaller bushes and garden clippings and anything else that would burn, were stuffed in and around the base. Miss Bridget gave us some old sheets and a mop, which we made into a ghost to sit on the top. Nan donated an old hat to put on top of its head.

The momentous night finally came. The sun was just about gone from the cloudless sky and there was a coolness moving in from the west. It was due to start half an hour after sundown.

Dad was late home again. It was becoming a weekly occurrence. We'd had our tea and bath and were lying on the verandah, watching for him to drive up the road. The build up for the night's events had made us all excited and jittery with anticipation.

Eventually we saw his car with its parking lights on, coming from the southern instead of his surgery at the town end of Main Street. As he drove into the driveway and parked under the house, we rushed the car.

"Well boys, this is a warm reception I must say."

He got out of the car with only his medical bag. Our hearts sank. In an instant we did our own check of both the front and back seats before running after him as he entered the house.

"What's up with you two tonight? You seem all worked up over something."

"We've had our bath and tea, and done all our chores –" Doug began.

"And our room's tidy," I added.

"Well that's very commendable of you both." He washed his hands in the kitchen sink as Nan got his plate of smoked cod from the oven.

"Have you forgotten what day it is?" Doug asked.

"No, we always have fish on a Friday."

"Stop teasin' 'em," Nan urged, adding, "They've been good all week." Dad smiled.

"Oh, Cracker Night. Here. You missed the boot." He tossed the car keys to us.

I caught them and ran through the hall, out the door and down the front steps. Doug followed so close behind, I could feel his breath on my neck. We grabbed two large paper bags from the boot and ran inside to the lounge room. We each scattered our bag's contents on the floor, running our fingers over the crackers as eagerly as a pirate drooling over stolen treasure.

There were sparklers, tom thumbs, sky rockets, Catherine wheels, flower pots, roman candles, volcanoes and various other coloured crackers. As we counted the exact contents, I could overhear Dad and Nan's raised voices from the kitchen.

"What am I suppose to do, just leave them?" he argued.

"Son, I'm not sayin' what you're doin' isn't the right thing, it's just that people –"

"I don't care what people say or think! I'm a doctor first. Hey fellas, you got everything you wanted?" We rushed in and hugged him around the neck. "Once I finish tea and changed my clothes, we'll go over. Done all your homework?"

"Yes!" we cried. We watched every mouthful he took. He seemed to be eating even slower than ever.

"Just this once, why couldn't he wolf his food down," Doug whispered.

"Here you two, stop breathin' down yer father's neck. You'll give him indigestion. Help me pack the sliced damper for the soup."

One of the great things about Cracker Night, Nan reflected, was that, "It brought everyone together", on both sides of the street 'cept Miss Kitty of course. Through the afternoon people had set up trestle tables and chairs. And even though it was Friday, we would be allowed to eat meat – only because it was such a special night. Nan had made a big pot of pea and ham soup to reheat on a separate little fire Dad had made, away from the main bonfire. She made the same every year Dad said since he was a boy.

"No pea and ham soup ever tasted as good as Nan's pea and ham soup with damper on Cracker Night," he declared.

❖

The air was clear and still as we waited for Dad and several of the other men to strike the matches at the base of the bonfire. First one of the dads poured some kerosene around the base then they struck matches and threw them at it. Whoosh! A feeling of something primal and dangerous began to grow inside me as I and all the kids stood around. Our eyes were the size of overcoat buttons as we watched the first flames grow then shoot up the height of the bonfire. We all cheered as they reached our ghostly figure, for only then could we start lighting the fireworks. All the crackers were pooled and placed in an old bathtub normally used to hold water for stock, who like pets, were moved far away from the night's activities. Honey was locked inside the Symonds' house.

Parents stayed with their children to supervise the selection of crackers. We were allowed to choose the coloured firework we wanted, but an adult had to put it in the mound of dirt specifically constructed for the night and light it. We were free to light our own sparklers though. What you usually did was get one ready to light off the one you were holding, before it went out; like the men that spilled out onto the street at the pub did with their cigarettes. We'd wave the sparkler about, making letters and numbers and words in the blackness.

Buckets of water were on the ready in case the fire got out of control and all shooting fireworks were pointed away from the creek and the wheat crop beyond. Bungers were to be saved for one last big noise. The older boys were allowed to join in with the men and light them, but they had to throw them well away from everyone. You had to be at least ten years old. They were also the only ones of the kids allowed to let off tom thumbs. That was how it was suppose to be, but they'd always pinch bungers early in the night and go off into the street and let them off. Steve let one off on purpose near the group and got yelled at, but no one took it too seriously.

In the distance, further into town, you could hear other groups of people celebrating around their bonfires. Wearing gloves, some men held the roman candles at arm's-length and had a contest to see whose one shot the coloured balls out the furtherest. Eric Horan the blacksmith, won. Dad was third.

At one point, looking away from our fire over to the creek, I could see through all the cracker smoke the hazy outline of a group. There were maybe eight or ten, men, women and children around a smaller camp fire, but without any crackers. They just stood and looked toward our bonfire.

Sky rockets whizzed high into the sky from the milk bottle launching pads, exploding into the darkness and filling the sky with more stars, while Catherine wheels placed on nails in fence posts spun out their bright colours. The flower pots and volcanoes were placed into the mound of earth then lit. It was so exciting watching from the safety of one of Nan's cuddles, Dad light the paper taper then stand aside as it slowly burnt away until a gush of sparks and colour spewed out the top. I loved Cracker Night. It was magic! It was just a truly magic, magic night I'll always remember. A night we never wanted to end.

And when there was nothing left in the bathtub, when the last bang, the last eruption of colour was over and the smell of smoke hung heavy in the damp air, we gathered with our mates around the tables to eat. Nan gave her permission for us to eat as much as we liked.

There were about fifty people I guess, all up. The women had pooled the food and gathered around the tables placing people's selections on plates for them. Nan ladled out the soup into mugs and placed them on the table next to the damper for people to help themselves. The men stood and ate with us before drifting off into little groups, drinking beer and talking. Mrs Symonds didn't disappoint either. All the kids waited to see what would be revealed from under her tea towels this time. It was a large tray piled high with coconut macaroons, with a small dot of strawberry jam on top of each one.

"I don't care if I don't get to the front of the class and get picked to do Benediction. I'd even happily go to Hell a native heathen, as long as they had coconut macaroons there," I declared to Barry.

At one stage I copped a sneaky elbow to the ribs from Steve. It caused me to drop my plate, as he and two of his mates pushed in between Barry and me. They laughed their heads off. While I picked up my plate and unbeknown to Steve, Doug dropped a golly in his trifle to pay him back. Only Mrs Symonds saw Doug do it. She made no fuss, just gave him a little wink. We all held our composure until we were at a safe enough distance, then cacked ourselves laughing as we watched Steve eat it all up. He and his mates just looked at us like we were morons.

There was more than plenty of food for everyone. Dad stayed with Mr and Mrs Symonds and us at the tables, helping Nan butter the still warm damper slices. Later, I wandered over with my replenished plate to where a group of the women clustered together. They were whispering amongst themselves about Mrs Wood's no-show, even though Steve brought along a sliced jam roly-poly she'd made.

"Three guesses and they all relate to her husband," stated Mrs Horan with a knowing look to the other women.

"If I was Pam I'd leave him. It can't be pleasant livin' with him and his drinkin'. He's alright through the week mind, sober as a judge. But come knock-off Frid'y through Sund'y, he just writes himself off. You know I'm not one to gossip, however, bein' right next door, you can't help but hear the rows over his pay packet, after he's come home from the pub. Have a look at him over there tonight and you'll see what I mean," sniffed Mrs Grady.

"She'll cop a gob-full tonight then for sure," observed Mrs Horan.

"Oh my Lord. I have to close me window it gets so bad," added Mrs Grady. "And a man that hits a woman is a bloody mongrel in my book. Pardon my French. You know I asked her once about some bruises on her arm and she covered by saying, 'Oh I must've bumped into some furniture.' Furniture my foot. It was like a handprint. And she had a swollen bruised eye another time. But you can't interfere in people's domestics. Up to them to sort it out, isn't it? And young Steve looks like he's following in his father's footsteps," she predicted.

"You should hear the language he uses to his mother. Even in the street," confirmed another.

"Needs a good kick up the bloody bum, if you ask me. Pardon my French," responded Mrs Grady.

"I guess the apple doesn't fall far from the tree," added Nan through pursed lips. I wanted to find out more but Nan caught me eavesdropping and gave me one of her 'what are you doing here? This is none of your business' looks. I moved away.

At Nan's urging Dad decided to join the men. Doug stayed at the table but I tagged along. In one group Mr Horan was telling a joke.

"– So this woman gets on the tram with her baby and the conductor takes a squiz at the kid and says to the woman, 'That's the ugliest baby I've ever seen.' The flustered woman is lost for words and just moves to the back of the tram and says to the man she sits next to, 'That conductor just insulted me.' To which the man says, 'Why don't ya go back up there and give him a piece of yer mind? I'll mind yer monkey.'" The group all laughed themselves silly. We moved between them and another group where the men were all nodding and agreeing with Mr Green. Mr Symonds poured Dad a glass of his beer.

"Well I won't have 'em in my store. Black hands over everything. There's some things you just can't wash and resell. Not to mention pinching things, and that's what they'll do if we let them get any closer to town," Mr Green concluded. Then Mr Wood said his bit.

"They're not only doin' up the Hudson place, but the news is they're buildin' two fuckin' new fibro places for a mob from the Reserve as well! All bringin' 'em closer to our houses an' families. An' this lettin' 'em walk around town without being arrested will spell trouble. Mark my words. Look, there's a fuckin' mob of 'em over by the creek. Been watchin' us all fuckin' night. Won't be able to leave yer door open at night soon."

"I keep the door closed this time of year to keep the heat in, anyways," Mr Symonds stated matter-of-factly.

"You know what I fuckin' mean."

"I just don't see them as a problem Bob, is all," sighed Mr Symonds, adding, "I mean they've closed down the Reserve. Where are they s'posed to go? I mean, we're responsible, we white folk. We put them there in the first place."

"For their own good. Well now they can bloody well go back to the bush and live off the land. Won't fuckin' hurt 'em."

"Hey Bob, watch the language, there's kids –" interjected Mr Green. Mr Wood continued,

"They've been doin' it for centuries anyways. And leave us honest folk in peace," a heated Mr Wood ended, backed up by a loud "yeah", from his son Steve, who'd been sneaking sips of beer from one of his dad's bottles throughout the night.

"Exactly. They're filthy. I won't have 'em smelling up my store and driving customers away. I'm a Christian man and I know they're not all bad, but that's only a few. I'll serve 'em if they've got money – at the door," added Mr Green. Dad had been listening but looked like he'd heard enough and was about to leave, when Mr Green called out to him,

"Doctor, I mean Harry, you're an ed'jucated man, what do you think?"

"I agree." Mr Symonds looked at him in amazement. "They are filthy. And they smell. It's disgraceful."

"See, even the doctor agrees," assured Mr Green, jumping in.

"You'd smell too if you couldn't wash because your water had been turned off, because your toilet and shower had been boarded up, hoping you'd move on. Let alone having any soap – or food.

Their conditions are a shame – on all of us," Dad argued.

"Sergeant Farrar had his orders," Bob Wood declared, taking a wide stance.

"You better leave, this could get heated," Dad suggested to me while Mr Wood staggered right up close to him and pointed his finger in his face.

"No, I'm stayin' with you," I insisted, to Dad's surprise. He paused, then continued,

"I'm fully aware of Sergeant Farrar's orders. We should, however, as human beings, ask ourselves how following orders takes precedence over the observance of moral decency. Giving them proper housing is the least we can do." Mr Wood looked confused at first over the words Dad used and then a bit self-conscious of his ignorance I guess, in front of the other men.

"We don't have to ask ourselves nothin'," Mr Wood began. "You haven't had to go through fuckin' half what we have with droughts and debts and... Only to have them fuckin' Abos come along and pinch yer remainin' stock. Let 'em eat bloody 'roo. I tell ya, they're fuckin' lazy and they won't work. My brother had a mob of 'em workin' for him once, and in the middle of harvest, in the middle of bloody harvest mind, they go on bloody walkabout! Cost me brother a fuckin' fortune. No one ever gave me a house for free, neither."

"The Hudson place has been derelict for years. And it's not free, they'll be paying rent," Dad assured the group. Mr Wood seemed to ignore that point and continued over Dad with his rant.

"And the women are only good for one thing." He turned to the rest of the men with a salacious leer. I could see Dad balling his fist at his side as he finished his middy of beer.

"But ya gotta be fuckin' pissed to put up with the smell," said Mr Wood, finishing with a laugh. I pulled hard on Dad's pants leg to get his attention as he handed his empty glass to Mr Symonds. He took a step toward a swaying Mr Wood.

"Your attitude disgusts me," Dad enunciated slowly and clearly.

"An' your kind McNally make my blood boil. Fuckin' bleedin' bloody hearts. An' yer helpin' 'em only encourages 'em ta stay. Oh yeah, we know what you've been up to." Dad brushed Mr Wood's prodding finger away.

"What, ya want a fight McNally? Sure, I'd be only too fuckin' happy ta knock ya down a few fuckin' pegs. Come on, I dare ya," taunted Mr Wood, the veins in his neck bulging. The others rushed to him and held him tightly to stop a fight. I pulled again on Dad's trouser leg.

He bent down as I cupped my hand to my mouth and whispered,

"Walk away."

Dad looked at me and paused in thought, then smiled and ruffled my curls with his hand.

"Come on son, it's getting late. Goodnight, gentlemen," Dad stated as he took my hand and we headed back to Nan. Doug was sitting on a log, stuffing a miniature meat pie in his mouth as we approached.

I counted up with Doug. I had one mug of soup, three sausage rolls, some of absent Miss Kitty's trifle, a chocolate brownie and four coconut macaroons. I could have had five as there were heaps, but I could hear Nan's voice inside my head admonishing me with 'don't be a guts.' Doug had as much as me, but managed to fit in an extra sausage roll and another meat pie.

Toward the end of the night, I saw Mrs Symonds disappear into the darkness, heading toward the camp fire of the group by the creek, with a tray of leftovers. I shook Doug's arm and pointed. We followed after her, remaining at a short distance away. She went up to the group and offered the tray of food. We got closer and saw they were indeed a group of Aborigines as Mr Wood had stated earlier. I recall thinking at the time, with their faces lit from underneath by their fire, that they looked as savage as the ones holding spears in the drawings in our social studies book.

"They're just like the ones that killed the first white settlers. Let's get outta here," Doug whispered. Mrs Symonds didn't seem a bit worried, though. Later she slipped back to our group with the empty tray. I saw Mr Symonds and her exchanging a smile and a nod, and then noticed Steve whisper something to his dad and point out Mrs Symonds as she rejoined the women clearing up the food table.

Doug and I were getting sleepy. My eyes were stinging a bit from all the smoke and I was blowing steam from my mouth into to the cold air. I circled the tables one last time with Barry and Raymond. The glow of the dying bonfire was still reflected in Raymond's glasses. Some of the men made sure the fire would not flare up after we left by pouring the buckets of water over the embers, before kicking dirt over the lot. Still half a dozen macaroons left. I looked at them for a long while before I took one last one. Cracker Night – mmm, magic.

CHAPTER FIVE

Next morning before anyone was up, we crept out our window and down through the yellowing leaves of the jacaranda. Autumn was upon us and by mid winter all the leaves would have fallen. Joined by Barry and Raymond, our eyes scoured the bonfire site, trying to find any unexploded bungers. We collected five, of which Doug found three.

Barry had got his dad's matches and we sneaked off to the edge of the creek, about two miles down stream. At that distance the sound couldn't be heard back at our homes and no one would see us letting them off. The creek there was shallow enough for us to walk out ankle deep on a sandbar to a dry mound in the centre.

Raymond brought along a length of piping and wedged it between rocks to make a cannon. He sat behind it and held on to the shaft. Doug demanded he be the one to light the bungers and drop them in the pipe as he'd found the most. Spotting an old tin can at the side of the sandbar he told Barry to collect it, with the instruction to quickly place it over the top of the pipe once he'd dropped the lighted bunger in. I was happy not to have either role in what I thought was a dangerous albeit exciting game.

Raymond held the bunger while Doug fearlessly lit it and dropped it in, followed by Barry's quick capping of the pipe with the can. I put my hands over my ears and waited – nothing. We waited some more, just to be on the safe side. The tension built as Doug kicked off the can with his foot, just in case the bunger suddenly exploded. Raymond counted to ten out aloud then lifted the pipe to retrieve the bunger. It was declared a fizzer. Luckily all the others weren't duds.

When the second cracker did explode, it made such a loud reverberating 'Boom!', that a whole gum tree of sulphur crested cockatoos took flight in one screeching curtain of feathers as the tin can soared about twenty feet into the air before dropping into the water. I waded barefoot into the shallows and retrieved it for the next explosion. It turned out to be great fun.

Further down the creek we could hear other bungers being exploded. Barry worried that we best get going. He had to return the matches before his dad noticed them gone. We all well knew, if any of us were caught playing with matches, let alone bungers, we'd be in for the hiding of our lives. Doug and I raced back home and out the back, making out we were up early to collect the chook eggs.

After breakfast, we went around trying to find if any of the sky rockets landed in our yard. None had, but climbing up the jacaranda, Doug could see one lying on the ground in the front yard of Miss Bridget's and Miss Kitty's and I saw one caught up in the lattice attached to the side of their house, near the back. They had a choko vine climbing up it. We had to get those sky rockets, for they were the prize finds of Cracker Night. We'd be heroes if the others at school couldn't find any, and we could have not one, but two to show off. Out came my lucky 1936 halfpenny.

"I'll toss," Doug declared, taking charge. "Heads I get the one up the lattice, tails you do." I agreed with some reluctance and handed over the coin. He tossed it high and missed the catch. It landed on the ground. We clambered down the tree like monkeys to see how it landed. It had come up tails. Doug quickly took off, pushing aside the three loose palings and keeping low to the ground. He was back with the first sky rocket safely in hand within seconds. My turn had come. I felt my palms getting sweaty.

"S'pose Miss Kitty catches me and tries to suck my blood 'cause she's used up all the cats'?"

"You're just chicken."

"Am not," I lied, trying to get up the courage. "But what if she does see me?"

"I'll go up the tree and make a sound like a crow if I see anyone coming. Go on."

"Maybe you could just knock on their door and ask."

"You know Dad said we can't bother them. This way, no one needs know. You'll be back before anyone knows you were even in there." My feet felt glued to the ground. "I'll go then, ya big baby."

"Alright, I'll go. But you as much as see a curtain move and ya gotta crow."

I waited until he was up the tree and in place before I pushed aside the same swinging palings and squeezed myself through the hole. My heart was fit to explode through my chest as I made it to the side of the paint-worn weatherboard house. I looked back at Doug. He had climbed out on a far limb that hung over into their yard, but still managed to keep most of himself covered behind the leaves. Taking a deep breath, I tiptoed as quickly and as quietly as I could to the bottom of the lattice. Right near the top, I could see the wooden shaft of the rocket. To get to it I had to pass an opened window half way up and to the side.

I glanced once more at Doug before putting my first foot on the lattice, then the other. The structure gave a little groan under my weight. My feet were just able to get a hold between the latticework. Soon the top of my head was in line with the bottom of the window. I made an effort not to look to the side and into the house, but to just concentrate on climbing. Something caught my eye though, and I just had to pause and look. Through a lace curtain I could see a shadowy female figure. It must be Miss Kitty, I thought, because Miss Bridget's car wasn't anywhere to be seen. Miss Kitty, the vampire!

Swallowing deeply, I moved slightly to get a better look and lost my footing. I was hanging only by my hands, making scrambling noises with my feet as I tried to regain my foothold. Looking up I saw her moving quickly to the window. I panicked, lost my hold altogether and crashed to the ground with a thud, landing on my bum – and it hurt.

A woman's voice came from behind the lace of the opened window, but I couldn't see anyone.

"Are you hurt Patrick?" she inquired in a concerned tone. How'd she know my name?

"I think I hurt me bu… bottom."

"Don't move. You may have broken something."

I stayed put, only moving slightly to crane my neck and glare at my 'crow'. There was the thwack sound of the back screen door then this mysterious woman appeared around the edge of the house carrying a wet washer. My heart started racing. She wore a long floral dress with long sleeves and white gloves that left her whole arms covered. But I couldn't help staring at her face, even though I tried not to. Her skin was the colour of Nan's good bone china and her hair was white as well. It was parted in the centre leaving only a small gap to form two flat saucer-like sides covering her temples and cheeks and pinned at the back. She wore large sunglasses and was like no one I had ever seen before. She knelt down beside me. I started to tremble. She rolled me over and pressed gently on my tail bone.

"Does it hurt here?" she asked with a voice as soft and soothing as a butter menthol.

"No."

"Tell me if you feel pain anywhere when I press." Her hands made their way bit by bit up my spine. I shook my head with every press.

"Can you stand up?" I did. "Well it appears you haven't broken anything. Now, tell me what you were doing up there in the first place?" she asked as she stood up and held the cool washer against my forehead, studying my face at the same time.

"I was after a sky rocket," I confessed, pointing up into the choko vine.

"Like this one?" She picked the spent firework up and handed it to me.

"I must've loosened it when I fell." Somehow she had put me at ease.

"That was a very dangerous thing to do. You could have been

seriously injured." I felt a bit silly. "Never mind. Would you like to come inside? I'll get you some milk and biscuits." I looked in Doug's direction, a bit unsure now of what to do next.

"No, I better not. My brother's waiting for me." I was trying hard not to look like I was staring at her so I diverted my gaze everywhere else. She moved her hand to my hair and gently stroked it.

"In future, if ever you need to retrieve anything ... a ball or whatever, just knock on the door. No climbing up lattice, okay? Promise?" she smiled.

"Promise. Are you going to tell Dad?"

"I don't think he needs to know, do you?" she proposed with a little laugh. "After all, you're not hurt and the lattice is intact. It can be our little secret. Bye-bye Patrick."

I started off in the direction of the fence, a bit confused.

"Are you a vampire?" I turned and asked, once I was a safe distance away.

"Whatever gave you that idea?"

"Barry says you suck the blood of cats at night." She gave a little chuckle.

"Do I look like a vampire?"

"I've never seen one up close. So I don't exactly know what one really looks like."

"No one has, because they don't exist. Just make believe in Hollywood pictures. Tell young Barry Figgins, he's wrong. And that what he said is a very hurtful thing to say about anyone, especially behind their backs."

I felt bad at what I had just asked and how it had hurt her. When I got to the fence Doug whispered from the safety of the tree.

"Did she try and suck your blood?"

"No."

I looked back around to her house, still a bit confused. She was standing there watching me as I slid back through the fence. She gave a little wave before making her way around the back of the house.

Doug shimmied down the tree as I entered our yard through the fence.

"Well?" I handed him the sky rocket. It didn't seem to be that important to me anymore.

"Well what?" I asked as he tried to check my neck for fang marks. I brushed his hand away. "She's not a vampire. She told me. Barry's wrong. They're only in pictures."

"She only said that 'cause she knows we're on to her."

"She didn't bite me. She even offered me milk and biscuits."

"Only so she could get you inside, then throw you down into her dungeon and perform evil experiments." His dark brown eyes widened at the thought.

"Dungeon? Their house is on stumps like ours. You can see right under it. I think she's nice. An' anyways, she's not gonna tell Dad."

After securing our sky rockets, one in each of our school bags, we wandered back out front. Adopting our customary stance of leaning over the pickets of our front fence, we waited for something, *anything* to happen as we watched the powdering of dust on the road blow up the street.

"What d'ya wanna do?" Doug sighed. I was still thinking about my encounter with the enigmatic Miss Kitty. What was it with that weird hairdo?

"Dunno."

Flies glided on the breeze. Even they seemed bored – not even bothering to be a nuisance. Now we lived here all the time, we kept on running out of things to do. Lunch was hours away.

Within a few days, Doug pointed out a big bruise that had come up on my left buttock. Neither of us uttered a word about it to Dad or Nan.

CHAPTER SIX

The seasons changed. It was now winter. The yellowed leaves of the jacaranda were all but gone. The overnight temperatures dropped dramatically. Lighting the gas stove for a hot breakfast helped warm the house from the buffeting of the cold westerly winds. Of an evening Dad would light the large log fire in the lounge room as soon as he arrived home. The heat it generated would last until early morning.

This night we started the evening meal as usual, with Dad saying Grace – all eyes closed and heads bowed.

"For what we are about to receive, Lord make us truly thankful."

"Amen," we all responded.

Nan had made lambs fry, ox kidney and bacon. She dollopped the mash potatoes then spooned the meat with its rich gravy over our plates followed by the peas Doug and I had shelled earlier. Once we'd finished talking about our day at school and Nan had given us the date of her next CWA afternoon tea, Dad went into a serious mood. I had this strange feeling we were about to cop a talking to, but for the life of me I couldn't work out why.

"Fellas, this Saturday morning, I want you to come with me. I've got something to show you."

"Where to?" asked Doug, just before me.

"You'll see."

Doug and I looked at each other and wondered what it could be. The tone in his voice meant it was something serious, but we were too afraid to ask. At least there was no 'Dougal' or 'Patrick' so we weren't in any trouble.

"Then after, I've heard some pictures have arrived in town." We let out a high pitched squeal.

"Lord Almighty. Quieten down. You're not outside playin' now," snapped Nan.

"One's an old Errol Flynn one, *The Sea Hawk*; and one's, oh …" It seemed like he was acting dumb on purpose, but we hung on every word. "A Tarzan one." I opened my mouth to give another squeal, but luckily Doug's kick to my shin stopped me in time.

"Owwh!"

"What did I just say to you two?" Nan warned. I looked daggers at Doug.

"They've got a Bette Davis double on at night. *Now Voyager* and *The Letter*. Give you a night out," he put to Nan.

"I'll ring some of the girls."

"After the matinee, how about I pick up some takeaway from the new restaurant? Something different for a change. Give you a break from the cooking and time to get ready," Dad offered.

"Lovely," she struggled out, barely hiding her misgivings.

"Wonder what it tastes like – Chinese food. Just don't pick anything too spicy." Doug looked at me and miaowed softly as Nan was talking. My excitement over going to the pictures took a bit of a dive. One of my favourite meals, beautiful velvety rich lambs fry and kidney was becoming harder to swallow.

"You feelin' a bit off colour?" Nan inquired, as I fell behind everyone at the table.

"Just not that hungry."

"Might need a good dose of castor oil. What do you think, Dad?" Nan suggested.

Appetite restored, I finished everything on my plate, much to Dad and Nan's amusement.

As soon as we had permission to leave the table, we raced into the lounge room, talking non-stop about Saturday's programme, trying to guess what the stories might be and letting out a Tarzan call every now and then until Dad called out.

"If you two don't keep that noise down in there, there'll *be* no pictures." We continued in excited whispers, beating our chests and doing silent Tarzan calls, lion roars and mimicking the bow-legged walk of Cheeta, Tarzan's chimpanzee, while they talked on at the table – just loud enough to be overheard.

"You should be takin' someone ta the pictures. You should."

"Mum please. I've told you, I'm not interested in dating."

"It's a small town, love. Everyone knows yer circumstances. You'd stand a better chance with that ring off ya finger."

"I've no intention of taking it off."

"Then you're a fool."

"That it? I'll join the boys inside."

❖

Saturday morning couldn't have come fast enough. Dad had told us to rug up as it was going to be cold. We realised we must be going to visit one of Dad's sick patients, because he was loading a heavy metal pot full of casserole and two dampers I saw Nan make the day before, onto the back floor of the car. We were almost ready to leave, when Mrs Symonds hoyed us from across the road, before running over and handing Dad a box with some old blankets, a tin of powdered milk, bars of soap, as well as two loaves worth of sandwiches.

"I think we're going on some sort of picnic," I whispered to Doug. But what was Poppie's old water drum that he used to fill stock troughs with, doing in the boot, we wondered.

"Here Harry, take these."

"That's very kind of you, Esme. I'm sure they'll be much appreciated – especially the blankets." She gave a small smile.

"Hello boys. He's a good man, your dad. Well you are. Let me know if there's anything else I can do, Harry," then she darted back to her house.

It wasn't long before we were at our destination. Dad got out with his medical bag and we followed over the brown sandy loam.

Before us was this big fenced in area and in the distance several large gum trees and just a few others scattered around. We entered the enclosure. Some of the fencing looked like it had been deliberately pulled down.

"This is the old Aboriginal Reserve or Reservation, boys." Doug and I both dropped open our mouths at the same time, with anticipation. We were a bit apprehensive, but felt safe with Dad.

My fear and excitement soon dissolved into disappointment. Where were all the tepees and horses like the American Indians on Reservations we saw at the pictures? Where were all the bare chested men with feathered headdresses and women with papooses on their backs? We made our way further onto the Reserve. Sheets of corrugated iron were lying on their sides on an angle, sticking into the air. They were propped up by tree branches, and other twigs and smaller branches formed sides to them. What passed as a dwelling looked like it could so easily be blown away. They were empty, but each had a small fire near it that hadn't been used for some time.

"What are they?" I asked.

"They're called humpies. That's what some Aborigines sleep in."

"Where are the tepees and horses?" Doug asked, echoing my very thoughts. Dad stopped and came down onto his haunches to our level.

"Fellas, you're thinking of American Indians. These are Aborigines. Just like those near the creek on Cracker Night. The tribe in this area are mostly the Wiradjuri people. Here thousands of years ago. Old as cavemen." We couldn't hide our disappointment, and though still curious to explore, kept very close to Dad as we moved on.

"Don't the Abos get cold?" I asked. Dad jerked my arm roughly.

"Don't *ever* let me hear you use that word."

"That's what Mr Wood calls them," I reasoned meekly.

"Bob Wood is living proof you don't have to have a long neck to be a goose. He calls them that as a put down. How'd you like it if someone kept calling you, 'whitey' or 'shortie'? You wouldn't like it would you?" I could feel by my bottom lip starting to quiver that tears were close.

"It's okay, I'm not having a go at you, mate," putting an arm around me and pulling me to his side. "They're called Aborigines. And it's important we respect them by calling them by their right name. Now, you asked me whether they got cold. Well, that's why there's all those little fires near each humpy. There used to be a lot of people living here, but a lot have moved on. Sergeant Farrar, Penny's dad, was in charge until it was closed down. We, or rather the white authorities, put the Aborigines here in the first place."

"For their own good," I offered, quoting Mr Wood again. Dad put a hand on my shoulder.

"Son, look around. How could living under these conditions be for their own good?"

As we continued on I could see that in the centre was a bathhouse with its two water tanks – a disused small wooden building with a gap of six inches all around at the base of the walls and a dirt floor. It was partitioned into 'men' and 'women'. The windows and doors were freshly boarded up. Close to it was a small timber and corrugated iron shed bolted and padlocked. It looked like it had been a store for provisions. Next to it was an old water pump with a shiny new padlock on it as well.

Nearby was an open-faced shed like structure built of iron and bush timber with an earthen floor that had rows of rough-hewed wooden benches like church pews but without backs to seat about fifty people. At the front was a small wooden table or altar and behind it, attached to one of the poles, a plain wooden cross.

There were a number of separate houses, or single rooms to be more precise, made of bits and pieces of rusted corrugated iron and old metal advertising signs, dotted over the area. They only had three sides and a hessian curtain for the front, and didn't look like they could keep out the cold, let alone any rain. Most had old mattresses on the ground; a few had iron beds as well. Dad came to a stop again.

"I'm sure there were some in government who thought they were doing the right thing," he continued. "But others just wanted to get them out of the way, because they were black, because they looked and behaved differently to the rest of the community. I'd imagine the owners of the new Golden Sea restaurant are doing it tough as well. People not going there, even though they'd like to taste something new, just because they're Chinese."

Dad was passionate but remained calm as he tried to explain it all to us. I looked into his eyes as he spoke. There was sadness behind the passion. It was obvious he had been thinking about some of these things for a long while, maybe even before he went to the War. He'd served in both the European and Pacific campaigns, but never wanted to talk about any of it or march with the others on Anzac Day. He began to smile.

"Someone even started the rumour that they serve cat, just to harm the business. Can you believe people could be so stupid as to believe such rubbish?" I gave Doug an 'I told you so' look.

"I guess it doesn't seem right."

"No Pat, it doesn't. That's why I'm out here now, to try and help these people the only way I can. You see fellas, I took an oath. That means I made a promise when I became a doctor, to help anyone in need of medical help – be they black, white or brindle. Oh there are other Reserves all 'round the country marginally better than this. Ones where they get food and schooling and shelter and doctors visiting and they're looked after a lot better. But not this one. Do either of you think you could live here?"

"No sir," we both freely admitted. He began walking again towards the centre.

"They only got basic food, water and shelter. No vegemite or cream cakes, just things like sugar, flour, tea, salt, barley and a couple of tins of powdered milk. Barely enough to survive. If they've earnt some money they can buy meat from the butcher but they usually get by on meat and fish they've had to hunt for themselves. They were here ages before Captain Cook and the white settlers, roaming all over Australia freely. Then they're virtually told by the white authorities, 'the land inside those fences is the only land you can have. You must stay there.'

"We took the land and gave them our white man's diseases in exchange. Herded in here out of the way like they were some sort of unwanted livestock you wouldn't even waste a bullet on. Just like your American Indians on their Reservations. That was supposed to be for their own good as well. Same with the Jews in the War.

"Saying it's for their own good though boys, is often the way people make themselves feel less guilty about what they are doing to them. Not seeing Aborigines about town lets people like Bob Wood out of any sort of responsibility to care or treat them just like any other human being. Those very same people, who do nothing to help them or turn away, would be the first to kick up a fuss if it happened to them and their families. And now, the government's decided that it doesn't want to run this Reserve and others, any more."

"That's good then, isn't it?" Doug offered.

"They can roam the land again," I put forward.

"But where do they go, boys? First they've had the land, their freedom, everything taken from them, then placed in here. All the good land with watering holes has all pretty much been taken over by white people. And the new owners don't want them squatting on their land. When this place was still up and running, they had to get permission to leave to work the land for the white owners of a day for little money just to eat, when their rations had run out. And they had to be back here by dusk. And now they're abandoned completely. Good enough to fight as brothers beside us in the War, but not good enough to live as brothers with us in peace time."

"That doesn't seem fair."

"No Doug, it doesn't. You wouldn't do it to a dog. And people like Bob Wood and Mr Green don't want them anywhere near town, so where do they go?" Dad came to another stop. "You know, my best mate in the army was an Aborigine. We fought and slept side by side."

"What's his name?" I asked.

"His Aboriginal name was Girra. He said it meant 'creek'. The officers called him Trevor, but he was always Girra to me."

"Was?" Doug and I asked together.

"He died – on the battlefield – in my arms. He was my best friend. And I miss him." Dad's eyes were getting watery, his thoughts drifting to the past. This was the first time he had made any mention of Girra or the War.

"Are Mr Wood and Mr Green bad people?" I asked in an

attempt to bring Dad back.

"Not bad son, just ignorant. And ignorance comes from fear. They're scared they might have to share – to live alongside these people. Boys, there's been a lot, *lot* worse things done to these people over the years, but that's something to learn about when you're older. Come on, history lesson over. They're expecting me," he finished, ruffling my curls with his hand.

We went further to the small circle of humpies and more hessian or canvas curtained iron huts with their basic tree trunk frames, built around the main fire, near the clump of large gum trees.

A group of about thirty or so men, women and children gathered to meet us. All they had on were thin worn out clothes and no shoes. Many seemed listless, apathetic – not moving much at all. One tall old man sitting cross-legged got up and approached Dad. We hid behind Dad's legs and peered out.

The old man's face was like dried, blackened cattle hide. He had a broad flat nose and a beard as long and unrestrained as his mane of coarse white hair. His feet were splayed, the soles thick and weathered and he had large brown eyes. He smiled and shook Dad's hand with his larger strong hand.

"These are my boys, Doug and Pat. Fellas, this is Ganan. 'Ganan', means he's 'from the west'," Dad gestured. "And he's what we call the elder, or chief of his people." It *is* just like the Indians, I thought. Ganan gave us a big welcoming grin. The whites of his eyes with their red spidery veins stood out against his dark skin. I noticed the milky film of a cataract was beginning to cover his left pupil.

"Fellas, you go off and play with the kids. I've got some food and supplies in the car for you," he told Ganan. Ganan then called out a directive in their language and four men immediately came forward and went with Dad to the car.

Doug and I saw a group of children playing hopscotch in the reddish brown dirt. Another boy had an old busted metal toy truck, moving it along a road he'd drawn with a stick, while two little girls played jacks with some animal bones. They were the only toys we saw. The flies didn't bother us so much, but they seemed to always be around the other children's eyes, noses or mouths. Some had runny noses like Snotty Norris.

"If this is a Reservation, and s'pose they are like Indians, what's to stop them scalping us? Didn't you see the big knife in that rope holding up that old chief's pants?" Doug whispered. I pointed out a pile of spears leaning against a tree.

We ran quickly after Dad and the others, watching our backs in case of an ambush, and feeling I guess that if we were to be killed, at least we'd all die together.

"What if some fur trapper has sold them guns?" Doug puffed. We eventually made it to the relative safety of Dad and the car, but if something did happen we felt we were outnumbered and unarmed.

We all came back as a group, Dad looking a bit annoyed at us for running after him and not playing with the children as we were told. Two of the men set down the large metal drum full of water. It had a little tap attached to the bottom. When the children saw the box of food, they all clustered around it. One woman got two enamelled cups and measured out some of the powdered milk. She filled them to the brim with water from the drum before giving both a good stir. Another lined up the children and as the cups were past down the lines one would take a large two-handed sip, while another shooed away the flies as they drank.

Mrs Symonds' spam and pickle sandwiches were handed out and quickly eaten. Two boys offered us a bite out of theirs but we declined as we'd already had a hot breakfast.

At first we stayed close by Dad, thinking we'd be safer if anything did happen – but not so close as to be a nuisance. After all, we didn't want to ruin our chances of the double feature. As the time past we became more relaxed. One man let us hold one of the spears and touch its stone spear head.

Dad had brought an old tarpaulin which he laid over the small altar in the shed. He used it as a makeshift examination table for the patients to sit on. In front of it he tied off a sheet between two poles to act as a screen for privacy. The people sat in the pews waiting their turn. He started examining the women and children first and then the men. Ganan, on the other side of the sheet partition to Dad, acted as interpreter when Dad asked the patients a question. Dad gave some medicine on a spoon and to others, a tablet or two. Some got medicine and tablets. All received an injection in their arms. The adults comforted the children as Dad gave them all saline eyewashes with their injections. But after each jab the children got to choose a lolly from Dad's bag for being brave. Any tears soon evaporated.

The wind started to come up a bit, swirling the dust about in circles. The last to get checked out were two kids and their mother. Ganan said a few sharp words and they came forward from the back. We'd noticed early on that they played and ate apart from the others, some distance from the main group in front of their little tin shack. These two children, a boy about five and a girl about seven, weren't like the others. Their skin was darker than Dad or Doug's, but not the dark brown almost black of their mother and the rest of the group. The little girl had blue eyes and they both had light brown almost blonde hair. When Dad finished with their examination and the injections, they returned to the front of their house with their mother, to suck on their lollies and play by themselves.

It must have been three hours since we arrived to when Dad packed up. The casserole had been placed at the edge of the fire and the dampers under a cover away from the flies and the weather. Dad made a point of walking through the group before giving one of the larger blankets to the woman and her two children. Behind the curtained front of their shack was a filthy mattress flat on the ground and one worn blanket folded neatly at the foot of the bed. The mother seemed a little suspicious and cautious of accepting his gift at first, but took the blanket nevertheless. The other women looked on, none to pleased.

"I'll be back again through the week. I want to see how things are going. Take care, my friend. And remember, only put creek water you've boiled to refill the drum," Dad instructed, shaking Ganan's hand. The old man placed his other hand over Dad's in a tight grip and shook it vigorously.

"Thank you Doctor Harry."

As we made our way back to the car, I turned and looked at the dusty group. It seemed strange. They were all smiling and waving, despite their situation. At the time, I thought that bringing the food seemed to be a good idea, for it stopped them from killing and eating us and using our skin for slingshots.

Driving home, Dad asked us how we felt about what we just saw.

"They weren't like I expected," I stated, a little disappointed.

"What, no bows and arrows and war paint?" Dad replied with a grin. He'd read my mind, again.

"That and, I don't know ... they were friendly and that I guess, but ... how come their skin's so dark?" Doug chimed in.

"Everybody's different. Some people are tall, some short, some skinny, and some fat – all different. And some have dark skin, some pale, and others every shade in between. But underneath, we're all the same."

"What about those two lighter kids?" I asked.

"They're called half-castes. Half black, half white."

"Like black and white cows?" I asked.

"No, but I understand your thinking. No, in their case it's where their mother was black and their father was white." Then Doug piped up with a really good question, I thought.

"Well why aren't they living with him in his house?"

"That's very complicated. The upshot is the father doesn't want the kids even though they're his, because he had them out of wedlock and in all probability he's already married to a white woman." Dad noticed we were struggling to understand.

"But if he was already married, isn't he wedlocked?" Doug offered.

"To another woman, not the mother of these two kids. You can't be married to two women at once. And these kids were born to another woman other than his legal wife." Dad tried to explain but our faces showed we weren't comprehending fully. "The woman you're talking about is Ganan's daughter. And as you both saw, they live separately in camp. For some reason, they're not fully accepted by all of the tribe – especially the women. I think its got something to do with the fact she's Ganan's daughter."

"That's not fair," reasoned Doug.

It all seemed very confusing to me at the time. Doug and Dad both had light olive skin that tanned, while mine was white and freckly like Nan's and burnt easily. But no one was mean to us. I sat there thinking for a bit.

"I'm glad we live in a warm house with plenty of food and that. I'm glad we have you Dad," I eventually added.

He patted my leg as he looked across at Doug and me with affection, before going into one of his quiet thinking spells.

"Boys, remember when I talked about taking an oath to help everybody who needs my help?"

"Yeah," we sung in unison.

"Well a long time ago, a very important British religious leader called William Penn once put it something like this: 'I expect to pass through this life but once …'" he paused to remember the exact words. "'If therefore, there be kindness I can show, or any good thing I can do for any fellow being, let me do it now, and not defer or neglect it, as I shall not pass this way again.' Don't you think that's a wonderful way to live your life, being kind and doing good to everybody?"

"It's hard being good all the time," replied Doug. Dad fought off a smile.

"Well I guess as long as we try, eh fellas? As a matter of fact, it was Poppie who first told me that quote years ago." The mention of Poppie's name gave it more importance to us.

"Say it again," asked Doug. Dad did so, slowly and with clarity.

"I agree and that, but if ya don't do anything but spend all your time being kind and good to everyone, how do ya get anything done?" I put forward.

"It's not something you do or think about all the time, its just in the back of your mind so that when something happens, you automatically choose to do good and be kind rather than nasty and 'orrible to people," Dad counselled with a grin.

We continued on home for lunch. Once there Dad took us aside.

"I have to apologise fellas. I shouldn't have called Bob Wood a goose. Like I've told you before, it's not nice to call someone names."

"That's not name callin', you're just statin' facts," called out Nan from the kitchen.

"Mum, please. The sad part is, it's hard to change people like Bob Wood, boys."

"They're gonna hear a lot worse words than that as they grow up. You protect 'em too much at times. It's time they started learnin' that everythin' in the garden isn't always lovely," Nan emphasised. Dad mulled it over.

"S'pose you're right. Come on fellas let's wash for lunch."

"The sandwiches are fantastic, Nan," I enthused.

"What's got into him? You usually turn yer nose up at brawn."

"After this morning, I think for what they have received, they *truly* are thankful," Dad summed up.

"That's good, 'cause I'm thinkin' of doin' curried sheep's eyes Sund'y, with tripe sponge for puddin'." Dad and Nan guessed our response and joined us in a collective,

"Urrh."

Chapter Seven

The wait was over. We met Barry and Raymond out the front of the School of Arts for the pictures. All the kids in town and the surrounding districts were there. Sitting with a group of the girls from our class was Penny Farrar, now with a plastic mouthguard to help push back her top teeth. Steve was with his mates and at the back of the hall the older teenage boys and girls sat in pairs. Throughout the audience were various parents keeping an eye out for any shenanigans. Anyone caught throwing boiled lollies at someone's head would be immediately ejected. The ladies of the CWA sold the tickets as well as refreshments, just inside the entrance. Dad sat at the end of our aisle, far enough away so as not to seem like he was babysitting us, in front of our mates.

We all stood and sang *God Save The Queen* to Gwen Grady's piano accompaniment then took our seats. There was much talking and manoeuvring nervously in our seats in anticipation until the red velvet curtains jerked open and the white screen descended from above the stage as lights faded.

From the moment the musical fanfare began, and an old sailing ship glided behind the titles for *The Sea Hawk*, we were mesmerised. After interval and *Smitten Kitten*, a Tom and Jerry cartoon, we were taken on an adventure into deepest darkest Africa with Johnny Weissmuller as Tarzan, in *Tarzan and The Leopard Woman*. We sat with our eyes straining at the screen, cheering and calling out whenever a baddie was dispatched, while crunching on our chocolate crackles and Smith's chips, or sucking on homemade toffees – mmm, magic.

Afterwards we all hung around outside talking excitedly over what we'd just seen with our mates. Penny smiled at me as she nervously played with her hair, but I didn't smile back even though I liked her, because I was shy. Snotty reckoned she was keen on me.

"Pat and Penny sitting in a tree, k-i-s-s-i-n-g." He kept on singing as he wiped his nose on his shirt sleeve. I gave him a nipple cripple. That shut him up.

The Golden Sea was just a short distance up the road. We'd never seen inside before. A little bell attached to the door tinkled as we entered a wonderland of red and black carved and lacquered screens, wall plaques and statues. From the back came Mrs Chang, shuffling to the front counter in her tight fitting blue cheongsam.

"Table for three?" she enquired with eagerness.

"Just some takeaway please," Dad replied. She handed Dad the menu as my eyes and Doug's took in all the shiny painted red and black surrounds. Hanging over the light bulbs dangling from the ceiling were different brightly coloured paper lanterns that gave the room a soft diffused glow. Dad and Mrs Chang exchanged friendly smiles as he studied the menu. Doug and I peered at it from the sides, not convinced cat wasn't hidden somewhere in the listings. If you haven't eaten cat before and it *is* served somehow, how would you know, we surmised in whispers to each other.

"I'll have eight fried dim sims, a beef with oyster sauce, a chicken chop suey and a large fried rice. Will that do four people, Mrs Chang?"

"How about sweet and sour pork as well? Should do."

"Fine."

After fifteen minutes of banging and clanging of utensils, Mr and Mrs Chang came out from the kitchen with a box containing our order. Dad paid the bill and Mrs Chang rang it up on their old cash register. Handing Dad the box Mr Chang added,

"I put in some soy sauce for the dim sims and some fortune cookies. No charge. Thank you. Please call again." Both of them gave several little bows.

"My boy Shen goes to school with your boys. You're Doctor McNally, yes?" asked Mr Chang.

"Yes. And these are my sons, Pat and Doug." They smiled at both of us.

"Shen's a little older. Ten. Different class."

"I didn't see him at the pictures. He's not sick is he?" Dad enquired.

"No not sick, but the other boys make fun of him because he's Chinese. Actually, Aussie Chinese. Third generation. Born here."

"Do they make fun?" Dad asked of both of us. We nodded.

"Steve Wood and some of his mates," offered Doug.

"Why doesn't that surprise me? What do they do?" Doug and I squirmed like worms thrown on a camp fire rock.

"They call out when he goes past, 'ching chong Chinaman'. And pull their eyes like this," Doug demonstrated, finishing with a little laugh.

"You find that funny, Dougal?" 'Dougal' – okay he might be in for it, but that didn't immediately mean me as well. I made sure I kept a serious look on my face.

"No sir. It's not as if they bash him up or anything."

"Doug, do you call him those names?"

"Sometimes. Everyone does." I waited. Was Doug going to dob me in as well? Dad looked at me, but said nothing. My red face was always a give away.

"I'm very sorry that this is happening to Shen. Is he here?" Dad asked.

"He's in the kitchen," replied Mrs Chang before calling out something to the back of the shop in Chinese. Shen peered through the thin strips of beaded curtain that separated the restaurant from the kitchen before parting them and joining his parents. Dad moved close to Shen, who remained looking at the ground.

"Shen, I'm Doctor McNally. You already know Dougal and Patrick." O-oh he used both our full names. We waited.

"Dougal would like to apologise, wouldn't you, for calling you names. Dougal?" Doug shuffled his feet a bit then spoke.

"I'm sorry I called ya names."

"Patrick?"

"I'm sorry as well."

"Now shake Shen's hand, but only if you truly mean what you just said." Doug moved first and shook Shen's hand, followed by me.

"I think we'll see some different behaviour from now on," Dad confidently predicted to the Changs. Mr Chang got a bag of prawn chips from under the counter and gave them to Doug.

"For your honesty and kindness." Both he and his wife bowed to Doug and me.

The bell had tinkled and the door just closed behind us when Dad turned to both of us.

"I want you to go out of your way to include Shen in your games at school."

"He's not in our class," I answered.

"Doesn't matter. Do you forget so quickly what happened to you when you first went there, just because you were different? And how *you* felt?"

He was right. He always was. I hated that sometimes, back then. But we were both thankful that if we didn't have to get home with the tea before it got cold, we would have copped another on-the-spot lecture, for sure.

We breathlessly filled Nan in on the pictures and the restaurant's interior as Dad placed each meal on warmed plates with serving spoons for us to help ourselves. It tasted great and different to anything we'd ever eaten. It wasn't too spicy and not cat as far as Doug and I could tell. Dad suggested we could make it a regular thing, say once a month, or try the Italian restaurant for a change, and Nan agreed. She especially liked the fried rice with its bits of ham and egg and peas. Doug and I loved the dim sims but even more, we liked playing with the glutenous sauces of the other meals that set like jelly on our plates as the food cooled. The fortune cookies finished off our meal. Dad explained the meaning behind my insert's saying, 'A journey of a thousand miles starts with the first step' and Doug's, 'Look not over your shoulder to find happiness'.

We drove Nan to the pictures then spent the rest of the evening curled up at Dad's feet in front of the fire, eating the prawn chips and listening to serials on the wireless. It was the one thing about winter I liked the most. It felt … good, and cosy. Later in bed we each gave him a big hug before he kissed us both on the forehead and tucked us in securely.

"I love my boys."

"We love you too, Dad," we chorused.

"It was the bestest day, Dad. And I promise I won't be mean to Shen again," added Doug.

"Me neither."

"I'm pleased with both of you. I think you've learnt a lot today. Now close your eyes and get some sleep. I'll see you in the morning."

Chapter Eight

By the time our ninth birthday on the 27th September arrived, buds were beginning to appear on the jacaranda. A football and a set of miniature golf clubs for Doug, a junior encyclopaedia and a toy doctor's kit for me, were our gifts from Dad. Nan gave us clothes and underwear. Mr and Mrs Symonds had us all over for birthday cake and Miss Bridget and Miss Kitty gave us Airfix plastic plane kits to assemble.

Our watering and the chook poo had done the trick for by late October our jacaranda tree was covered in clusters of purple flowers. Doug and I would lean on our bedroom windowsill on uneventful days and watch as they fell like snowflakes from the branches above. The roof and gutters were thick with fallen petals. Each day the crush of them underfoot was like walking on purple snow. Our tree now also had a rope swing attached to one of its higher branches thanks to Dad.

Down the street the mulberries were ripening slowly. We must have driven Mr Elliott crazy inspecting it every other day and asking when the fruit would be ready. It was always the same answer. 'A few more days.'

Our lives at Kilkenny in general settled down to regular routines as we got more familiar with our surrounds and our neighbours, although Miss Kitty remained a mystery.

Dad was able to get himself a receptionist, who was also a qualified nurse. Single and in her mid thirties, she was Susan McKenzie, a niece of Mrs Symonds. She lived in Sydney, but wanted to move out of the city. She not only booked appointments and assisted with patients but helped Dad with the accounts and ordering of stock. Staying with the Symonds until she got herself established, Dad would drive her to work and unless he had a callout, home as well. She took a lot of the burden of running the practice from Dad, allowing him to get on with just being a doctor.

He also surprised us with his carpentry and handyman skills, taking over Poppie's shed and tools. We'd sneak a peek through the window on those weekends he'd spend many feverish hours working away. These were usually the times he told us that the 'Black Dog' had come to visit and that he was best left alone.

'Battle fatigue' or 'gross stress reaction' were the terms used to describe a range of symptoms including depression and aggression experienced by troops returning from WWII. Now in the 1980's after the Vietnam War, there is much discussion in medical journals on what is being labelled 'post traumatic stress disorder' and its treatment. Whatever name you give it, it overcame Dad for hours. His working hard physically seemed to be his therapy to deal with it until the 'Black Dog' had left.

During these periods he made and replaced flyscreens for

windows, restored awnings and sanded back and painted the house. He even made new chairs for the kitchen using the lathe to turn out the legs and their supports. As he had learnt from Poppie, he promised when we got older and could handle the tools carefully, he'd teach us as well.

The best thing he built as far as Doug and I was concerned, was the wooden platform high in the jacaranda tree where two branches ran parallel to each other. It was only five feet by six feet of timber flooring, but to us it was our jungle treehouse, our flying carpet, our fort, our Sherwood Forest, our ship's deck, our castle. He even attached a long rope ladder to a branch above the platform that dangled to the ground, for us to use. Suddenly we were Errol Flynn and John Wayne. One day we were outlaws robbing the rich and giving to the poor, another, cowboys or pirates – all fighting the baddies and winning.

Although Doug found schoolwork a struggle, Dad never let him give in and become lazy. After the completion of our homework, Dad would check how we both went, and more often than not, sit with Doug and try to work through his mistakes. However, Doug didn't have his assistance in class or in exams.

While my occupations for when I grew up changed from a fireman, to a priest, to a teacher, Doug's went from a cricketer, to a farmer, to a policeman. Dad accepted our differences and limitations and praised our individual skills. Doug was never going to be a priest or a teacher and I could never be a cricketer or a farmer. Twins, but different and both equally loved by Dad.

❖

The old Reserve now only held about a dozen or so Aborigines. Eventually it would be abandoned by them altogether and the land sold off. But for now these remaining ones just didn't know where to go. For them the Reserve had been their home and the proposed three houses set aside by the Aboriginal Welfare Board could not accommodate everyone. The men would go off and search for food, only to return to the Reserve every few days. Dad still visited, now with Susan and sometimes Mrs Symonds, bringing food, clean drinking water and medical assistance. Occasionally Doug and I would go as well.

We weren't scared anymore. We even brought some of our toys we'd outgrown and left them for the kids to play with, along with fresh eggs and vegies from our garden that Doug and I had picked ourselves. Several times we saw Father Prittenden assisted by Sister Mary Placid saying Mass in the shed with the wooden cross and giving Holy Communion as we arrived. Other times they were distributing used clothing and shoes or conducting school lessons using a portable blackboard. All of us really, I suppose, in complete disregard of directives given to Sergeant Farrar to abandon the Reserve and its inhabitants altogether.

Ganan and most of his mob now lived on the outskirts of the town in small camps as Mr Green and Mr Wood had predicted that Cracker Night. They lived off the land as best they could. The men would occasionally pick up seasonal labouring or farming jobs and the women domestic duties on wheat stations to supplement their living conditions.

Allowed to move about freely by day was one thing, but shopkeepers had the discretion whether to serve Aborigines or not. By enforcing a strict night curfew on them entering and leaving the town proper, Sergeant Farrar managed to give some amount of protection to them while pacifying those worried white townspeople. These measures managed to keep a lid on any simmering tensions between a growing gang of anti-Aborigine white men in town and the Aborigines themselves, especially some young men, tired and growing resentful of their treatment by the whites and the white authorities.

These were harsh measures placed upon the Aborigines but as I found out later, when I began to see more of Australia, our town at the time was in actual fact more moderate in its treatment of them than the wider white population – a sad indictment of the times.

These small groups on the edge of town were often joined by others that drifted through the area. Now more regularly of a Saturday, fuelled by a day at the pub, some of the men from the white gang would go 'huntin' for boongs' as Gwen Grady once put it at one of Nan's CWA afternoons. They'd find out where a mob of them were camped, and then using a truck, drive through their camp firing shots into the air to scatter them so they'd get the message they weren't welcome and run off. One night while we were in bed, Doug and I even heard shots coming from as close as the creek, followed by a lot of whoopin' and hollerin' then more shots, then quiet.

"I've got me suspicions some of our men, full of grog after closin' time, are bloody, you know, foolin' 'round with them black gins. Pardon my French," Mrs Grady also suggested once. Nan told her she didn't approve of that kind of name calling or swearing in her house, especially in front of us kids.

"Huh!" Mrs Grady exclaimed as she left in a huff. Once she'd stormed out, screen door banging, down the front steps and out of sight, the other ladies of the CWA congratulated Nan.

"The old bitch had it coming," declared Nan. The whole lounge room erupted with laughter. "I meant *witch*, Lord, truly," she added quickly with a trace of a smile, before joining in the laughter herself. "Well she is. And we all know it. Sour old cow. Got a smile onna like a bleedin' eclipse. Ya only see it every once in a while." There was more laughter all around. Nan always had a funny slant on most things. Her motto was: 'If ya can laugh at life, it won't get ya down.'

One Tuesday after lunch, Sister Mary Placid instructed me to go outside and mix up the powdered ink for the afternoon's writing lesson. I was in the wash shed when through the wooden wall slats, I saw this gangly barefooted Aboriginal boy about thirteen or fourteen years of age, crawl out from under one of the buildings. He started ravenously picking through one of the garbage bins. I hadn't seen him at the Reserve, or near the creek, or anywhere else in town before. His clothes were worn and two sizes too big for him. At first he didn't see me, being more intent on picking through the lunch scraps. He dragged out and devoured half an eaten apple and the discarded crusts of someone's sandwich. I stepped out from the wash shed with the full bottle of made-up ink.

"Hi," I began, putting my hand on his shoulder. It startled him so much, he dropped the garbage lid with a loud clang as he span around to see who it was.

"I'm Pat." He just stood there saying nothing. He had sun-bleached straight brown hair, big brown eyes and a button nose. "Cat got ya tongue?" He looked scared and panicky. Sister came out onto the verandah.

"Patrick McNally, what *are* you doing out there?" she boomed. He ducked out of Sister's sight, around the side of the wash shed.

"I accidentally knocked the lid off the garbage, Sister."

"Well stop mucking about. We're waiting on that ink."

"Yes Sister." Once she'd turned her back, I looked around. "All clear." He wasn't going to take my word for it and checked for himself before edging his way along the walls of the separate classrooms, then bolting out of the school yard once he reached open space. I quickly returned to class before I copped another tongue lashing from Sister.

❖

And that was the first I saw of him. I told them all at home, but no one else. I didn't want to get him into any trouble for being on school property without a reason. Every day afterwards, I'd look out the classroom window about the same time, and more often than not he would be there, going through the bins for lunchtime scraps. Shortly after that I asked Nan if I could have an extra sandwich for lunch.

"If it'd make ya put on some weight, ya could have the whole bleedin' loaf! Look at ya, all skin and bone."

At the end of lunch, when no one was watching, I'd put the extra sandwich on the top of the rubbish in the exact bin so that he could get it. I kept my routine a secret, not even telling Doug, which was a first. I'd sneakily watch out of the corner of my eye from inside class as right on time everyday, he'd come into the school grounds and retrieve it.

I'm sure he knew it was me, because one day I saw him through the window smiling and waving at me as he helped himself to lunch. I remember wondering how he fed himself when school was closed over the weekends and holidays, before being brought back to reality by Sister, squeezing on my earlobe and telling me to pay attention.

❖

One Saturday morning, there was a knock at the back screen door. Dad went to answer it. It was that same Aboriginal boy from school. He smiled and held up his hand in acknowledgement of seeing me.

"Yes son, how can I help you?" Dad asked. The boy held out a tattered piece of paper in his long slender fingers and handed it to Dad. "'I am Johnny August. Can't speak but not deaf. Looking for work,'" Dad read aloud before looking at the teenager as he handed the note back to him. Now I realised why he hadn't answered me back in the schoolyard. I stood there shamefaced, knowing now how my innocent remark to him at the bins was actually very hurtful. I smiled at him, hoping he would forgive me.

"Well Johnny ..." Dad began, as he caught at first the disapproving shake, then the reluctant nod of agreement of Nan's head. "Let's see, there's a load of wood out there for the fireplace that needs chopping and stacking under the house. Do you think you can handle that?" Johnny flashed a broad grin. "You take a look, and then we'll work out a price." Johnny did and eventually held up one finger. Dad countered with, "There's a good hour's hard work there. We'll make that five shillings instead."

Deal done, Johnny removed his shirt then set about chopping the wood. Doug and I sat on the top step of the back stairs, watching as he laboured away furiously.

While he worked, we could half-hear Dad and Nan from inside the house.

"I just don't know if it's such a good idea, is all. We don't want any trouble," Nan warned.

"There won't be."

"You know what I mean. People'll talk. Before he's finished, the whole town'll be abuzz with the news we've got a black boy working for us."

"He's done the right thing. He's knocked on the door and rather than asking for a handout, he's willing to work for a few bob. I'm surprised at you. A good Christian woman who helped many a traveller on the wallaby during the Depression, now turning your back on a young boy. You can see by the look of him, he lives pretty rough."

"I'm not turning me back son, it's just that I'm worried about the repercussions. Ya know what some people are like."

"I won't live my life worrying about what other people might think. You brought me up to look out and care for those in need. And you *know* the kind of conditions these poor buggers live under."

"You're right," Nan conceded. Dad came out to view the progress.

Johnny's build was lean but surprisingly muscular. The muscles in his arms were taut as he swung the axe down over the top of the log that rested vertically on a sawn off tree stump. Most times, with only the one attempt, the log would split easily down the centre. By the time he had finished with the stacking of the chopped wood under the house, he was dripping sweat. His hair stuck to his face. Nan came out onto the back verandah.

"Here's a towel love, ya can wash up in the laundry sink under the house." As she handed it to him Dad gave her a little smile. "I'll have a cool drink ready for ya," she added as she went back inside.

Freshly washed, he hung the towel on the line and put his shirt back on before knocking on the back door. Dad asked him to come inside, but he wouldn't and moved slightly back from the screen door remaining there with his head bent. Dad came out with his money and Nan followed, putting on a tray the jug of lemonade and some sandwiches she'd originally set out for him on the kitchen table. Dad counted out the coins and shook Johnny's hand, thanking him for a job well done. Johnny looked longingly at the refreshments but seemed to be waiting for permission to start.

"Well go on lad before the lemonade gets warm," encouraged Nan. With that, Johnny wolfed it all down like he hadn't eaten for a month. Nan and Dad looked sympathetically at him over his actions.

"If you come back next weekend, there's some mowing of the front and back that needs doing, as well as the edges," Dad offered. Johnny smiled and shook Dad's hand. "Say, six shillings?" Johnny's broad grin confirmed his agreement.

"There'll be a hot lunch with yer name on it as well," added Nan. After he'd gone Nan pulled us aside. "And you two, next time, don't keep staring at him while he's trying to work. You'd give anyone the heebie-jeebies."

The very next day Doug and I saw where under the cover of night, someone had painted in lime wash over Dad's surgery window ABO LOVER. Dad didn't bother to explain and we thought nothing of the words, just wondered why someone would put them there in the first place. We helped as Dad calmly set about cleaning it off.

Sure enough, Johnny came the next weekend as promised and continued on a weekly basis to do the lawns, tidy up the yard and do the gardening. As much as Nan wanted to tend to Poppie's labour of love herself, she was finding it too difficult to maintain.

One time I introduced Johnny to Miss Bridget but led off with how he couldn't talk, to save her thinking he was ignoring her. He carried several loads of cuttings around the back and burnt them off, refusing any payment. But Miss Kitty wouldn't let him go without a drink of milk and a couple of pumpkin scones instead, to settle the matter.

CHAPTER NINE

Finally, in early November and much later than usual, we knew Elliott's black mulberry tree was ready for harvesting. Nan's exchange of some of her tomato relish and choko chutney, always guaranteed a couple of bucketfuls of fruit in return. Doug and I were given the task of taking the jars of preserves to the Elliott's and collecting the coveted mulberries.

Before we entered their gate, we placed the jars on the ground and began to scoop up and eat the plump ripe mulberries that had fallen over the fence. We were stuffing our faces with the rich flavour of the berries when Mr Elliott came around the side of his house with an armful of empty buckets.

"Hi Mr Elliott," I called out. "Nan's given us these here preserves to give to you for some of your mulberries. She's gonna make some pies and jam this year. There's two of the tomato relish that you like and one choko chutney as well." He didn't respond.

"She told us to ask how Mrs Elliott's arthritis is," Doug added as we entered the yard.

"Er fine, fine," Mr Elliott stated, finishing his sentence with his usual upward inflection that turned each statement into a sort of question. He seemed distracted, not looking at us as he picked the fruit from the tree and placed it in one of his buckets.

"There's no mulberries this year."

"But there's plenty on the tree, see?" pointed out Doug.

"Well they're for them that don't um, fraternise with blacks. You can tell ya gran that from me." We started to leave, feeling hurt and confused.

"What's fraterise?" I asked, as I hadn't ever heard the word before. He repeated it again so that I got it right.

"Fratern-ize. F-r-a-t-e-r-n-i-z-e," he spelt out, with that upward finish.

"But what does it mean?" I asked.

"I'm not here to give no English lesson. Ask yer gran. Now go and take them preserves with ya."

"Is it okay if we collect a few of the ones that've fallen on the ground?" asked Doug.

"Didn't you hear me? There's no mulberries for you lot 'til you come to yer senses. I'm sorry, but we've um had a meetin', and well um, we're not prepared to turn our beautiful town into a Mission, for the likes of that black boy you lot are so keen on and the rest of 'em."

"You'd like Johnny if you met him. He's really friendly, and ..."

"Pat, I can't stand here all day listenin' ... Look um, it was decided at the meetin'. I'm not s'pose to even be talkin' to youse." Mr Elliott seemed a bit rattled. "Oh for goodness sake, stop lookin' at me you two with them big eyes. Go on, ya can fill two buckets, but no more." Doug and I wasted no time picking up the fallen fruit and putting it in the buckets.

"Not them ones, the better ones from the tree. But be quick about it. I don't want no one seein' me fraternisin'." We filled the buckets. Mr Elliott added a few handfuls to the top. "Now go before anyone sees ya. And um, thank yer gran for the preserves. Much appreciated."

We raced back to the house without dropping a single berry. Johnny was raking the leaves on our front lawn as we got back.

"Here Johnny, have some mulberries. There's heaps," I offered.

"Heaps," Doug restated. Johnny took a few then got back to the raking.

"What are we gonna tell Nan?" I whispered, as we went up the front steps.

"She doesn't have to know. It'll only get her upset. We delivered the preserves and got the mulberries – simple."

Doug was always able to see through a potential problem and find a simple solution. We convinced Nan to let us give the fruit a rinse, so that she wouldn't see the dirtier ones on the bottom – problem solved.

I looked up Dad's thick dictionary secretly that night, but was none the wiser as to what we did that could have got Mr Elliott so upset. He seemed angry that we were mixing with Johnny. The first meaning of 'fraternize', for they did indeed spell it with an 'ize' back then, indicated that we must have associated in a fraternal or friendly way, which was fair enough. It was the second definition of the word that must have riled Mr Elliott and the people at his meeting – the fact that we 'associated intimately with citizens of an enemy or conquered country'. Johnny wasn't our enemy, and yet I recalled Dad telling us at the Reserve that they were the first inhabitants of this country and that the white man took the land for themselves. Trying to work out what was what confused my young brain, but I kept it there at the back of my mind. We dropped the buckets back over the Elliott's front fence when Mr Elliott wasn't about.

Nan made three thick mulberry pies and still had fruit left over for jam. While Doug went off to Barry's place to play, Nan gave me one of the pies covered in a tea towel to take next door for Miss Bridget and Miss Kitty. I went the right way around this time, through their front gate and not the swinging palings. I banged on the front screen door and waited. Miss Bridget was off cleaning for the Patterson's still, so Miss Kitty came up the hallway.

"It's me Miss Kitty, Pat. Nan baked this mulberry pie for you."

"Oh isn't that nice of her. Please come in." I hesitated a bit, but as she held the screen door back, I looked at her smiling face and continued. Her hair was pulled tightly back off her face and pinned in a bun at the nape of her neck.

I placed the pie on the kitchen table then she removed and folded up the tea towel for me to return.

"Oh my, isn't it a beauty? Please, take a seat. Would you like some homemade ginger beer? My father's recipe." I agreed with a nod. On the table was a plate of veal and the ingredients to crumb it. I looked around the kitchen. The higher kitchen cupboard doors had some of their leadlight inserts missing and the whole place seemed to be so old and in need of a paint.

The ginger beer was cold and strong and I could tell the jam-centred biscuits came from Mr Green's corner store. Nan sometimes would send Doug or me down to his store to get sixpence worth of broken biscuits as a treat. Miss Kitty's were the dearer unbroken ones. As she continued flouring then dipping the veal slices in egg before crumbing them, I knelt on the chair and watched. With her hair done the way it was, you could clearly see a large port-wine birthmark covering almost half of the left side of her face from the temple, a bit over the eyelid and down over her cheek and ear. Even with the mark her white skin had almost an ethereal glow. At one stage she caught me staring.

"It's a birthmark."

"I'm sorry. Nan says its bad manners to stare." But I wanted to ask her some more things and I guess she felt it because she smiled.

"What's on your mind?"

I hesitated then asked how come she was so white and how come her eyes were a funny red colour. She smiled when I said, "funny red colour."

"I'm an albino. Do you know what that is?" I shook my head. She continued preparing the meal, placing the crumbed veal pieces in a frypan of hot dripping on the stove as we talked.

"Your father has an olivey skin that browns in the sun."

"So does Doug's."

"And you burn if you stay out too long, don't you?" I nodded. "Well, an albino like me can't go out in the sun at all, unless we're fully covered, 'cause we burn even quicker and blister then peel. The thing that makes other people's skin turn brown, albinos don't have. We're also born with reddish eyes that can't stand the glare of the sun. Does that answer everything?"

"What about your sister? How come she's not – ?"

"She's pale, but not as pale as me. She can take a bit of sun."

"How did you go outside and play as a kid?"

"Like you saw me the day you fell off the lattice – gloves and sunglasses and usually a hat. And dresses that covered my whole body. It wasn't very pleasant."

"Why?"

"Well, besides the heat from all the clothing, children can be very cruel. Adults even crueller – when they see someone who looks different. Different to them." She turned the veal over in the frypan.

"What did they do?"

"They called me names. Hurtful things – especially to a child."

"What did you do?"

"I ran inside and hid. I vowed I'd never go out and be laughed at again. Of course eventually I did. Mother put makeup over the mark so I'd look just like everyone else. Except I didn't. I was still an outsider, just not as noticeable."

I could see by her face, that remembering it made her sad. I squirmed in my seat a bit before getting the courage to say what I felt I had to get off my conscience.

"I should apologise too."

"Why's that then?"

"Thinking you were a vampire."

"It's not your fault. You only believed the story you were told. If I chose not to retreat from the world, maybe the stories wouldn't have started up. Who knows?" She gave a weak little smile. I smiled back and her eyes sparkled like the red rubies in Nan's engagement ring. She put the cooked veal on a plate before placing it in the oven to be warmed up later.

"More biscuits?"

"No thanks. I want to leave room for a big slice of pie later. I better go."

"Let yourself out. Thank your Nan for the pie. And Patrick, you're welcome to call in anytime."

"I'd like that. You can call me Pat, if you like." I leaned over and gave her a little kiss on the cheek, right on the birthmark. It took her by surprise. Her white eyelashes fluttered as she touched the spot where I kissed her. She watched as I skipped, tea towel swinging in my hand, back up the hall and home.

CHAPTER TEN

Our Christmas school holidays only had a few weeks to run. Since our arrival in town, Con's Chicken and Hamburger Takeaway opened, construction had begun on a second bank and a small block of four flats – the first in town. A motel was in the early planning stages as well. It caused a lot of interest, because it was going to have a swimming pool – another first for the town.

More often then before, Doug and Barry would take off by themselves. They'd either go to Barry's and play board games or scale the rocky outcrops that lined part of the creek, three miles upstream. Every now and then I'd join them, with either Snotty or Raymond, but mostly I preferred to stay around the house reading or playing school teacher. Dad had let me use the fibro walls of the shed as a blackboard, provided I cleaned off the chalk each day. Honey sometimes would act as my class of pupils, happily agreeing to stay put on the old fruit crate I had placed at the front of my class in the sun. She'd curl up and sleep for several hours at a time.

Around lunchtime one particular day, I had run out of things to teach a sleeping dog and was just carrying Honey back home when along the road came one of the two town taxis. It stopped in a cloud of red dust right outside our gate. A slim lady in a white dress with big red roses printed over it, got out and went up our front steps. She wore a white turned-down brim straw hat obscuring her face, with matching white handbag, shoes and gloves. As the taxi turned and headed back to town, I could see Dad's car coming down the road with Susan inside. Most days they'd both come home for lunch.

I dumped Honey quickly on her verandah and raced back to the side of the road and waited for them. Nan had already answered the lady's knock at the door by that time and was having a heated exchange. Doug got out of the back seat. Dad had picked him up while he was walking home for lunch. Susan alighted from the front passenger seat and headed for her house. Carrying a patient's payment of a dead rabbit on some string Dad, followed by Doug and me, walked up the front steps. Across the road, Susan lingered on her verandah, looking over from time to time before going inside.

"Harry, there's someone here to see you," Nan announced with a twist of lemon in her voice. The lady turned and faced us. Nan, all five foot nothing of her, stood behind her, barring the doorway with her hips almost touching its sides. Her arms were folded resolutely in front of her.

"Hello Harry," the woman said in a husky tone.

"Claire!" Dad looked surprised but pleased, as he reached behind her and handed Nan the rabbit.

"Boys, do you know who this is?" Dad smiled. We shook our

heads. I noticed Nan heading back inside muttering to herself. The lady leaned her head forward as she unfastened a hatpin. Her light brown hair fell to her shoulders in soft curls as she removed the hat. Though beautiful, she appeared very pale and tired.

"This is your mother." Dad and she looked at each other as she proceeded to remove her gloves and awkwardly shake our hands. Her fingernails were long and matched the bright red of her lips and the roses on her dress. Both Doug and I were wide-mouthed, speechless. My only memory of her had faded to a featureless shadow in a doorway. Dad tried to kiss her cheek, but she shied away. Doug and I looked at each other. We were owed an explanation.

"It's good to see you, Claire."

"Likewise," she replied with a nervous self-consciousness. "I can't stay long."

"Please come inside."

"I think under the circumstances it might be best ..." She indicated Nan now hovering inside near the front door.

"Please have a seat," Dad offered as he went inside to talk to Nan. We sat down opposite her on the cane furniture.

"Well boys, it's good to see you looking so well."

Nan's raised voice could be heard over Dad's whispers.

"I won't have that woman in my house."

"Keep your voice ..."

"I won't shoosh! You tell me what sort of mother walks away from a marriage when there's kids involved. And the sooner you stop carryin' a torch ... I don't care whether she hears me or not. What she want anyway? Turnin' up here like a bad penny after all these years. Why she's nothing more than a tramp."

"Now that's enough!" Dad exploded. We could see Nan's words had registered heavily with Mother. She fidgeted with the red bangles on her left arm, distracted by the commotion inside. Dad came back out and took a seat beside her.

"I think it best we have our sandwiches out here."

Doug couldn't hold in his thoughts any longer.

"You told us she was dead. You lied!" he spat out. It could have been me stating the very same.

"No son, I didn't lie. I never said your mother was dead. I said something like 'your mother's no longer living with us'. Not dead. I'm sorry if I ... All this time you thought ... Oh fellas, I'm so sorry. I was trying to explain as best I could to two three year olds what had happened between your mum and me. I should have put it better. I'm sorry."

"Look I don't want to stir up any trouble, Harry. I just came back to ..."

"You came back," Dad smiled. "That's a start." She looked away and took a packet of 'Craven A' cigarettes from her handbag and lit one nervously as Dad disappeared inside again. We all just sat there with nothing much to say, Doug and I staring at her face through puffs of smoke. I felt awkward sitting there. This was our mother, but we didn't know her at all.

"You're very pretty," Doug ventured. My thoughts exactly.

"Why thank you," she smiled coquettishly with a tilt of her head. "But time and the weather are a woman's worse enemies. So tell me, how are you doing at school?" she faltered, looking around while trying to make small talk.

"I topped the class in spelling and arithmetic," Doug boasted. I looked at him but said nothing to destroy his lie. She gave him a dimpled half smile.

"That's excellent. And you, Pat?"

"I topped it in writing and social studies." I hadn't but wasn't about to let Doug get away completely with big-noting himself, without adding my own fabrication. But as I finished speaking, a smirk came over Doug's face. She saw it too.

"Oh I see. I don't know whether I'm talking to two geniuses or a couple of wise guys," she smiled. And we smiled back. We couldn't think of anything else to say so we just sat there looking at her as she puffed on her cigarette. To us she was strange and exotic, like some star in a Hollywood picture.

After a while Dad returned with a tray of mixed quartered sandwiches and four glasses of cordial. The three of us ate in awkward silence but she didn't even take a bite. Dad was the first to speak.

"You're looking well."

"You've done a great job with the boys."

"We've plenty of room if you'd like to stay."

"With her? Thanks, but I'm booked in at the Exchange. I'm leaving on the morning train."

"Tomorrow?"

Dad looked confused and she very uncomfortable, moving about in her seat as she stubbed out her cigarette on her plate before lighting another straight away. Nan would have been furious if she saw what she just did to her good plate. Doug noted it as well. Dad suggested Doug and I go inside so they could talk.

"I hope you will stay. Pat and I would like it if you would," Doug said as we got up.

Once inside, we got as close as possible to the window to hear what was being discussed, while remaining out of sight. Nan was already standing there. She didn't say a word, just put a finger to her lips and let us stand there with her, listening.

"Harry, the reason I came ..."

"You're still as beautiful as ..."

"Harry please. Just listen. I'm not coming back. Neither of us could make it work. And we both tried." There was a moment where neither of them spoke. I looked at Doug. We both felt an empty sort of ... sadness, I guess. It would have been nice if she had said 'yes' and stayed, I thought.

"Things'll be different, I promise." There was an anxious plea in his voice.

"I could never be the wife you need or deserve. And I'd die out here."

"You'll never know, unless you give it a try. Please."

"I did that, remember? The old bag's right about one thing, you can't keep carrying a torch." Nan bristled, narrowing her eyes and setting her jaw.

"The boys need a mother," Dad argued.

"I've met someone." It went quiet again for a second.

"Who?"

"Richard. You don't know him. He owns the pub I work at. He loves me and wants to marry me." We were waiting for Dad to speak, but only she continued. "I only came because I didn't just want to post them without explanation. I've got these papers I need you to sign and lodge. I've also written out the details about the – well, you've got sufficient grounds. It's all in there. I'm not after anything from you. I'm sorry. I know you're strict Catholic, but a divorce is the only way for both of us to move on with our ..."

"Divorce?" Dad sounded stunned. "Claire, I still love you. We can make …"

"And I loved you – once."

"What about the boys? You can't just waltz back into their lives, then – Claire, they need you in their lives." There was another pause. "So, if I sign and whatever, can they at least visit you from time to time, say school holidays?" There was another silence.

"Richard doesn't know about them. He thinks I'm single. He doesn't want kids. If he knew I had kids, I'd lose him. And I need *someone*. Someone who'll stay." Her voice trailed off.

I felt like I was going to blubber as I glanced over at Doug. He had a stony look on his face. Nan looked down at us and placing her hand on my shoulder, whispered very gently to us.

"You boys go and play in your room for a bit." We both walked slowly with our heads bowed to our room.

An hour or so later, Dad appeared at the door. We were both just lying on our beds gazing out the window through the branches of the jacaranda to the drained summer sky.

Dad began awkwardly.

"Your mother said she was sorry, but she had to go. I drove her into town."

"We heard. She doesn't want us," Doug mumbled, barely holding in his emotions.

"It's not that she doesn't love you, it's just that – well, your mother has got her own life, and..." We both just looked at him. No words could cover the fact she didn't want us. "Look, she left this for you both," he said, trying to give excitement to the words.

We watched as he searched through his wallet to find two five pound notes. Our mother had never sent us as much as a card on our birthday and now she wanted to give us each five pounds? The three of us knew she hadn't. Neither of us would take the money he was holding out. Doug rolled away on his side.

"What does divorce mean?" I asked. Dad paused in thought.

"Well, that's where um two people decide not to be married any more."

"I wish she *was* dead," Doug muttered as I swung my legs over the side of the bed and sat up. All I could do was look at the floor.

"You don't mean that, son."

"I do."

"Then that saddens me a great deal." Dad put the notes back in his wallet before quietly leaving the room and heading back to the surgery with Susan.

"I'm never gettin' married and never havin' kids. Never," Doug later proclaimed to me.

❖

As tired as we were from the whole events of the day, we found it hard to get to sleep that night. Laying with our hands behind our heads we both just stared up at the dark ceiling.

"Doug, you awake?"

"Yep."

"You want to get in with me?" He didn't answer. "Can I get in with you?"

"No."

"Okay."

But it wasn't. And although we were best of mates and still did things together, that part of our lives Doug had outgrown before me. It made me unhappy for a long while, because I wanted everything to stay the way it was between us.

Around the same time, I started to get more involved with schooling and achieving better marks that put me only five desks away from assisting at Benediction. Doug, on the other hand, was always a day late and a penny short when it came to school work. He much preferred kicking a football around with mates rather than concentrating on lessons or doing extra work to better his grades. As a consequence, he stayed in the lower quarter of the class, and getting further and further away from me.

"Are ya mad at me or somethin'?" I asked once. "Ya never want to mess 'round any more."

"I'd muck 'round with ya, but most the time you've got ya nose stuck in some book." He was right. We were different and neither about to change – we couldn't. It marked the beginning of our independence from each other and the development of our own individual personalities – but we still remained close, just in a different way from before.

Later that same night of our mother's visit, when I got up to get a drink of water, I thought I could hear Dad sobbing in his room. When I paused outside his door on the way back from the kitchen, there was no sound. I didn't mention it the next day, to anyone.

In the days that followed, everyone was a bit quiet. Nothing more was said about our mother's visit 'cept I overheard Dad say to Nan a few weeks later, that his solicitor had filed the papers with the Court. Nan was as nice as could be to all of us, especially Dad. There were times we'd come home from a game of forcings back and Dad would be sitting on the verandah daydreaming, just staring into the distance at nothing in particular. When we found him like this, we left him alone as much as possible and tried to be on our best behaviour.

"It's harder on Dad I guess, knowing she won't be coming home. At least we've got Nan," Doug once reasoned.

"I think we're better off without a mother," I said, trying to convince myself we were. Doug didn't reply.

Dad was still Dad, finding the time to take all of us on car trips out of town for picnics and bird watching. And soon he started mucking around with us again. He'd wrestle and play 'tickle torture' with us on the front lawn on warmer nights, or join us on the verandah sleep-out. On the stillest of those nights you could hear the distant croaking chorus of frogs from the creek or the voices of neighbouring kids also sleeping out with their parents. We'd fall asleep all curled up around Dad, looking at the stars as he told us stories. The stars seem different here than in the city – brighter and closer, like you could almost reach up and pluck them from the inky sky.

"Dad, you know how there are other planets spinning 'round, just like Earth –" began Doug.

"Well not *just* like Earth, but yes, other planets."

"Well, just like we're lying here looking up at the stars, do you think that somewhere up there amongst all the planets and stars, there could be people lying there as well, staring back at us and wondering the same thing?"

"Yeah, back at us," I repeated.

"Could be. It's possible I guess. Who knows?"

We all just looked up at the night sky in silence for a moment. It was almost a spiritual experience, contemplating the overwhelming enormity of the universe. It was another magic moment, lying there with Dad's arms around us. My feelings of being abandoned by our mother diminished to a degree. Snuggling up to him, I felt loved and secure – and wanted. And I wouldn't trade how I felt for one hundred pounds. Doug didn't want to talk about her ever again.

CHAPTER ELEVEN

It was late one Sunday afternoon. Dad, Doug and I had just come home from a weekend camping trip, when Nan almost fell over running down the stairs with Dad's medical bag. She told him to go into the Walshe place immediately – there'd been a terrible incident.

"You two stay here and unpack the camping gear," he instructed as he took the bag and rushed next door. We waited until Nan had gone back inside, then Doug and I sneaked through the palings and ran around the back of their house before tiptoeing up the steps and onto the verandah. Through the flyscreen door we could just see into the lounge room, where they were all standing around looking at someone lying on their stomach under a blanket on the lounge. Dad was in front of the person and Miss Bridget and Miss Kitty were standing to the side, blocking our view. Miss Bridget was speaking.

"I was coming back from the Pattersons when I saw him naked, tied by the wrists between two trees with a sugar sack over his head – a bit back from the road. I drove straight towards them blasting the horn. They soon scattered."

"You saw who it was."

"There was a group. At least four men. All white. They jumped into the one truck and sped off. We were both churning up the dust, me just trying to get to him, so much so I couldn't make out who they were or the truck's rego either. His little tin hut was strewn all over the place. I untied him and mopped the blood on his back as best I could, Harry, with a hankie. Then I laid him on the back seat and got us outta there quick smart, in case they came back. God knows what they had in mind."

Dad bent down to examine the patient. Miss Bridget and Miss Kitty completely blocked our view of what Dad was doing as they moved in closer as well.

"Don't worry son, I won't hurt you. If I could ask you ladies to leave the room, I'll give him a thorough examination."

The sisters hovered outside the door. From within were several cries of pain and Dad's voice saying, "Sorry mate, but I have to do this." After about twenty minutes Dad opened the door and let the women back in.

"Those are whip marks on his back," he stated.

"One of them was waving something about in his hand."

"Several are quite deep, indicating a fair amount of force."

"Who'd do such a thing? Poor lamb," Miss Kitty sighed.

"Some mongrel," growled Dad. "I've cleaned up the lacerated flesh and applied some iodine and dressings. I've also given him a shot in case of any infection and something for the pain. He's an excellent patient, aren't you Johnny?" All Doug and I could do was look at each other, our hearts as leaden as sacks of flour when we heard his name.

"We'll pay any –" began Miss Bridget.

"I wouldn't hear of it ladies. Johnny's a mate of ours. Have you given Sergeant Farrar a call yet?"

"No, I thought it best you see him first before the Sergeant starts asking him a whole lot of questions," reasoned Miss Bridget. "Besides, how can he tell him anything?"

"I'll give him a call when I get home. Whoever did this needs locking up. Would you prefer him coming home with me?"

"Oh no. Please, we can look after him, can't we Biddy? I'm sure he won't be any bother," Miss Kitty pleaded with some urgency.

"Son, these ladies will take good care of you. I'll see you tomorrow. Bye ladies."

Dad started to leave the room, which meant it was time for us to get back home as soon as possible. We shot down the steps, through the fence and waited for Dad in the front yard.

"Everything alright, Dad? Nothing wrong with Miss Bridget or Miss Kitty?" I asked. Dad said nothing, just headed up the steps. He turned calmly as he reached the top and looked back and forth at both of us, with a stern expression.

"I thought I gave you two an order. I'm disappointed in both of you." I looked quickly at Doug. "And next time you listen through doors, make sure it isn't a see-through flysflcreen."

"We didn't hear anything, honest," rushed Doug to cover.

"But he will be alright, won't he?" I asked as Doug trod on my toe. "Owwh."

"We're sorry," Doug stated in our defence.

"I'm sure you will be when you go without pocket money this

fortnight. Maybe then you'll take notice that when I tell you to do something, you do it. Right?"

"Right," we both answered, with hung heads.

"Get that camping gear stowed under the house and the table set. Now." We ran to the boot of the car. "In answer to your question, 'yes' he will recover."

We wasted no time in emptying the boot and had the gear stowed in minutes before flying up the steps to set the table.

Later, after we had our wash, I made an attempt to salvage our pocket money.

"It was only a white lie," I suggested to Dad.

"A lie's a lie son, no matter what shade." I continued putting on my pyjamas, thinking on what he had just said.

Later that evening, Dad rang Sergeant Farrar and he came around. Dad took him into his bedroom and closed the door. Nan kept an eye on us in the lounge room, so that we wouldn't listen in. I made an excuse to go to our bedroom to get a book and heard a bit of their conversation.

"We can't let this sort of thing happen. Someone has to be brought to justice," Dad argued.

"There's a group that get a belly full at the end of the week and go stirrin' up trouble with the blacks, but what can I do? No one wants to be a witness."

"It's Wood and his mates, isn't it?"

"Until I have proof …" Sergeant Farrar replied in a way that seemed to suggest he knew who it could've been, but didn't know for sure. "Every town has to have a troublemaker. We must be lucky, seems we've got bloody three or four. Don't worry; I'll keep an eye out closin' time to see there's no mischief brewin'. Let's go see the boy."

At that stage, I quickly scooted back to the lounge room as they wound up their talk and opened the door. They left the house, saying nothing.

It was only a half an hour into the first of our serials, when Dad came back up the front steps and entered, supporting Johnny. His arm was over Dad's shoulder and he had a blanket wrapped around his waist. Doug and I jumped up from the floor.

"Mum, can you make up the spare room? We've got a guest," Dad called out from the doorway to Nan, still cleaning in the kitchen. She entered, wiping her hands on her apron.

"How is he, love?" Dad set Johnny down in his armchair. He winced in pain then sat upright so that the wounds on his back didn't touch the back of the chair.

Dad then pulled Nan aside into the kitchen doorway and explained that Johnny was starting to run a temperature. He thought he'd be better off here, where he could keep an eye on his recovery. I turned the serial on the wireless down to a low whisper so that we could hear what was going on. Johnny just sat there, fascinated by the wireless, like he'd never seen one before. I looked over to Dad and Nan.

They kept their voices down but I managed to hear most of what was being said.

"… And Sergeant Farrar can't or won't do anything about it," Dad concluded.

Johnny could hear as well, and was trying to get up to make a bolt for the door. As he shuffled to his feet they walked back in and Dad grabbed Johnny firmly by the arm. He cowered as if he expected Dad was going to hit him, before getting all wobbly.

Trying to regain his balance he let the blanket slip, revealing his nakedness.

"Oh son, no one is going to hurt you. Sit yourself back down. You're safe here," Dad soothed as he quickly replaced the blanket over Johnny's lap and legs. "We'll look after you until you're better."

"I'll fix the sheets. You two can give us a hand settin' up the spare room, seein' as ya don't seem that interested in the wireless this evening'," Nan instructed. Nothing escaped her.

Bed made, we all returned to the lounge room and Nan turned the wireless back up for us. Dad had completed taking Johnny's temperature. He helped him up and gave him a sponge bath before putting him to bed. When Dad returned to the lounge room, he reminded us we had school tomorrow and that it was time for us to go to bed as well.

Before he whispered 'goodnight' and turned out the light, I finally confessed the secret I had been concealing from everyone for so long – that I knew more about Johnny.

"He was the boy I saw at school, going through the bins for scraps."

"Goodnight boys," and he moved to leave.

"There's more. That extra sandwich Nan gives me, I put on the top of the rubbish in the bin for him."

"Oh I see," Dad deliberated.

"It's never wasted. It's just that he looked so hungry."

"That was a good thing to do, son," Dad affirmed then gave a little smile, his eyes crinkling up as he did so. "But not doing what I tell you, when I tell you, isn't. Now off to sleep the pair of you." As he was leaving the room he turned and added, "However, in light of what you've just told me, I might reconsider the issue of the pocket money. I'll sleep on it."

With the door pulled almost closed, Doug whispered in the darkness.

"Geez, ya can be such a crawler."

Next morning at breakfast, Dad told us we would indeed get our pocket money next Friday, if we continued our chores. It came with another lecture about 'obeying your father' and the reminder that we should mention the incident at this week's Confession.

"It's a good Christian thing you've been doin', feedin' the boy, and not turnin' yer back on someone in need. But you could have told me," Nan added, speaking to me but starting with a glance to Dad.

"I thought you'd get mad."

"No I wouldn't darlin'. But I want you to know, both of you, that you can always come to ya Nan and tell me anything. Alright? Now eat yer bubble an' squeak, you'll be late for school."

"Where's Johnny?" Doug asked.

"I gave him something to help him sleep. You can see him when you get home," Dad directed. I looked at the spare chair. Over it were some of Poppie's old clothes. Nan had stayed up late into the night, altering two shirts and a pair of trousers for Johnny to get around in.

That morning in the playground before school, we were telling a group about Johnny and how he was beaten and how he was living with us until he got better, when Steve pushed through the group.

"Your dad's an Abo lover." The same words painted on Dad's surgery window. "An' that makes youse ones too," he hissed. I couldn't make out what was his point, but by the tone of his voice, I figured to be an 'Abo lover' was something bad. Doug and I just stood there unsure of what he was getting at.

"My dad said your dad's a bloody do-gooder who don't know when to keep his nose outta other people's business, and some day he'll get his. So what are youse gonna do about it?" And with that Steve thumped me in the chest so hard, I nearly lost my balance. Doug hauled back a fist to land one on Steve. I grabbed his raised arm and pulled him aside, reminding him what Dad had said about no fighting – to walk away. We tried to and that's when Steve shouted out.

"Look at the two girls running away. Scared of gettin' yer nice new uniforms all dirty, girls?"

Doug was aching to punch Steve on the nose and it took all my strength to pull him around and lead him to the seats under the tree. He was boiling mad. Luckily one of the nuns came out into the yard and shook the handbell for assembly.

"Dad'd be proud of us, especially you," I whispered in Doug's ear so as not to get into trouble for speaking while in line. But Doug wasn't buying it, not this time.

"It looks like we're chicken."

"Not chicken, just smart. You want to get into a fight and cop the cane plus a lecture from Dad, not to mention losin' our pocket money, all over some drongo like Steve?" That calmed him down somewhat. He gave a begrudging shrug of his shoulders in agreement, but a showdown between us and Steve was always looming. Then I felt this hard thwhop to my ear and turned around. It was Sister Mary Placid's cupped hand.

"No talking at assembly. Now turn around and face the front."

CHAPTER TWELVE

By next Saturday, Johnny's swelling had gone down but he was still left with bruises and where the skin was ripped, scabs were starting to form. As we served ourselves breakfast, Dad reminded us to wait for Johnny before we start. By the time he came from the bathroom wearing Poppie's Sunday trousers and shirt, we'd already said Grace and were all sitting at the table with full plates of pikelets.

"Good morning Johnny," Dad said with a welcoming smile, to which we all added our own greetings. Johnny nodded shyly back at us.

"There's pikelets and syrup over there on the bench, love. Help yerself," Nan directed.

He only took one pikelet and the barest teaspoon of syrup then automatically headed for the back verandah to eat. Doug and I looked at Dad then Nan as to what was going on.

"Why doesn't he – ?" I started to ask.

"Shoosh," ordered Nan as Dad got up and went after him.

"Johnny, lad." He turned as Dad gently placed an arm around

his shoulder and motioned him to the empty seat at the table.

"Son, there's always a spot for you at our table." Dad waited for Johnny to ease himself into the seat before sitting himself. He looked at Nan in a way that suggested they both understood why Johnny had headed outside. Nan got out of her chair and reached out for Johnny's plate.

"Here, give me that. That wouldn't feed a sparra," she insisted, then proceeded to add another five pikelets in a stack and heaps of butter before pouring a generous amount of Golden syrup over them. "There. That'll put some meat on ya."

Johnny smiled like he'd just received the biggest birthday present ever. He ploughed through the stack as if his life depended on it. We'd never seen anybody put away that much, so quickly. Doug and I once got up to six each, but when offered, Johnny managed to fit in another three. Here was serious competition in the eating stakes I thought.

"Later, how about a stroll into town?" Dad suggested. "Then I thought you boys might like a milkshake, what do you say?" Doug and I nodded furiously as we stuffed our faces with the last of the syrupy pikelets and drank our orange juice. "That includes you, Johnny." He looked surprised, but nodded his thanks. Dad glanced at Nan again, who had a look of concern over Dad's proposal. "Boys when you're ready help Nan clear the table and then Johnny with his bed. After that, you can show him 'round the place. I've got a few telephone calls to make," Dad instructed, finishing with an exchange of looks with Nan.

After making the beds, we all went outside onto the back verandah where Doug had set up his train set. Johnny liked winding up the key in the locomotive then letting it run the length

of the track through the miniature town. I let him launch my balsa
wood glider off the verandah as well, then I'd retrieve it. Dad was
on the telephone for some time, so we got out our marbles to play
in the backyard. We thought everyone knew how to play marbles,
but Johnny had no idea. We had to show him how to play 'Bunny
Hole', but not for keeps this once. He preferred to hold the little
glass spheres up to the light and peer through their colours rather
than the game itself. Doug won, as usual.

It was after ten when the four of us started ambling up the street.
Johnny was lucky he didn't have shoes, because there was no way
Nan would have let him out of the house without them. We
stopped as Miss Bridget walked out onto her front verandah.

"Hello Johnny. Good to see you up and about. I'll be there at
two tomorrow, Harry," she called out as we moved on, Doug and
me in front, followed by Dad next to Johnny.

Most people's places we past, if they were in their front yards
or on their verandahs, airing rugs or bedding over the railings,
would give us a wave. There were others though who just looked
at us with a frozen expression. A few made the point of telling
their kids to 'come inside right this minute' once they saw our
group, even before we could get close enough to say 'G'day.'

Across the road up ahead, Doug and I saw Steve sitting on his
front steps. He was stroking and talking to his pet guinea pig in
his lap. Once he saw us his soft expression changed. He stopped
fondling the animal and dumped it back in its cage before running
up his verandah steps.

"Hey Dad, have a look what's comin' up the street," he called out. Doug and I stopped and so did Johnny. Mr Wood came onto his verandah unshaven and in a food-stained singlet with the newspaper in his hand.

"Don't stop boys, keep on walking," Dad directed. Mr Wood gave all of us the filthiest of looks.

"We don't want no Abos, or Abo lovers in this town McNally. Ya hearin' me?" he yelled out. I watched Johnny recoil a bit as soon as he heard the sound of Mr Wood's voice. We all looked to Dad.

"Move on," Dad urged as he ushered us, before replying to Mr Wood with the tipping of his hat and a neighbourly smile, "'Morning Bob," then walked on. That only seemed to get Mr Wood angrier. Steve moved the guinea pig's cage out of his way as he swooped down to the front gate.

"You'll be sorry McNally – you and yer family." Dad stopped in his tracks.

"Walk to the corner and wait for me. Walk. Now!"

Dad headed across the road to speak with Mr Wood. By this stage, Mrs Wood had heard the shouting and came out and down the first few front steps. She looked older than her years as she wrung her hands nervously.

"Bob, stop this," she called out as Doug and I grabbed Johnny by the arm to keep him moving along. He was shaking a bit.

"Go home Abo!" Mr Wood shouted in our direction.

"Yeah, Abo," echoed Steve.

We did as we were told, but only far enough up the street so that we could see and hear the exchange. Mr Wood opened his front gate then moved onto the grass verge as Dad approached.

"Bob, your ignorant racist taunts are one thing, but when you hurt an innocent young boy …"

"Who says? Where's yer proof?"

"Bob please," implored Mrs Wood. Mr Wood gave her a look that'd singe the hair off a rabbit and she withdrew.

"I know it was you. Or others like you," Dad stated calmly.

"You'd take a blackfella's word against mine? What did he tell ya then? Go on, what were his *exact* words?" he said with a sarcastic laugh.

Dad stood his ground, staring right into Mr Wood's face with one of those looks that made you feel he knew you were lying, and you knew he knew.

"S'pose it was me. An' I ain't admittin' nothin'-"

"Look at him. A defenceless … Why, he's not much older than young Steve here.

"You don't run this fuckin' town, McNally."

"Never said I did. Neither do you."

"There's plenty who think the same about 'em movin' in on us. We don't want no Abos … loit'rin' with intent. That's it, loit'rin' with intent. There'll be break ins and God knows what before ya know it, if we let them black buggers loose on our streets."

"I, like a lot of others, see no problem with law abiding people, walking our streets – regardless of colour." Dad started moving away with a dismissive look on his face that indicated he was wasting his time even talking to Mr Wood, who stood still for a bit, looking awkward, like he was struggling to think of something as a come back.

"Go on Dad, don't let him get off with sayin' all that," Steve urged.

"It's just I'd hate to see anythin' happen to you, or yer boys."

Dad stopped and went back.

"If anything happens to any of mine, or Johnny there, you'll have me to answer to. Except I won't come after you in a pack with a sugar sack and a whip. I'll have the law with me."

"It's just a friendly warnin'," Mr Wood offered with a grin.

"And I'm warning you. Keep your ugly opinions and your hands, to yourself."

"So now I'm ignorant and ugly. Ya here that Steveo? Just 'cause I don't live in no big house an' earn me livin' labourin' 'stead of some cushy doctor's job. An' it's my *right*, not to want no black or yeller shit walkin' our streets ... takin' over the town! Same goes for wogs." I could see Mr Wood moving closer to Dad, but Dad didn't move a muscle.

"Walk away, Dad," I warned under my breath.

❖

The next bit happened very quickly. We saw Mr Wood drop his newspaper then raise his fists, taking a boxer's stance. Doug seemed keen for something to happen, but I called out a bit louder.

"Walk away, Dad." He mustn't have heard me.

"Bob!" called Mrs Wood, timidly edging forward. But Mr Wood had up a full head of steam by now.

"Go get him Dad," encouraged Steve.

"Come on McNally, if ya think you're such a big man. Have a fuckin' go. Or do ya need the Sergeant to do yer fightin'? Come on, I fuckin' dare ya."

At around six feet, both he and Dad were of a similar height. Mr Wood was more muscular from all the labouring for the

Council, but had a big gut as well. Dad was in good nick though – lean but firm.

"Bob, violence never settles …" Dad had just begun, when out of nowhere, Mr Wood landed a right hand punch to the left side of Dad's head that sent his hat flying. Steve cheered his dad on.

It was only then that Dad put up his guard before landing a punch to Mr Wood's solar plexus. He followed it up with another quick left to the same spot, and then while Mr Wood was doubled over, Dad hit him under the chin with a right that sent him sprawling onto his back – out cold. I had to stop myself from cheering. Dad bent over and checked that Mr Wood was okay then slapped him gently about the face to bring him around. Steve raced over to his father, who was groggy but starting to sit up by this stage. Dad offered his hand, to help him to his feet. Mr Wood just glared at him, pushed his hand away and stumbled slightly as he got to his feet himself.

"Sorry. Now let that be an end to all this. Good morning Bob," Dad concluded. He picked up his hat, gave it a brush with his hand then tipped it to Mrs Wood before placing it on his head. He took a few deep breaths as he walked across the street to us. Doug and I finally managed to wipe the stunned looks off our faces. I pulled Doug around and got us walking back up the street with Johnny, acting like we'd seen nothing, as Dad crossed over to our side.

When he'd caught up to us, we just kept on walking like we were on some leisurely Sunday stroll. Dad put an arm around Johnny's shoulder. Doug and I were bursting to say something, but kept quiet. We had never, *ever* heard Dad raise his voice so strongly before, let alone get into a fight. He'd gone against his own words to us about fighting.

An explanation was due. We both waited.

"Everything okay Dad?" Doug prompted. I could have died. I held my breath in anticipation of Dad's reply.

"Yes Dougal." Enough said, we knew not to pursue the subject any further. As we continued on into town, I looked back to see Mr Wood arguing with his wife in their front yard. Steve stood alongside his Dad, yelling at her as well. Mr Wood finished the argument by slapping her hard across the face. She disappeared in tears up their front steps.

❖

Dad went into Renshaw's first. The three of us followed. The whole place smelt of his heavy-handed use of bay rum aftershave. He was serving someone else and didn't see us enter, so we just wandered around. When he was free, he came up to Dad.

"'Morning Harry, what can I do for you?"

"'Morning Sid. I'd like a dozen pair of 'Y' fronts to fit a boy about fourteen."

"Fourteen?"

"Johnny, come out here." Johnny appeared from behind a rack of coats. The colour drained from Mr Renshaw's face, as if he was going to faint. "And a pair of shoes and thongs." Where he'd normally talk Dad's ear off with his symptoms, trying to get a free consultation, it was clear Mr Renshaw was agitated about serving Johnny. Without a further word he quickly got the order together, keeping an eye out for any customers who might enter and see him fitting a black teenager.

"You better try the shoes on," instructed Dad, indicating for Johnny to take a seat. Mr Renshaw became very uneasy. "You have any old socks he could –?" Mr Renshaw quickly produced a mismatched pair he kept under the counter, for when anyone came in without socks to try on shoes. The shoes were a good fit. As Dad handed the socks back, Mr Renshaw began to stutter more than usual.

"No, you can k-keep them."

Dad looked him squarely in the eye.

"Thank you, but we couldn't," Dad answered politely but with a look that hadn't a trace of warmth. Mr Renshaw couldn't take the intensity of Dad's gaze, and turned away. "And you best give us a half a dozen shirts and socks in his size. Anything wrong, Sid?"

"N-nothing. N-n-nothing at all." Mr Renshaw spluttered as he saw Gwen Grady enter his shop. "W-w-won't be a m-minute, G-G-Gwen."

Mrs Grady just stood there in silence, observing the scene, with a look of outrage on her face, as if some stranger had just come up and pinched her on the bum. As the shirts were brought out and wrapped with the other things, Dad, flushed with victory over Mr Wood I guess, decided to tackle Mrs Grady's haughty demeanour head-on and introduced Johnny.

"Gwen, this is Johnny." Johnny gave a little nervous smile combined with a nod of acknowledgement.

"He's staying with us for the moment."

"Staying – with you. In the house. That's nice," she finished with a thin-lipped smile.

"'Til he fully recovers from the beating someone gave him. Johnny, show them your back." He did so, and for a moment they were lost for words as they winced at the sight before them.

"Of course you hear things, people will gossip, but that's terrible," she tut-tutted.

"Thanks son, you can put your shirt back on. Can you believe that in this day and age someone could do this to another human being?"

Dad settled the account and as we headed out the door, I heard Mrs Grady begin to natter with Mr Renshaw.

"A handout's one thing, but allowing them to stay in your *house* ..."

❖

The Parthenon milk bar was a totally different experience. Dad wasn't put off by the strange looks we got from two of the customers who got up and left without even finishing their food and drinks. He approached Mrs Pappas who was standing behind the counter.

"Eleni, will there be a problem of young Johnny here joining – ?" Before he could finish the question, Mrs Pappas interrupted, welcoming us all in with a wave of her hand. She let us pick whichever booth we wanted.

"I remember when I first come to Australie. 'Go home wog'. Please sit. Everyone welcome here."

While she filled our milkshake order, I flipped the pages over of our booth jukebox. Dad put in some coins and I picked one I knew he'd like. There were lots of strings and then Frank Sinatra started up with a slow 'Night and day, you are the one ...' Doug didn't want his turn.

"Just leave him be." Dad declared. "You pick another." So I

picked Bill Haley's *Rock Around the Clock*, and Johnny, who just pushed any button, came up with a band playing *Stardust*. My first choice ended up being not so good, as Dad went very quiet and distant until it finished while we slurped on our milkshakes. He'd settled for a short black from the strange espresso coffee machine that ground then bubbled and hissed, and some home made Greek shortbread.

After we'd finished, Dad called in to see Sergeant Farrar while we all waited outside. On our way home, Doug seemed still out of sorts, dragging his feet a bit behind the rest of us. I knew exactly what was on his mind.

As we walked, Johnny would stop every now and then and pick wildflowers that grew in clumps along the road until he had a good handful.

Mr Wood was lopping his trees when we went past his place, but on our side of the street. He didn't say anything or do anything, but I felt his eyes on us all the way home. I turned as I got inside our gate. Steve had joined his father in trying to stare us down. But I wasn't scared, not when I knew my dad had a knock out punch.

Nan was picking veggies from the garden for tea when we arrived home. Johnny presented her with his bouquet of flowers, his eyes warm with emotion. It was his way of saying thanks for her care of him during his recuperation. She kissed his cheek.

❖

We all went to bed early that night, ready for Sunday morning Mass. Dad had tried to get Doug to talk, but he remained sulky, hardly touching his tea. When Dad came in for 'lights out', Doug turned away on his side. Dad sat down at the foot of his bed.

"Got anything you want to talk about boys?" I shook my head.

"Doug?" He didn't answer.

"Let me explain about today."

"Are *you* going to Confession?" Doug finally demanded as he turned to face Dad.

"You think I should?"

"You're always tellin' us to walk away. Everyone at school thinks I'm chicken."

"Today I did something I'm not proud of. And if I could've walked away I would've. Fighting doesn't achieve anything, son. Bob Wood didn't give me a choice. I s'pose that's not altogether a satisfactory answer, but when there are important issues at stake, like people's right to live their life in peace, or threats against your family, well sometimes you have to speak up and take a stand. I still would've preferred to have talked it out with him, but as you saw, some people only know one way of resolving a disagreement – with their fists. And when that happens well, it is okay to defend yourself."

This got both our attention.

"Now before you two get all excited, I want you both to promise me you won't start fights and that you'll do your best to avoid them if you can think of another way out. Promise?" We both hesitated, looking at each other then answered simultaneously.

"Promise."

"Standing up for serious things, like today, and when you have no other choice but to defend yourself, is the only, and I mean the *only* time you might get into a bit of a scuffle. Not over some idiot calling you names. Having said that, I think it's time you both learnt the basics of self defence. Just so any schoolyard bullies will think twice before they push 'round the McNally boys."

He touched Doug's leg through the bedding. Great, I thought. Now we'll be just like the good guys in the pictures, flattening the baddies in the saloon and saving the town from the outlaw gang.

"We'll start tomorrow. Goodnight, boys," and he kissed us both on the forehead, before tucking us in.

"Goodnight, Dad," we replied. Before he got to the door he turned, smiled lovingly at us both then switched off the light.

We heard him go into Johnny's room. He talked for some time. I couldn't make out what he was saying through the door and we were both too sleepy to get up and listen. My straying thoughts before sleep were of Dad and John Wayne having a huge fight in a saloon. Dad won.

❖

I think Dad would've taken Johnny to church with us on Sunday and forced the issue of his right to be there as well, but when asked, Johnny didn't seem that keen anyway. He did join us in our boxing lesson with Dad afterwards, where we learnt the difference between a jab, a hook and an uppercut, as well as the importance of keeping your guard up. Dad partnered with Doug to demonstrate the punches to us. Johnny was my partner. It was all pretend boxing. Dad was teaching Johnny and me how to keep our guard up and protect our face, when Nan yelled out through the back screen door.

"When Jake la Motta and Sugar Ray Robinson have finished there, lunch is on the table."

It was shortly after this that Dad began his long campaign with the Shire Council to secure for our town a sports field. He believed that a sports field would help channel youthful energy away from bullying and other antisocial behaviour. He envisaged that fathers, instead of spending afternoons at the pubs could help train and referee the various sports. It would also relieve the boredom of living in a town with little to do beyond your own imagination. Everyone when approached by Dad agreed and signed his petition. It would be a long drawn out process with Council, but after a number of years of badgering from Dad we did get our very own sports field, complete with a modest spectator stand.

CHAPTER THIRTEEN

By two o'clock that same Sunday, neighbours from all over started coming onto the verandah. There was Mr and Mrs Symonds and Susan, the Smith's and Raymond from next door, Mr Chang and Shen, Miss Bridget, Mr Horan, Ned Spooner from *The Echo* and driving up in his police car, Sergeant Farrar. Johnny sat in the circle with the others. Dad stood behind him, his hands resting gently on his shoulders. Raymond, Shen, Doug and I sat in the jacaranda tree, our legs dangling over the platform.

"Thank you all for coming. For those of you who haven't met him, this is the boy I spoke to you about on the phone, Johnny August," Dad began. At that stage, our front gate opened and Miss Kitty entered. Everyone was as surprised as me to see her.

"Kitty, you came," smiled her sister, as Miss Kitty made her way onto the verandah. Both Mr Chang and Mr Symonds stood up to give her a seat. She quietly sat in Mr Chang's chair, looking out toward the jacaranda tree.

"It's good to see you, Kitty love," Nan whispered.

"Please, don't let me interrupt."

She bent her head forward as she removed her sunglasses. Her eyes, full of apprehension remained downcast flitting from side to side as she straightened her head. Her hair was pulled back tightly in a bun and she wore makeup to conceal her white skin and birthmark. She clasped her gloved hands in her lap. It was the first contact most people there had ever had with her, at least for a long while anyway. She looked scared and vulnerable, but determined to be there nonetheless. The boys couldn't take their eyes off her the whole time.

"G'day, Miss Kitty," I called out. She gave me a timid wave. I smiled back to let her know she had a friend on her side, as Dad continued.

"As I told you over the phone, Johnny doesn't know his father. He took off when he was a baby and his mother died after being hit by a car. He has no living relatives that he knows of, and walked a long way to get here from up north. Only to be set upon by a bunch of drunken thugs. I'm sorry, son. I know how going over things upsets you. He's trying to block things out of his mind which is understandable. Anyway, there appears little we can do about bringing the perpetrators of Johnny's injuries to justice," Dad cast an insinuating glance to the Sergeant.

"But we can do something for Johnny. Last night I talked over with him some possibilities. We could help him rebuild his camp, but as you can imagine, he's a little scared he might be set upon again. So with Mum's blessing, we're happy to provide a room in our house. Johnny indicated he'd prefer that, but that he wanted to work for board, not a handout. This to my mind speaks volumes for the boy's character. I asked you all here because I know you all to be decent people, who may be able to help. Sergeant, I know there's resistance by a lot of people to having Aborigines around town and in the shops. And I realise you're just doing your job by trying to keep them out of the main part of town to avoid any confrontation, however, the fact of the matter –"

"The fact of the matter, Harry, is a lot of people have had already, or fear they will have, things stolen from their houses or shops by them. There just isn't any work around for them. And I can sympathise with that. I can."

"Has anyone actually seen a particular Aborigine stealing, Sergeant? Have you arrested any?" queried Mr Symonds.

"No, but it's fairly obvious that –"

"Well Sergeant, surely then it's all unsubstantiated rumour. It could have been a white neighbour, a disgruntled white shopper or white kids, and the blacks are being used as scapegoats. Well couldn't it, if there's no proof?" asserted Ned Spooner.

"Gentlemen," Dad interrupted. "If I can get back to why we're here. Johnny, have you got that bit of paper? I want to read you all something." As Johnny handed over the tattered note, I noticed for the first time that Dad wasn't wearing his wedding ring. Dad read the note out and as he did so, all eyes looked toward Johnny.

"Here's a boy, if he was white would be in school. I'm hoping that between us we can at least find enough work for him, so that he can support himself and not be seen as a vagrant or threat to anyone. I'm prepared to pay him to do my hedges, cut my lawns and chop the wood on a regular basis." Dad searched around the group for someone to match his offer. Ned Spooner kept making notes.

"I'm getting too stiff to do gardening, and we could use someone who'll mow the lawns and chop the firewood as well," offered Miss Bridget.

"And the house could use a couple of coats of paint inside and out," added Miss Kitty in a jittery rush, hoping for and receiving Miss Bridget's smile of approval as she spoke.

"I think we've all got chores 'round the house for an eager lad," Mr Smith threw in. It was greeted by a lot of "yeses" and "mmms". Mrs Symonds whispered something to her husband.

"The missus was saying Harry, you've already got two boys to look after. What I mean is, we've got Esme's mum's old downstairs flat going to waste. We'd happily let young Johnny here stay with us, as a boarder – rent free. A few chores about the place will be payment enough."

"Well, what do you think?" Dad asked Johnny who gingerly agreed with a nod. Mrs Symonds looked on the verge of tears, even though she seemed very happy. Mr Symonds squeezed her hand.

"I need someone to help with new fences, if I'm ever going to get the missus off me back," smiled Mr Smith. "And as bank manager, I'm prepared to open up an account in Johnny's name so that he can deposit his earnings. I'll kick it off with two pounds." This was a very generous gift and it registered with those adults present as they looked about at one another.

"I give five shillings too," volunteered Mr Chang.

"Well Sergeant?" Dad asked.

"I can't see anyone having any grounds to object to the young bloke's presence in town, if he's employed and banking money. However, you'll always get those who just don't like blacks. You can't change people's way of thinking."

"Some folks always look to blame others when things aren't going their way. They look around to take it out on others less able to fight back – just like in the Depression. And some of us here remember that," Nan contributed.

"There's a bigger issue here, Sergeant," began Ned Spooner. "We're not talking about a theft. We're talking about a person, in this case a boy, being savagely beaten. What would the reaction of the good people of this town be if he was theirs? If he was white? You'd be out there interviewing likely suspects and maybe making an arrest or two." Sergeant Farrar was feeling uncomfortable and paced up and down on the spot several times. Everyone waited for his response.

"We need proof before we make any accusations, and unfortunately there is none, Ned. Look everyone, I'm on your side believe me, but it isn't easy being the only cop in town either – trying to keep law an' order and a lid on things. Sometimes it's best to let people blow off steam then move 'em on, just to keep the peace."

"This isn't some Saturd'y arvo dust-up at the pub, the lad's been beaten to within an inch of his life," argued Ned Spooner. Johnny looked like he wanted to take flight. Dad gave him a reassuring rub on his shoulder and he settled.

"The boy was ambushed. And from what I could make out from him, he didn't see who it was because they'd shoved a sugar bag over his head. We need proof before we start arresting people based purely on assumptions and then –" the Sergeant pointed out as Ned Spooner started talking over him.

"Exactly my point. We also need proof before we go around accusing the Aborigines for all the stealing in town. People see them with no belongings as such and immediately presume that they must be doing the stealing. If we have no proof, it's all assumptions and rumour. I bet half of what you hear is made-up anyway. But one thing we know for sure, no black man would do to another black man what's been done to this lad – for no reason."

"I'm sorry. All this is my fault. If only I could have made out their faces through the dust, but they were gone and far away by the time I got to him. But they were definitely white," an upset Miss Bridget tried to explain.

"Bloody cowards," interjected Mr Symonds.

"Johnny's confirmed Miss Walshe's suggestion, indicating that it was more than one, maybe three or four. What we don't need is different groups goin' off at each other 'cause they think so and so is responsible, and causin' more trouble. If there is any trouble, leave it up to me to settle. Don't go takin' the law into yer own hands," Sergeant Farrar emphasised as he looked around the group. "I won't stand for no breakin' of the law, and that applies to you as well Ned." He looked at Johnny, before putting his hat back on to leave.

"However," he started up again, "if you wish to write an article about this cowardly incident, by assailants unknown, and how these people here have responded in a positive way, that sort of action I would fully support. It'll highlight the matter, and hopefully, reach out to people's better side, so that it never happens again. Anyways, I've got police work to do."

Everyone sat there thinking for a moment, as Sergeant Farrar left and drove off. We remained quiet in the tree, waiting to see what would happen next. Eventually everyone seated stood up, and Johnny went around and shook their hands as a thank you gesture. His expressive face conveyed his pleasure at their show of support. Those left on the verandah then came up to Miss Kitty, including Mr Chang, and started talking to her like an old friend.

"I hope we see more of each other after this, Kitty," expressed Mrs Symonds and her wishes were seconded by the group. Miss Kitty seemed overwhelmed by the response.

"It was important for me to be here – for this lovely young man." She took both his hands in hers. "I know what it is like to be singled out and pointed at. I wouldn't want that to happen to anyone else. Never let anyone drive you away."

People started to make their way down the verandah steps and head on home. Dad moved to have a quiet word with Susan at the end of the verandah. While Shen and Raymond used the rope ladder, Doug slid down the tree so quickly he banged into Mr Chang.

"Dougal! Slow down! You could've knocked Mr Chang over," Dad reprimanded. I was still on my way down as Miss Kitty past by. She looked up at me and smiled, as she put on her sunglasses and followed her sister out through the front gate. I smiled back.

"Bye Miss Kitty," I called as I reached the ground.

When it was just Dad, Nan, Johnny, Doug and me left on the verandah, I mentioned to Dad as we helped him put the chairs back inside, that I really didn't want to see Johnny go.

"He's not going away, just across the street. You'll still see him as often as you wish." I felt a bit better. "Maybe you could still have a couple of meals here, eh Nan?"

"You're always welcome, ya know that," Nan indicated cheerily.

"When's he have to go?" asked Doug.

"That's up to the Symonds. Whenever they get the flat set up, I guess," Dad reasoned.

Doug gave me a thump on the arm then took off around the back.

"Owwh. Come on Johnny, we'll get him." And the two of us shot around the other side of the house.

"Play nicely you lot. No rough stuff," Nan called out after us.

❖

Ned Spooner reported Johnny's beating in *The Echo* under the heading COWARDLY ATTACK ON TEENAGER ENDS WELL. The article went into detail and only near the end mentioned that Johnny was of Aboriginal background. It spoke about tolerance and having respect for every person in the community regardless of colour or other differences and that the men who committed the crime were no better than a pack of wild dogs. It ended with 'Police have several leads and are conducting ongoing inquiries.' Those who hadn't already heard about the attack via Mrs Grady's grapevine, greeted the article with mixed response. On the whole though, most people were outraged that this could happen to anyone in the community, 'right under our very noses.'

Within a few weeks, Mr Symonds had repainted the downstairs flat and Mrs Symonds had put up new curtains. Johnny moved in on a Sunday and insisted he start doing chores around their house on the Monday. Late the following Saturday night the Symonds' place was pelted with a dozen or so rotten eggs from two speeding cars.

In the weeks prior to him moving across the road, a roster was drawn up between the neighbours. Over the next few months Johnny would be doing lawns and general gardening some days with special jobs like fence repairs and painting the Walshe sisters' house in between. Dad had taught him basic handyman skills and the use of Poppie's tools, allowing him to use them when he wanted, as long as he took good care of them. If he was stuck on anything, all he had to do was let Dad or Mr Symonds know and they'd give him a hand.

It struck me that Doug and I hadn't done anything for Johnny. I suggested we give him some of our toys, as we had heaps. So when he went over the road with his belongings, he also took with him two Airfix planes on stands, some metal toy soldiers, the wind-up train set he liked which we rarely played with now, as well as a selection of our marbles.

He didn't work weekends, which meant we had an extra playmate and another member for the cricket team. He became our best fieldsman and wasn't bad at bowling either. Nan arranged with Mrs Symonds for Johnny to come over for tea once a week and lunch Saturday followed by our regular saunter up town with Dad for milkshakes.

CHAPTER FOURTEEN

The incident with Mr Elliott and the mulberries and the egging of the Symonds house was not to be the last time some people expressed their dislike at having Johnny living in town. He still got hateful looks and called names from some passers-by. Others turned their backs on him in the street or spat in the dirt as he passed. Looking back, their behaviour was based not only on misconceptions and ignorance, just as Dad had said, but also fear. Fear perhaps that their jobs might be taken over by someone more willing to put in a harder day's work than themselves.

Sergeant Farrar was also right. Forgetting they were just people, like all of us, some folks just really didn't like Aborigines, for whatever reason. But as Dad told us many times, "You can't tell people how to live their lives. You can only live yours and hopefully set a good example." I wondered at the time how these same people would feel if they were Johnny – no mother or father or immediate relatives you know of. You're all alone in the world. And on top of that, the frustration over the fact you can't speak to express how you feel.

Thankfully there were others in the community who became more embracing and tolerant over time. As word spread that he was gainfully employed and had the support of a lot of us, his presence in town if not altogether accepted, became less of a threat.

❖

On Dad's advice Johnny always made sure he saw the owner of the house or property each day before he started his work and not just to wander in and get started. That way, no one could ever accuse him of being where he shouldn't. He also tried to stay in sight at all times, so that there couldn't be a repeat of the beating. If he felt someone was fixing to harm him, at the first sign of any trouble, he was to run as fast as he could home, or to our place, or the police station. I figured Johnny had the best punch out of the three of us now anyway, and it'd be a pretty silly bloke who picked on him.

Dad helped Johnny with the preparation of the Walshe place for painting but let him apply the primer and two coats of paint by himself on the outside as well as all the interior work. The Walshe sisters both praised his efforts saying it was the best their house had looked for a long while. Everyday during his time there, Miss Kitty made him lunch and they ate together in the kitchen. She'd play the piano for him as well. When I asked him about what he thought of her skin and the red mark on her face, he gave a nonchalant shrug of his shoulders.

"Yeah, so what," I agreed.

❖

With his weekends free, I took it upon myself to give Johnny an education. I thought that if he couldn't say what he wanted, he would at least be able to write it down in a note. Unlike Honey, I knew he wouldn't sleep through class and would be eager to learn. On the shed wall I began writing out the alphabet in capitals in chalk, then under each letter, the same in lower case. I got to 'C' before Johnny stood and held his hand out. I was a little perplexed but handed over the chalk. Not only did he complete the whole alphabet, but his letters were more perfectly formed. He smiled as he handed back the chalk.

"You've been to school." He shook his head then opened his hands up like the pages of a book then using his index finger, tapped on one of his opened hands.

"You learnt from books?" He nodded in agreement. "From who?" He drew both his hands down the side of his head to his shoulders, indicating a veil before clasping them in prayer in front of his chest. "Nuns. A nun." He smiled. "So *you* wrote that note. I just assumed … Well, don't I feel foolish. You can write better than me. How's yer arithmetic then?" I challenged in an effort to regain some face. He wrinkled up his nose. I started writing up some basic sums on the wall. He was so quick, picking up another piece of chalk he completed all the calculations I threw at him. In retrospect, how patronising of me, the whole exercise – presuming he was uneducated just from my perception of what his background might have been and the fact he couldn't talk. At an appropriate lull in our work I asked him,

"Johnny, I know you have an idea who beat you, don't you?" Write a name. I know you know." The colour drained from his face as I offered him the chalk. He wouldn't take it. "It was Bob

Wood, wasn't it?" He didn't move. A moment passed then he took the chalk from my hands. *Telling won't change what happened*, he wrote. After letting me read it he immediately rubbed it from the wall. "Can I tell Dad?" He shook his head. I honoured his wishes and let it pass.

❖

One of the first things we did together was to work out a new note of introduction in Johnny's handwriting for any potential clients.

"I think we should start with your name again and your address." He began writing his note up on the wall. "Then what jobs you can do, next. What do you think?" He gave a gentle wobble of his head in agreement. We discussed its contents then he'd write down what he thought was best. We'd work out between us the spelling of any difficult words. Most people knew who he was by sight and that he couldn't talk, so we left that bit out from his original note he'd presented to Dad .

"Then there's payment. Mmm. That depends on the job really, doesn't it? We could say you could work out a price, I guess." It took a couple of attempts to get it just right, but the final note looked really good. What we finished up with was:

My name is Johnny August. I live at 55 Main Street. Do you need any mowing, gardening, wood chopping, painting, fencing or any other odd jobs done? If so, we can work out a price and time. Thank you.

When we showed Johnny's completed handwritten note to Dad, he thought it was a terrific idea and that his printing was excellent. Johnny's pride registered in his expressive eyes and the broadest of grins.

❖

To begin with, Mr Symonds lined up his jobs and worked out costs and payment details so that he didn't have to worry about money and banking. In time he showed Johnny how to do his own accounts and look after his banking himself. With the Symonds providing free board, Johnny was steadily growing his savings, keeping out only a little for weekly incidentals.

Later, he produced another handwritten note and gave it to Dad. He read it to himself. He paused before he spoke.

"Thank you, Johnny. That's lovely."

"What's it say?" Doug and I pestered.

"Do you mind?" Dad asked of Johnny. He gave a small shake of his head. Doug and I read it out aloud together.

"Dear Sir I am very grateful for you and Mr and Mrs Symonds. I have a new mother and two new fathers now. I am very happy. Johnny."

"It's a very touching note. I shall treasure it always." With that Dad folded it up and put it in his top pocket, later to be placed in his Sunday Bible. He finished by putting an arm around Johnny's shoulder and giving him a good squeeze.

❖

Johnny was finding heaps of work and was able to get about without any hassles. The only incident that did occur was almost comical in its unfolding. It was a late Friday afternoon and Johnny was walking beside me up our street after finishing work for the day. A ute came down the road from town, did a U-turn then pulled up outside Mr Wood's place. Bob Wood stumbled out of the passenger's seat just as we were passing on the other side of the road. Once the car took off we could see that he was blind drunk. He was carrying a meat tray he'd won in the pub raffle and was weaving towards his front gate when he saw us.

"Don't ya get the message, ya black bastard? We don't want ya here. So bloody piss off!"

He was swaying from side to side like a flagpole in a strong wind. The next thing we saw was him wobbling about before falling over his closed front gate. Chops and sausages became airborne. We couldn't help but crack up. Johnny's hoarse, more rasping of air than a laugh, made me laugh even more, so much so I thought I'd wet myself.

Mr Wood struggled to get to his feet. He fell over twice before crawling around on all fours gathering the meat and replacing it on the tray. He managed to stagger to the base of his front steps and called out to his wife before collapsing unconscious backwards to the ground. Mrs Wood and Steve both came outside. She pulled the remains of his pay packet from his top pocket while Steve picked up the meat tray. They headed back inside, leaving him where he fell to sleep it off.

❖

The rain that began to fall that early October would keep up, on and off, through to the New Year and made the town look fresh and clean. Buds began to appear among the lacy green foliage of the jacaranda. By late October it would be a mass of purple once again. The creek was now full and the whole town and surrounds were green with spring and the colour of flowers. Magpies, sulphur crested cockatoos, kookaburras and other birds, filled the trees and sang their thanks for the spring rain as well.

Gone was the thin powdering of dust that seemed to get in everywhere and settle over everything. For once there was the absence of shop owners with millet brooms in hand, daily sweeping away the dust from their wooden verandahs. No one complained about the wet, because in no time we all knew we'd be back to dry hot days with no sign of rain at all on the horizon. With the rise in the creek water level, after school and weekends most kids, us included, would pick a favourite spot along the creek and just muck about or go swimming in the nuddy with your mates.

CHAPTER FIFTEEN

Dad didn't have tea with us one particular Saturday night. He got himself all spruced up in one of his suits while we were eating.

"Where are you going?" I asked as I ate my mashed sweet potato.

"Out."

"But where?" Doug asked.

"Just out."

"But where's out?" I pushed further.

"What is this, the thoid degree?" Dad sounded like an American gangster in the pictures, acting upset, but really just mucking around. "If you must know, I'm going to the dance in town."

"Who with?" Doug and I asked together.

"Listen you two, just eat yer tea and leave yer father be," instructed Nan.

Dad smiled and poked his tongue out at us when Nan wasn't looking, then proceeded to polish up his good shoes. We found out soon enough, because half an hour later, Susan knocked at the door. She was wearing a Schiaparelli-pink dress all stuck out with rope petticoats, black high heels and matching handbag. She looked like a princess, with her hair piled up on her head in a French roll. All done up she looked so different to the Susan Dad drove to work. Doug and I just looked at her with our mouths open.

"You two catchin' flies again?" Nan directed at Doug and me. Susan smiled.

"Oh hi," Doug said in passing, feigning disinterest.

"Look at you. Pretty as a picture in that dress," Nan gushed.

"Beautiful," I added. Doug felt so too, I knew, but he wasn't about to reveal his emotions.

"You certainly are," smiled Dad.

"This old thing? Bought it ages ago for a dance at the Sydney Trocadero."

"Well it's lovely. Really suits you that colour. Now you two head off, I'll see these two villains get to bed at the right time," offered Nan. Dad got his car keys and was about to leave.

"It's such a lovely night, let's walk," Susan suggested. Doug and I waved them off from the verandah.

"Dad's got a girlfriend, ewwh," I whispered to Doug.

"Ewwh, yerself," he mimicked before hitting me hard on the arm and running inside, leaving the screen door to slam. I ran after him and was close enough to give him a kick up the bum when Nan yelled out.

"You two aren't too old for me ta get out the wooden spoon to in a minute. And stop bangin' that bleedin' door." We both laughed, but not so that she could hear us, because we knew by now it was an empty threat. We wrestled in our room instead.

The rule was, if your shoulders got pinned to the floor you were 'held'. The winner was the one who successfully held the other to a count of three, two times out of three. We got to one each, and then Doug won the last. He pinned my shoulders to the ground with his knees as he sat on my chest. Then he leaned forward and held my head on either side with his hands so that I couldn't move. While in this position, he worked up this big gob and let it just ooze out of his mouth. I closed my mouth and eyes as tight as I could as it stretched to its limit before splattering on my face. I was mad, but didn't let on. I just wiped my face on my shirt and plotted my revenge.

I waited until he was asleep then crept to the side of his bed, pulled down the back of my pyjama pants and dropped a big smelly fart before jumping back into my bed, looking like I was asleep, but with my eyes all squinted up to see. It was loud and foul smelling enough to wake Doug up. He sat up all groggy and half asleep, then collapsed back onto his pillow. I kept my hand pressed over my mouth to muffle a laugh.

❖

I was still awake when Dad got home from the dance and wandered into his room.

"What are you doing up?"

"Couldn't sleep." I sat on the bed while he got changed. "Did you have tea at Shen's?"

"No, we went to La Roma and had pizza and spaghetti instead."

"Is she a good dancer?"

"Very good. And a lovely person as well."

"You gonna marry her?"

"Hey hold on matey, we've only just had dinner and a dance – that's all."

"You like her better than our mother?" Dad finished putting on his pyjamas then sat on the bed next to me, placing an arm around my shoulder.

"Susan is very different to your mother. There was a time when your mother and I first met, well, we were very much in love. We got married, and had you two boys, out of that love. But sometimes, people don't always stay in love. And that's why they get a divorce."

"They're not wedlocked any more. Can they marry someone else?"

"Legally, yes. If they wish."

"I'll always love you and Nan."

"And I'll always love you," he said in his soft reassuring voice.

"Dad, can I sleep in your bed tonight?" For a second, it looked like he was going to tell me I was too old for that and to go back to my own bed.

"Sure, hop in." He turned out the bedside lamp and I snuggled up to him.

"Doug won't let me get in with him anymore."

"Well, I guess he doesn't need a cuddle as much as me these days." We lay there for a few minutes as I got up the courage to ask what was on my mind.

"How did you and ...?" The word 'Mum' wouldn't leave my lips.

"Your mother?"

"How did you meet? At a dance like Nan and Poppie?"

"No." He took a deep breath. A moment passed. "Well, I'd just got back from the War …" I could feel he was finding it hard to talk about these things, but I wanted to know. He paused again to compose himself then continued.

"I wasn't in good shape I guess. Not for years. Not injured or anything, but some of the things you see in battle never really leave you and –"

"Like your friend Girra dying."

"Yes. And other things. Anyway when I got back to Sydney, I just felt I couldn't come back to Poppie's motor shop. So I decided to take up a scholarship I'd won before and go to university. Your mother worked as a barmaid at the pub nearby. We hit it off and one thing led to another and we got married. Then after a year, you two came along."

"Does everybody have to get married, 'cause Doug says he's never going to, and never going to have children, neither?" Dad stayed quiet for a while.

"Well, it's a long ways off yet. He might change his mind."

"Miss Kitty and Miss Bridget aren't married."

"Not everyone gets married. Not everyone meets someone they want to marry."

"If Miss Kitty didn't have that mark on her face, do you think she might have got married and had kids?"

"Even with that mark, Miss Kitty is beautiful – on the inside as well. People tend to only see the outside and make a judgement, never taking the time to learn how the person really is – on the inside. If people had've done that with Miss Kitty, she would most certainly have met someone and married, I'm sure."

"I like her, she's nice." I paused in thought. "Why didn't Miss

Bridget get married then?"

"Aren't you full of questions. Well, from what I understand, she was engaged once, but her fiancé died in a farm accident. Some people never get over the loss of a loved one."

"Nan still misses Poppie. She told me."

"She'll never forget Poppie, just like all of us. But don't worry, your Nan's strong. She believes in just getting on with it. And she's right. Now, you still want to stay here with me tonight, or feel you could go back to your own bed?"

"I'd like to stay here in the big bed."

"Alright, but get some sleep. Goodnight, son."

"Goodnight Dad. I love you."

"I love you too, mate." He kissed my forehead. I fell easily asleep tucked under his arm.

Chapter Sixteen

I seemed to spend more and more time with Johnny. It became so I'd rarely see Doug after school or most of the weekend. He was usually off riding his bike by himself or else playing games with Barry. He started to withdraw into himself. I'd only really see him around mealtimes.

Johnny would take me, and sometimes Snotty and Raymond or Shen, off into the bush and show us all these things only an Aborigine would know. Things like which berries and parts of plants you could eat, how to start a fire and eating ants and witchetty grubs he'd dig up from under the ground. The grubs were like large white caterpillars with yellowy heads. Johnny rolled them in the hot ashes of the fire to cook them. About three quarters of an inch thick and three inches long, they tasted like eggs and at other times like fish or mussels – once you got the nerve to chew them. Snotty spewed his up, but Raymond and I managed to keep ours down. I'd never seen let alone tasted anything like it before.

"Imagine the mess they'd make if a heap of 'em got loose in Nan's veggie patch," I wondered.

"Nah. They live underground. They mustn't like the taste of vegies either, like me," Snotty said with a grin followed by a wipe of his snotty nose on his bear arm.

When we went with Johnny, we'd all wait until we were out of sight then take off our shoes and socks and hide them somewhere, only to put them back on when we were going back home. It felt great, the dried grass crackling under our feet and the warmth of the red earth between our toes.

He even showed us how to catch and cook fish, using a spear. The creek was flowing enough to have fish in it, and on different days we took turns to try and spear a fish. Johnny could do it in one go, but us boys took ages to catch even the smallest ones. Then we'd cook them on a fire. Johnny showed us how to start one using a stick you spin between your hands while its point rested on a piece of wood. The friction would start a smoulder, which when dried leaves and bark from the paper bark tree were placed on top, turned to smoke then flame. Raymond reckoned it'd be quicker using the lenses in his glasses and the rays of the sun but the rest of us liked the traditional way.

I felt like a real Aboriginal bushman, cooking the fish I caught, on a stick, in the flames of a fire I helped make. Doug couldn't do that. I tried to tell him about our adventures, especially the eating of the witchetty grub and making the fire. He wasn't that interested, so I just left it.

Another time, while Doug was off somewhere with Barry I got Nan's permission to go with Johnny all day. He told us he was going to show us something exciting. He led Raymond, Snotty, Shen and me off along the creek bank where we met up with a couple of his Aboriginal mates tending a fire over an open pit. Beside them was a dead kangaroo with a single spear hole in its neck. We all stripped down to our shorts and went barefoot like Johnny and his mob and sat there spellbound as Johnny helped with the methodical ritual of preparing the animal for eating.

First the fur was singed off in the flames. When the carcass started to swell, the kangaroo was then gutted. They did this by cutting a hole in the skin on the gut, taking all the innards out then cutting the abdomen open and cleaning it with water from the creek. The sight of all the insides being pulled out made me a bit squeamish at first, but it passed.

Then Johnny got a hard stick and used it like a big skewer to stitch the skin together. The tail and feet were then removed and placed with the kangaroo carcass onto the hot coals in the pit. More coals were placed on top and the whole thing covered over with soil.

While the kangaroo cooked we all just mucked around in the creek before ripping off some bark from the paperbark trees and taking it back to the fire. Johnny and his mates uncovered and removed the cooked kangaroo with sticks. Using the paperbark as mats Johnny proceeded to cut the animal up. Snotty and Raymond couldn't even bear to watch. Shen was alright with it though.

Once dissected, we all chose a cut and started eating. It was underdone to my liking but still tasted great, like really strong flavoured mutton or venison. We washed it all down with a cup of strong black tea and flat flour and water johnnycakes cooked in the ashes of the fire. After we'd eaten his mates started practising their dancing for a big ceremony that was coming up for them. They danced around imitating various animals, stirring up the dust as they stomped about. Us boys were enthralled and clapped along to the beat of their feet on the ground. The remainder of the kangaroo was wrapped up and taken back by Johnny's mates to feed the rest of their mob.

All dressed again and on our way home, the four of us told Johnny that the day was the biggest adventure we had ever been on. He looked pretty chuffed with himself. Dad and Nan were impressed as well. Nan said she'd often had kangaroo tail soup when they had the farm. Doug listened but didn't seem to care one way or the other.

In bed that night waiting for sleep, I decided I'd had enough of Doug and his moods. I got up and went over to him. I asked him straight out,

"Doug, what's up? You never want to hang 'round with Johnny and me. Why?"

"What's the use? Ya start to like someone and then they're taken from ya. An' yer left to get over it."

"Johnny's not like our mother. He's here to stay," I offered, touching him gently on the back with my hand. Doug turned, punched me in the abdomen then got up and went over to the window and out, to seek solace on our platform in the jacaranda tree.

"Shut up! She's nothin' to me," he yelled as he went.

"Just let him be for the time being," Dad said, sticking his head around the door. He must have heard us talking as he passed our open door.

Doug, in time, resumed a type of friendship with Johnny and would come away with us every now and then, but there was always an emotional distance between them. It would apply to the girls he would meet later on as well. Things would be going well between them until they wanted a serious commitment. Doug would never again risk his heart to another. Sad, but that was Doug and Doug's decision.

❖

In the playground that Monday morning before school Steve overheard me telling some mates the news of our adventures with Johnny. He yelled out to me, just to impress his mates.

"We'd all be better off if he hadda carked it. One less boong." Then he laughed.

What he said was disgusting and cruel. I started towards him. My blood was on the rise. I could feel my face going red with rage. We stood there toe to toe. My legs were shaking as I waited for him to start it and throw the first punch, so that I could block it then fire off a punch myself. I wasn't any prize fighter, but by now, I thought I could get in a solid punch or two. I stared as menacingly as I could into his face.

He was sporting the remains of a black eye. I remembered Nan saying about the apple not falling far from the tree and thinking that Steve was just like his dad, all angry and ugly inside – and that was sad really. His dad could've given him that black eye I speculated. I wondered what it must be like for Steve and his mum, living with his dad.

Something happened as I looked him in the eye. My hatred

toward him vanished. Somehow I felt … sorry for Steve.

A self-conscious almost wavering look came over his face. He must've sensed what I was thinking. Then not wanting to show any sign of weakness in front of his gang, quickly changed his expression back to a scowl before stepping out of my face and calling to his mates.

"Come on, let's go," and he just walked away. I turned to find Doug and Snotty were right behind me, to back me up. Doug placed his hand on my shoulder as if to say, 'Good on ya' and that we were still mates – mates, twins, but different. And that was okay too.

CHAPTER SEVENTEEN

One day after school, I was just about out our gate and on the way to see if Johnny was home from work, when Miss Kitty called me over to the side fence. Her face was fully made up.

"Pat, do you think you could do me a favour?"

"Sure, what is it?" She drew a deep breath.

"I've got some shopping I –"

"No worries. Give us the money and I'll get it for –"

"No. I want to get it. Will you come with me? I'm a bit nervous." Her eyes searched my face.

"Sure." I took her basket and we strolled slowly up the street. Everyone we met on the way who had known her long ago was surprised at first, but said how good it was to see her about again. She took in the smallest details of the scenery as we went. Kells' Butchery was first, with a half a pound of blade steak, followed by the Green's for some milk and groceries. The reward for my companionship was a penny's worth of broken biscuits. Mr Green allowed me to serve myself from the broken biscuit tin at the end of the wall of rectangular biscuit tins stacked on their sides. I got as many different types as I knew the penny would stretch. Meanwhile, Miss Kitty had handed him her list of items. Mr Green bunged it on a bit heavy though, even more than normal for Miss Kitty as he set about filling her order.

"A proper lady like yourself is a welcome sight in this establishment Miss Walshe. You've no idea the likes of them that tries to come through them doors. I like to think I'm a Christian man, but I draw the line at vagrants and them that just wanna nick stuff when yer back's turned."

"That's terrible. How's Mrs Green?"

"She's well." But Mr Green had something on his mind and Miss Kitty was gonna hear it, whether she liked it or not.

"This town Miss Walshe is goin' to rack an' ruin. Rack an' ruin. Good Christian folk like you and I are going the way of the dinosaur. You're lucky you've been holed up in that house of yours all them years. The changes I've seen. Why just this morning mind, I'm going out the front to bring in the milk delivery, an' here's these two skinny piccaninnies, boy and a girl, couldn't be more than five or six, finishing off a pint each! Can you believe it?"

"Mr Green – " she tried to interrupt, as he just continued to rattle on over her.

"As brazen as all get out, laughing to themselves as they did it. I grabbed me broom and managed to sneak up on 'em from behind and give the girl a good crack on the head with the handle before they could run away – "

"Mr Green."

"Warned them that if I catch 'em at it again, they'd go to gaol. Two smashed bottles I had to clean up mind, but they'll think twice before doing that again. Then there's that whole mob of 'em been moved into the old Hudson place. All done out by the Government – fresh paint an' all. We're stuck with the bloody lot of 'em. Anything else I can help you with while you're here?"

"No. Thank you."

"I'll just put that on your sister's account then shall I?" he finished, smiling.

"No, I'll pay for it now." She hadn't flinched throughout his speech, just let him go on, as he tallied the purchases. "And I'll finalise our account as well," she added calmly.

"End of the month'll be fine."

"I'll pay it now. You see, my sister and I won't be shopping here any longer."

"Selling up?"

"No."

"But ... Have I done anything to offend you?" Miss Kitty remained unruffled.

"Mr Green, it's people like you, with your mean-spirited, bigoted outlook, that offend all mankind."

He was dumbstruck. I couldn't believe it either. His jaw dropped open and a sheen of perspiration broke out on his bald head. She calmly took the account from him, checked its accuracy then paid it. As she did so, her voice rose in volume.

"Did it *ever* occur to you that your milk might have been the *only* nourishment they've had? That they were *forced* to steal, to survive? And you call yourself a Christian. You could have *killed* that little girl. Here, that's for their two bottles of milk!" She slammed the extra coins on the counter. I just picked up her basket from the counter and followed as she headed out the door, thumping her heels into the wooden floor as she went.

Miss Kitty muttered to herself most of the way home.

"Don't go gettin' yerself all upset Miss Kitty. He's always steamed up over something."

"The sanctimonious little twirp. Like to see how *he'd* feel if the shoe was on the other foot. Whew. Come on, I think we both could do with a cuppa, eh Pat?" She smiled down at me as she took the basket from my hands.

"You should be runnin' for Council, Miss Kitty."

"Me? Too honest. I'd have 'em all booted out." She let out a hearty laugh. I think she enjoyed telling Mr Green off.

We had our cup of tea and some of the broken biscuits, on the front verandah. We talked about the weather and school, then she gave me the news that a relatively new John Wayne picture was coming to town in a few weeks. She'd read in *The Echo* that it was only a couple of years old.

"*The Searchers*. Didn't say what it was about. Probably a western. I used to love them the most as a child. Do you like westerns?"

"Sure do. I'll remind Dad." I waited then asked what was on my mind, "Nan says neither of you two've been married and..." I stopped, thinking it was none of my business.

"And?"

"And Dad says people just looked at that mark on your face and never bothered to get to know you. That's not nice."

"Your dad's almost right." She placed her cup down on the saucer, letting her thoughts flow back to the past. "When I was young, I was good at riding horses – as good as any boy. Won sashes and everything. I wore the makeup to hide my shame, so it didn't matter as much. There was one boy, not from 'round these parts. His name was Kevin. Tall and handsome with the sweetest smile, bit like yours. We met at a gymkhana. His horse was a brumby he'd broken in himself. From the very moment I saw him, I liked him. He was different. No sly jokes about my appearance behind his hand, like the others. For him I didn't have to wear the mask. He loved me for me. And we fell madly in love. I was seventeen. We'd meet in secret and go riding, or swimming in the creek together. But nowhere where anyone would see us."

"Why?"

"Father wouldn't have approved. One day, someone must have seen us together and told Father. No matter how much I swore my love for Kevin, it didn't matter. I was locked in my room while Father and some other men went out to find him. The very first chance I got, I snuck out of the house after they'd all gone to bed and rode off to be with him." As she stared into middle distance, her eyes slowly began to fill with tears.

"Funny. I've never talked about this to anyone except Biddy, before today."

"Did you find him?"

"What? No. No, I learnt from his friends at his camp that he'd been beaten, then put on his horse and told never to show his face 'round here again or they'd kill him. I never saw him again. I don't blame him. He was only seventeen himself. And scared I guess."

"I don't understand. Why didn't you take him to meet your parents? Let them get to know him. Then they might have let you get married." She blew her nose then took a long sip of her lemon tea.

"There was no way that was going to happen. You see Kevin

was an Aborigine – a full blood like Johnny. And like today, white folks just didn't want anything to do with them, let alone let their daughter marry one. We talked about eloping once. I was going to climb down that lattice and he'd be there at the bottom with his horse and we'd ride off together." She fell silent. I sat there for a bit, picking at the icing on a broken iced vovo biscuit.

"What *did* you say to your dad?"

"I didn't argue. In those days, you obeyed, or else copped a beating yourself. But we didn't speak that much after that. I stayed home more and more until I just didn't want to face the world. I became known as Poor Kitty, like the 'poor' was a part of my name. Visitors to the house would whisper thinking I couldn't hear. 'How's Poor Kitty?' they'd ask. It wasn't long after that Mother became bedridden, then later Father. So it was easy for me to be the one to stay home and look after them and run the house. Years past and now I'd hear tradesmen inquire of our housekeeper, 'How's Poor *Miss* Kitty?' I had become an old ..." she paused. "But don't pity me. I've had a good life, of sorts. I'm not sad or anything. I'm not. Really. Biddy's right. I talk too much."

"Nan says it's good getting things off yer chest, 'stead of bottling it all up inside." She gave me a warm smile.

"Biddy was the lucky one. She got away. Became a governess on a cattle farm for a while and nearly got married ..." She pulled herself up. "But that's her story. And I have no right to tell it." I didn't know what to say. I just sat there nibbling evenly around all the edges of my biscuit.

"How long have ya been playin' the piano?" I finally came out with.

"Since I was eight. Why?"

"I like the sound."

"Would you like me to teach you?" I thought it over for a bit, wondering what the other guys would say, but we'd all played recorders at school and everyone had to be in the school choir as well, so ...

"Yes please." Over many months I'd learn all the scales and could play *Chopsticks* and *Heart and Soul* with two hands. Some days I just liked to sit there and watch and listen, sometimes with Miss Bridget. Miss Kitty would play tunes like *Clair de Lune* and sang along as well to *Someone to Watch Over Me*.

❖

Feeling awkward, because I'd run out of things to say, I saw Dad's car coming up the road and used that as my excuse to leave. I felt bad I made her tell me all her secrets, but it seemed at the same time, she felt relieved by talking about it. I stood up.

"Thank you for the biscuits and the afternoon tea."

"Take the rest of them home for Doug." I scooped up the remaining pieces from the plate. "You let me know when you want to start learning the piano."

"Next Sund'y, after church?"

"That'll be fine."

"Anytime you need shopping done I'm happy to carry the basket. But don't let people like Mr Green put you off getting out. And you don't have to buy me biscuits or nothin'. I'm happy to do it for free, 'cause I like you. If you want, you could come to the pictures with us. If you want. Bye." And I hurtled down the steps to meet Dad.

They didn't see me, but I saw Dad put his bag and a dead rabbit on the roof of the car before giving Susan a kiss on the lips as he took her hands in his. She pulled away a bit, but with a look to show she liked him doing it. I went through the hole in the fence, around the back of the house past the water tanks and through the back door so that they wouldn't see me.

Over our tea of rabbit casserole I mentioned what happened at Mr Green's and what Miss Kitty revealed about herself. As I told them though, I felt guilty at revealing her confidences, but I couldn't help myself. Looking back, I can see that my betrayal of sorts was brought about by my youth and inexperience. It's hard for a boy of ten to keep such things bottled up inside. I hoped she didn't mind. As I got older, I learned to respect the trust people had placed in me to not reveal their confidences. They would tell me things they wouldn't even tell their priest. Nan said that's because I listened and let people get things off their chests. It meant that they trusted me. "What you've got is good listenin' ears – like yer father. It's a gift from God," she'd say.

"Such a shame though," Nan summed up about Miss Kitty at the time. "A lovelier person you wouldn't meet. And as for that weasel Green, we'll do our shopping in town as well in future." And from then on, we did.

"He kissed her on the lips – honest," I whispered to Doug in bed that night. He looked at me like he didn't believe me. "May I drop down dead here and now if I'm lyin'. It was like a peck, right on the lips. Have you ever seen Dad kiss anyone on the lips? I haven't.

And he held both her hands in his. And that ain't the way you take a pulse."

"So?"

"So, Dad's got a new girlfriend. He doesn't wear his wedding ring anymore either," I offered as evidence to support my claim.

"So?"

Dad stuck his head around the door.

"What are you two still talking about? Lights out and go to sleep, school tomorrow."

"Yes, Dad," we said together. I fell asleep thinking about what Doug had said after meeting our mother. The bit about starting to like someone and then them being taken from you. I wondered whether Dad might marry Susan. What would it be like with her as our mother, as if it was already a certainty.

CHAPTER EIGHTEEN

All the boys at school, and even the girls, were keen on seeing *The Searchers*. Almost everyone liked John Wayne and even if you didn't, there was usually an Indian fight that was exciting enough all on its own. I remembered my offer to Miss Kitty. She hesitated, but agreed to come, declaring it would be her first picture in over forty years. I also asked Johnny to join us.

"I don't know whether that was a wise thing to do," was Dad's initial response to Johnny's coming.

"But why?" I asked.

"There's no reason why he shouldn't, I just don't want to stir up any more resentment towards him. He's been through enough."

"It's only a picture," Doug tried to reason.

"A picture," I reaffirmed. Dad had a second think.

"You're right, boys. And he's got just as much right to see it as anyone else."

When the Saturday rolled around we all walked into town – Susan, Miss Kitty, Doug, Johnny, me and Dad. Miss Bridget was staying the weekend at the Patterson's cattle farm, helping to sew new curtains.

We passed the Wood's place as a frazzled Mrs Wood, wearing a simple cotton shift, belted her rugs on the clothes line. We waved at her. She smiled and waved back. Steve and his Dad weren't about, at least not in the yard. Wearing her makeup, Miss Kitty got little attention from the crowd, but people were looking at us and started to whisper to each other as we approached the School of Arts. Dad deliberately put his arm around Johnny's shoulder to make him feel safer. Susan had got our tickets along with packets of Smith's chips for the three of us boys and a box of coconut quivers for the adults.

It was always exciting waiting around outside for them to open up the green velvet curtains that separated the foyer from the hall itself, for us to enter. We met up with Barry, Shen and Snotty as well as other mates from school. Just before it was time to go in, the Symonds arrived after closing the tearooms. The Smiths with Raymond and his sister, and Ned Spooner from the paper joined our group as well.

"It doesn't look like there'll be any trouble," Dad speculated, looking around, "But thank you all for coming and giving support."

"This your first picture, Johnny?" asked Mrs Smith. Johnny nodded.

"I'd like to get a photo out the front here for this week's *Echo* if I could," suggested Mr Spooner. This is a first. A black person actually inside the School of Arts and not forced to peer through the back window."

"You happy with a photo Johnny?" Dad enquired. Johnny's Cheshire cat smile said 'yes'.

"Okay folks, those that want to be in it stand 'round the young fella," directed Mr Spooner.

He took a couple of shots just in case one didn't turn out. As he was taking them, I could see Steve out of the corner of my eye. He was with his mates and was all worked up over Johnny's presence. I pulled the leg of Dad's trousers to get him to look in Steve's direction.

"Don't worry mate, I've got him in my sights, and I'll handle his father if he turns up and causes any trouble." I was almost hoping he would show up just to see Dad flatten him again. But any hope of that happening disappeared when Sergeant Farrar and Penny came up the street and joined us.

"Itth tho exthiting," lisped Penny through her new dental mouthguard as she smiled at me.

"Looks like you didn't need my backup, Harry. Got a posse of your own I see," commented Sergeant Farrar.

"Thanks for coming," Dad and Mr Symonds replied together.

"I'll make sure I'm seen so's no one gets any funny ideas. Looks like some have already changed their minds," remarked Sergeant Farrar, indicating a couple of parents who had been waiting in line for tickets, but on seeing Johnny, were pulling their disappointed kids by the arm to go back home. "So's not to get too many noses outta joint Harry, how's about you all sit up the front. Easier to keep an eye out if there's any trouble."

Dad agreed as he could see Johnny getting uncomfortable at being looked at by everyone. It suited all of us kids just fine, as the front rows were the best anyway.

"See you inside," stated Sergeant Farrar as he and Penny went and got their tickets and eats.

Sergeant Farrar was right. People stopped their whispers and just got on with enjoying going to the pictures. But just to be sure, he sat down right behind Steve and his mates. They quietened down considerably. So much so, they could have been sitting in church. Penny joined us and pushed her way in, so that she was sitting right between me and Doug. Johnny was on my other side. Dad, Susan, Miss Kitty and the Symonds sat directly behind us, five rows back. Three young black kids stood on crates outside the opened back window and watched the show for free.

The picture was something else. We'd been expecting a western and weren't disappointed. As soon as we saw John Wayne all the boys cheered. It didn't seem such a strange story to us then – that of a Civil War veteran tracking down his niece who had been kidnapped and raised by Indians to such an extent that she thinks she's one of them. To a ten year old boy, what more could you want? It was a western, it had John Wayne and Indians.

Johnny just sat there, his eyes the size of two bob pieces but facially emotionless. At one stage, when we cheered at Indians 'bitin' the dust', I looked at Johnny and he had this frightened look on his face. At times he even covered his eyes. I returned to watching the picture, but my mind was now distracted slightly by Johnny's reactions. Then all of a sudden he bolted for the exit. Dad quickly followed. While the other kids around us were still intently watching the picture unaware even of Johnny's leaving, my attention remained split between wanting to know what had happened to him and what was about to happen next on the screen.

When the excitement became almost unbearable, when our hearts were beating hard in our chests, Penny grabbed my hand. I wanted to pull it away, but didn't know whether I should or not. She eventually loosened her tight grip, but still held onto my hand. She must've been really scared I thought at the time. Once the lights came up though, she pulled her hand away quickly and acted like nothing had happened. 'Cept she kept on looking at me with this stupid grin on her face, as we all forwarded out of the hall.

Johnny was standing next to Dad out the front of the building eating an ice cream cone.

"What happened, Johnny?" I asked.

"All that violence was too much, wasn't it son?" Dad answered for Johnny. "To him it was real. But I explained, didn't I son? What's on the screen is just pretending. No one really gets killed. Still, my fault. I should have known better."

"Like to come again, but maybe something not so violent, eh Johnny?" enquired Mrs Symonds. Johnny gave one of his toothy smiles.

"Biddy heard there are two comedies on in a few weeks. The Three Stooges and a Bud Abbott and Lou Costello one. You'll like them better, I think," offered Miss Kitty.

When we all started to leave, I saw Steve and his mates head over in the direction of the Exchange Hotel and pointed him out to Dad.

"Great atmosphere to bring up kids. Playing on the footpath while their fathers get drunk inside," Ned Spooner commented sadly to Dad.

"At least there wasn't any incident here, which is a step forward. As for Bob Wood, if he wasn't in the pub getting a skinful, he'd be causing problems somewheres else," replied Sergeant Farrar.

No takeaway that night. Nan made bacon and corn fritters using leftover boiled bacon from another night, with boiled vegies. They were great, all smothered in tomato sauce. After that it was serials on the wireless. Dad went over the road after tea and sat with Susan on her front verandah, sharing a bottle of beer. Whatever was said between them, he wasn't too happy when he got home within half an hour.

"You'll lose her if ya not careful," was Nan's only comment as Dad passed her in the kitchen on his return.

The Searchers became one of our games for weeks as we'd fire our toy guns and pretend to scalp each other with our rubber knives. The lot of us climbed and swung on the rope ladder or scrambled over the wooden platform in the jacaranda tree. Doug was John Wayne as usual and I was Jeffrey Hunter. Our mates were the other white men or Indians. Penny played the Natalie Wood part of the white girl the Indians kidnapped. Raymond had a bow and arrow set so he played Scar the Comanche chief. We used flour and water mixed up into a paste as war paint.

"Come on, you can be an Indian too, if ya'd like. It's only a game," I called out to Johnny a second time, after he just stood there on his verandah, watching us play. He didn't want to join in and never did. He just shook his head and I noticed for the first time a serious adult expression on his face. I felt it must have been something more than just the picture. I wondered as I looked at him whether the relatives that Johnny no longer had were also attacked like he was and maybe killed like the settlers in the picture or the Indians that John Wayne's character, Ethan, tracked down.

All our hooting and hollering and agonised screams of death were too much for Nan.

"Right that's enough of all that noise. You'll drive me to me grave you lot, with all that shoutin' and scalpin' nonsense," she called out to us through the front flyscreen door. We were banned from playing it anywhere within her earshot.

Many years later *The Searchers* was shown on television and through adult eyes I saw my boyhood hero John Wayne's character once again, but in the true light – playing Ethan Edwards, the veteran Civil War racist that he was. As I grew older I became more familiar with Aboriginal beliefs and customs through Johnny and his mates. I came to understand for instance that in many ways they have a deeper relationship to the cycle of birth, life, death and grieving through rituals that is much more complex than Western culture – and taken more seriously than our boyhood games.

CHAPTER NINETEEN

Christmas brought a passing shower and crushing humidity. It was our second Christmas lunch without Poppie. Like he'd done the year before, Dad ordered a turkey from Kells' Butchery, rather than the usual chicken we'd always had the years before. And for the second year in a row, miraculously, none of the chooks ran away or got taken by foxes as used to happen around Christmas Day, when Poppie was alive.

At the time, Nan told us this was due to Doug and my efforts at looking after them. That made us feel special. However talking later with Raymond at our usual Christmas/New Year's Test match of cricket, we were wised up. He told us how this year he saw for the first time his dad kill one of their chooks for Christmas lunch.

He said he snuck under the house and watched as his mum held the chook down on the wooden chopping block and his dad swung the axe. He actually saw the headless chook running around their backyard and both his parents chasing after it. His dad dived for it and missed, hitting the dirt with a thud. His mum managed to trap it up against a fence. Raymond said it was the funniest sight he'd ever seen.

"Poppie must have done the same with our chooks every year as well," I stated to Dad.

"What about him telling us they got out or foxes took 'em," added Doug.

"He only said that so as not to upset you both."

"He lied to us," Doug interjected.

"Lied. And a lie's a lie, no matter what shade. That's what you told us," I pointed out. Dad squirmed a bit.

"Yes, that's true son but ... See on a farm, where Poppie grew up, chickens and cows and sheep are killed to provide food for humans to eat. That's what God put them there for. Poppie knew that you two not growing up on a farm, might get upset at seeing − "

"I just thought he must've got one from Kells' each Christmas," I said. "And believed that they did get out or that foxes did take one each year."

"He lied," Doug restated.

"Yes, alright, he lied."

As I got older I came to understand Poppie's reluctance to name the chooks was based on the fact that it was easier to kill and digest them if they were nameless. Looking back, I'm grateful that we never in the preparations for Christmas lunch witnessed the slaughter and plucking of our pets. It was all carried out while we were off somewhere playing. Dad's swapping to turkeys from Kells' kept the mortality rate of our pets down. Every Christmas, now years later, when I think of that and Poppie, it always makes me smile inside and sends me back to happy memories of the day itself.

This Christmas was also our first year without a visit from Santa. Dad decided that at ten years of age, it was time to tell us the truth, and we sort of felt he knew we knew anyway.

We both got Malvern Star bikes. On Christmas morning, we rode them all around on the wet roads, until our leg muscles burnt with pain and our shirts were soaked with sweat from the high humidity.

Dad also gave us a new toy gun each complete with holsters and a bow with rubber-tipped arrows of our own to add to our armoury. Normally against weapons even if toys, he gave in to our pestering but only after he received a lecture from Nan on them being harmless fun that even he enjoyed as a child and wouldn't lead to us becoming crazed killers later in life.

Johnny came over after lunch and joined us for the slicing of the fruit cake Nan had made. Mr and Mrs Symonds had given Johnny a small chestnut gelding with a white blaze and riding gear including a leather saddle and bridle. When I asked Johnny its name, he pointed to Dad sitting on the verandah reading.

"Dad?" I queried. "That's a strange …" Johnny shook his head.

"Harry, ya drongo," Doug guessed. Johnny shook his head more violently then acted like he was Dad, carrying his doctor's bag, and then imitating him using his stethoscope.

"Doctor," I finally came up with and Johnny nodded with a toothy grin. Doug thought it was hilarious but I made no comment because I knew it meant a lot to Johnny to name it after Dad.

When Doctor was first brought into the Symonds' paddock,

Honey started yapping and snapped about at his heels, but settled down in time. Johnny and Mr Symonds built a large wooden stall with a corrugated iron roof to house the horse of a night.

As time went by, if ever Honey went missing, she could usually be found sleeping with or near Doctor in his stall. It was like Honey had adopted him, or vice versa.

Sometimes Johnny would put Doug or me on Doctor's back, and lead us around the yard.

Once Johnny got more confident in riding, he was allowed to take Doctor into the scrub for exercise. Soon he went riding all about the area, making sure he kept well away from trouble. Some weekends, he'd have the Symonds's permission to 'go bush', and he and Doctor would be gone until Monday morning.

The kangaroos that had moved closer and closer to town during the drier months and used to lie in the long dry grass, took off whenever Doctor got too close to them. 'Cept some of the males especially the Big Reds who continued to lie on their sides, scratching their bellies, not showing any sign of fear or panic. Some of them were heavier and taller than a good sized man.

Poppie once told Doug and me that when a travelling boxing troupe passed through the area he saw a boxing match where a Big Red took on a local man – courage born after one too many beers and at the urging on of his mates. He said people came from everywhere to see it. They put boxing gloves on the Big Red so that he couldn't do any harm with his paws, then taunted him a bit with a cattle prod before his opponent lined up to see if he could win the purse. The man had to be careful, because even with gloves, a Big Red was so powerful, it could disembowel a person with its hind legs.

"Who won, Poppie?" I asked for both Doug and me.

"No one. After all that tauntin' with the prod, the 'roo started gettin' too aggressive. Went wild and headed for the crowd of onlookers. So they shot him."

❖

The holidays were galloping to a close. In an act of desperation, not wanting the dying days of our freedom to end, Barry, Raymond, Shen, Doug, Snotty and I decided to build a raft like Huckleberry Finn. We were going to ditch school and sail all the way to the Spanish Main in the Caribbean and dig for pirate treasure. We all promised to keep the raft and its location secret and took an oath, that "If I reveal our hideout, may I die a horrible death – my body covered in pussy boils with maggots eating my eyeballs." Once you took the oath someone had to spit in your hand and you had to eat it.

For hours we sat around drawing up plans for the raft in the soil with a stick. What started out as a good idea soon fizzled when we realised the amount of materials, tools and work necessary to build such a craft to carry all of us. Instead, we played pirates on the creek bank. A large eucalyptus tree's branches hung out over the water, giving us the means to march whoever were the mutineers for that day's game out over it, as if 'walking the plank'; before they dived or were pushed into the water. We wrung so much fun and life out of the remainder of those days that we fell like dead men into bed each and every night.

Chapter Twenty

Events of the following year seemed to move very quickly as I recall. Now in fourth class, we had a new lay teacher called Mr Carroll. He was the first male and the first non-church teacher at the school. It was all brought about by the death of one and the retirement of another of the teaching nuns, and a shortage of replacements within the order. Mr Carroll had red hair but with pale skin like mine and covered in freckles. He came from England and was a mad cricket fan. If an important match came up, he'd put on his bakelite radio and let us listen while we did our work.

If the number of Aborigines in the main streets of town of a day was more evident, they were tolerated, rather than accepted by the majority of white people. Ganan and his family from the Reserve we'd often see and talk to. Dad, always concerned for their health and welfare, often got supplies for them from the shops. He'd take them to them as they sat in a group along the creek bank or under the trees on the outskirts of town.

One Saturday around lunchtime, Dad, Doug, Johnny and I were on our way back from The Parthenon when we saw on the corner just outside the Exchange Hotel this Aboriginal woman sitting cross-legged on the dusty wooden verandah. Her young son, just short of two years of age and wearing a dirty nappy, played beside her. Dad stopped to talk to her as we passed.

"Hello Ruby. How's young Tommy there?" It was clear the woman had been drinking, but she smiled on recognising Dad.

"Hello Doctor McNally, sir. Him much better," she slurred. 'Cept he wasn't – he was malnourished and flies swarmed around his eyes and runny nose.

"How 'bout you come and see me tomorrow, and we'll examine you both."

"Oh I fine. Little one has cough." Dad eyed the boy from head to toe.

"I think it's very important that we take a good look at Tommy as soon as possible."

"Doctor McNally sir, could you spare a little change so I can get him something to eat and drink?" Dad looked her squarely in the eye.

"No I can't." Ruby was taken aback.

"Any smokes?"

"I don't smoke, Ruby. Now, you know where I live. If you want to come with us now, I'll give you both something to eat and drink and clean up young Tommy here. But I won't give you money to spend on grog or cigarettes. Understand?" She looked at him sheepishly before replying,

"No money then?"

"No money, no smokes." Dad began to move on. She started

to get to her feet.

"Okay Doctor, we go."

Dad playfully placed his hat on Tommy's head before picking him up and carrying him on his hip. Doug and I looked around us. We were getting hostile looks from some of the drinkers standing on the pubs' verandahs. 'Abo lover' was shouted out from a couple of the men to our backs as we headed on home. But Dad walked tall and straight as usual. I kept an eye out in all directions just in case. Some people stopped and stood aghast, passing whispered comments of disapproval once we'd walked by. One was Gwen Grady and a friend.

"Ignore them, boys," Dad commented. "They're not worth worrying about." Yet there were others who'd call out 'Hey Doc' and wave and smile at us as we passed. Ruby kept her head down and stayed close to Dad's side. Johnny, particularly Johnny, as well as Doug and I, were so moved by Dad and his caring for this woman. Later Dad spoke to Doug and me.

"Always do unto others, as you would have them do unto you," followed by an explanation and the further comment after, "There but for the Grace of God, go you or I." He was good at quotes from the Bible and other sources, and equally good at explaining them in context to us, so that our young minds could understand.

Once home, after first feigning dismay by rolling her eyes at Dad over this latest act of kindness, Nan welcomed them both inside. Dad took them into the lounge room for a check up, closing the door after them. Nan cut up a towel for a nappy. While she did that, she instructed us to get out of the fridge the ingredients for a brawn salad.

We heard the boy scream and cry from within the lounge room and then after a while Ruby and a tear-stained, lolly-eating Tommy emerged. His nose and eyes were clean and clear. Nan took Tommy from Ruby and handed her another fresh towel before showing her to the bathroom. Throughout her visit, Ruby looked a little apprehensive, coupled with I guess a sense of disbelief that this was being done for her and Tommy – the fact they were not only allowed in to someone like the doctor's house to use the bathroom and wash, but to also have lunch.

At first the boy resisted being taken from his mother, but Ruby said something to him in her language that had a soothing tone. After that he was quite happy to go to the laundry, holding Nan and my hand down the back steps, while Ruby showered upstairs. Dad, Doug and Johnny stayed in the kitchen preparing lunch.

A freshly washed and diapered Tommy sat on Nan's lap at the table while Ruby ate her salad. He ended up having some fresh milk, orange segments and a small slice of Nan's date roll with butter. Dad made Ruby promise to visit his surgery in two days time, with Tommy.

"I can't pay you Doctor," she said at the end of the meal. Dad smiled.

"There's no charge. Just promise me you'll look after the both of you. And stay off the grog."

"I'll try. Thank you Doctor. God bless youse all" she struggled to get out. It was heartfelt and very moving.

The next day she was drunk and back outside the Exchange

Hotel with Tommy, but she did keep her appointment with Dad as promised. Nan left a little bag of sandwiches and oranges and a bottle of milk with Dad to give them when they turned up. She did that for every appointment they kept, until Ruby moved on to somewhere else with Tommy in tow.

❖

The Aboriginal population in town were still generally looked upon with suspicion, though I never witnessed or heard of any incident that would warrant such alarm. The majority caused no bother. Compared to the behaviour of the regular white drinkers at the two pubs, those like Wood and his drinking mates, they were saints. But being black, a lot of people were quick to criticise them to their face with terms like 'what would you expect from a dumb Abo' and worse, if their actions deviated slightly from 'acceptable' white man's dictates. So they had to always be on their best behaviour, keeping out of the way of white folk as much as possible. They'd keep their heads bowed to avoid eye contact and the invariable intimidating 'what are youse lookin' at?' from some of the whites that'd follow after them heckling, and just go about their business.

Two households on the other side of town had taken in a half-caste Aboriginal girl each. This and the setting aside of a number of houses for the Aborigines was all part of the Aboriginal Welfare Board's policy to disperse them into the white community.

The girls were both around thirteen years of age. One you never saw about much. The other girl could be seen around town following after her new mother, carrying her purchases for her from the various shops she'd visit. Whenever you saw either girls with their new white families about town or at Church, although they were always well turned out in freshly washed and ironed dresses, white gloves with matching socks and shoes, nothing could mask the emptiness in their eyes.

Work was still difficult to find. Jobs the Aboriginal men had successfully carried out on farms while the white men went off to war had been quickly taken back by the returned servicemen. Many blacks followed the crop seasons, hoping to pick up temporary work. Some farmers fed their Aboriginal workers well and paid them fairly. Others though were merely given food and shelter – if you could call it that, or cigarettes and grog in exchange for an actual wage.

Later another afternoon, long after Ruby and Tommy had left town, Raymond, Barry, Snotty, Shen, Doug and I were riding about on our bikes when we saw some of the regular white drinkers, including Bob Wood, outside the Exchange Hotel. They were buying one group of black men hanging around outside the hotel because they weren't allowed inside, free beer – not out of kindness but for sport. They'd get them drunk on just one or two schooners because they had lower tolerances to alcohol than the whites, then laugh at them as they staggered around or fell over.

Then Bob Wood and his mates, drunk themselves, but not as legless as the Aborigines started pushing them about and tripping them up. They formed a circle around one young man, no more than twenty, and started pushing him from one to the other of them like he was a side of lamb. Then the pushing got more violent and resentful. You could hear them calling out and taunting him.

"Come on, stand up ya black cunt," then chanting, "Abo, Abo, Abo …" As he fell to the ground Bob Wood laid the boot in.

"We gotta do something," I shouted at the other guys as I dropped my bike on its side and ran across the road. Doug and Shen came after me trying to pull me back but I broke free. "Stop that! I said stop that!" The men interrupted their game and looked in my direction.

"Well look who we have here eh, McNally's boys," slurred Bob Wood.

"You're hurting him."

"What's it to you?" I helped the young black man to stand by supporting his elbow as he made several attempts to struggle to his feet.

"Please, Mr Wood, he's done nothing to you."

"He's an Abo. That's reason enough. Isn't it fellas?" His mates mumbled some sort of agreement.

"Then you'll have to fight me," I threatened.

"Yeah," chorused my band of merry men, who had by now joined Doug, Shen and me on the pub's verandah. I took the pugilistic stance Dad had taught us.

"Hey fellas, looks like we got us a young Tommy Burns here."

I stood there grim-faced and determined with my fists raised but not really knowing what to do next as the men started laughing, all bar Mr Wood. He moved towards me rolling up his sleeves and with a menacing scowl on his face.

"It's about time someone put you McNallys in ya place." He

reached out and held my head firmly with one hand as I took several wild air swings, all missing the mark, before he let me go. The men laughed even louder through all this which made my blood boil. While he wasn't looking I scored a weak punch to his abdomen and with that Mr Wood positioned his right arm high across his chest, about to follow through with a backhander to the side of my head. Then he stopped as if he had a change of mind as he looked up over our heads to across the road.

"Come on fellas, we're wastin' precious drinkin' time. The fourth race'll be on soon. If you'll excuse us Master McNally," offered Bob Wood with a sarcastic smirk.

"Well alright then," was all I could come up with. As the gang of thugs went back inside the pub, my fellas slapped me on the back. I went and checked the young man over – no blood. "There ya go mate, you'll be right." He thanked us then staggered off, assisted by his mates.

"What woulda ya done if he took ya up on the fight?" Snotty asked me as he wiped his nose on his arm.

"Well, we all woulda stayed and fought, wouldn't we?"

"Oh yeah. Sure," the group all replied, perhaps a little too immediate and strong to be totally convincing, but reassuring none the less.

"Well boys, what are you doing here? Bit young for drinking, aren't you?" The voice came from behind. We turned around. There was Sergeant Farrar coming toward us from his police car across the road.

"We were just –" I started.

"I pretty much saw the end of what happened and can work out the rest. I won't have any public fighting in my town."

"But Pat was only –" Doug began.

"Now you boys, on yer way. I think a night in a cell for one or two of our drunken vigilantes might have them thinking twice about their little games. At least I'll know who to come to if I ever need some back up. See ya fellas."

He gave us a friendly wink, then waited until we were back on our bikes before heading into the hotel. I knew 'drunken' sure enough and 'vigilante' I found later in the dictionary. When we told Dad about it after tea, he took his time to respond while we both waited.

"Mmm," was his considered summation of the events.

"Is that all?" I asked.

"Don't get me wrong. I'm pleased you went to someone's aid, but Sergeant Farrar's right. Leave the policing to him. You could have got on your bikes and reported it to him and he would have–"

"By then the bloke might've been dead," Doug argued.

"Mmm. Fellas I'm afraid the way things are going, there could be a lot worse than a drunken dust-up coming our black brothers' way."

"It's the bleedin' drink that causes all the problems," Nan offered.

"Anyway, that's a problem for the grown-ups. And you're a little too young to be taking on men three times your size." I thought I saw a trace of a pleased sort of smile quickly vanish from his face once I looked up at him, before he directed us to get changed for bed.

Once Dad had done 'lights out' we crept from our beds, out through the window and clambered onto the jacaranda branch. The air held the false promise of rain.

"We would've been better off keeping it to ourselves," Doug sighed. "No fight'd get his approval, no matter what."

"He did say he was pleased we went and helped him. It did stop the beating. Or maybe he's saying it's alright to defend yourself, just take on people your own size."

"Yeah. Steve's not that much bigger," reasoned Doug. We felt good again. We didn't get into or start a real fight that afternoon, but were prepared to if needed. And to me, and the rest of us, it left us feeling like John Wayne. It also proved just how strong the mateship was between us that in a time of crisis, we all stuck together.

"Shh," I whispered, my finger to my lips as the front screen door gave a gentle thud and Dad walked down the steps and across the road to the Symonds. We were about to climb back through the window, when Dad and Susan emerged from inside her house. There was an awkwardness between them as they walked down the Symonds' steps before stopping at the bottom. The night was so still, we could just pick up bits of what they were saying.

"Harry, what am I supposed to do? Do you expect me to just wait 'til somehow you get better and – ?"

"No. I'm ... It's hard to talk about ... the War and things. Things I'd rather forget."

"Harry, I want to help, but I can't if you won't let me in. Let me know what happened that causes these black moments. I want to understand. Please." She sounded exasperated. Dad didn't reply.

"I'll say goodnight then."

She started walking back up her front steps. When she reached the top he called out.

"I love you, Susan."

"I know," she replied, turning back slightly before entering the house.

We made ourselves as small as we could as Dad entered the front yard. Once he was safely inside Doug and I just looked at each other before crawling without a sound back through our bedroom window.

CHAPTER TWENTY-ONE

February marked the start of a series of dramas climaxing in a tragic sequence of events that no one could foresee. It would have repercussions not only on our family, but ultimately Johnny – indeed the whole town.

The first I s'pose on the scale of events was minor and involved Doug. He and Barry had got an empty forty four gallon drum from the service station and were taking turns standing on it and, moving their bare feet, rolling it forward along the street. They had a tree branch for balance. Its thinner tip rested on the ground and they held onto the fatter end, moving it forward bit by bit as the drum rolled along. Barry with his broad feet was really good at it and he was flying along.

Doug on his turn wasn't as well balanced on the drum and had to often jump off whenever it hit an uneven bit of bitumen.

"Ya better get off. You're gonna break ya neck," I called out as Barry and I ran beside him to keep up.

The older he got, the more stubborn Doug got. You couldn't

tell him to do anything he didn't want to. Even Dad had problems getting him to follow his directions. Only warnings that he'd dock his pocket money or stop him from seeing our mates for a period of time would see Doug back down and do what he was told.

He was becoming so headstrong with no thought for his own safety, always taking risks and now he was determined not only to conquer the new toy, but go even faster than Barry. He was barrelling along at one stage. We were less than one hundred feet from where we hid our shoes when the tip of the branch broke and Doug took a nasty fall. He went over the front of the drum. Putting out his left hand to break his fall, he fell heavily on his arm. You could hear the bone snap. He cried out in pain as we got him to his feet. Barry stated the obvious.

"You've broken it." Tears were already forming tracks down Doug's dusty cheeks. There was nothing I could do 'cept take him along to Dad's surgery. Barry shot through so I was left to help him on my own. An hour later, after dressings on his grazed knees, the painful resetting of the bone and another lecture, Doug ended up with a plaster cast on his arm and a sling around his neck. Dad telephoned Nan, explained what had happened and said he was taking us for a milkshake to get over it. Before we arrived home he asked us where our shoes were and we retrieved them, getting us out of another lecture, this time from Nan.

"Oh it's all fun and games 'til someone loses an eye – or breaks an arm," Nan commented on hearing the whole story. "Thank God Pat here's got more sense."

"This'll get me outta school for months," Doug boasted that night in bed.

"If it was your writing arm maybe, but it isn't. Dad won't let you stay home."

"We'll see."

I was right. He not only had to go to school but suffer the humiliation of being taken and picked up by Dad in the car because he couldn't ride his bike or carry his satchel on his back. Dad still let me go by myself and come home the same, riding my bike with our mates. My grinning and waving at him when I cycled off, while he waited in the car for Dad, had Doug fuming. It often finished with me poking my tongue out at him. I knew once the cast was off I'd pay for it, but at the time I remember thinking, you have to take advantage of these situations as they come your way.

Everyone in the classroom signed the cast, including Mr Carroll. Nan wasn't impressed when she discovered the cock and balls Snotty had drawn on the underside and covered it over with white sandshoe polish.

Doug hated every minute of his loss of freedom and privacy, especially having to have Dad wash and dress him. His complaining stopped once Dad stated that if he didn't like him doing it, Nan would be happy to take over. I helped by getting him into his pyjamas of a night and putting his shoes and socks on for school. He had to have his meals cut up for him as well, but managed to feed himself with just a fork or spoon in his right hand.

Months later, once the cast was removed, my retribution for the teasing I gave him came quickly and without warning. A blue-tongue lizard secreted in my bed, which had me screaming like a girl and running from the room to the sound of Doug's laughter, evened the score. Needless to say, only weeks after the cast's removal, Doug and Barry had climbed up on top of a wheat silo and were skylarking about. They both stood on the top with arms outstretched and cooeeing at the world.

"Come down! You'll kill yerselves!" I yelled to no effect.

"Why don't ya run home and tell Dad. Go on, I dare ya," Doug shouted down at me. I went home alone and never did tell Dad. I was surprised and a little disappointed that he thought I would.

❖

Johnny secured a full time job with Mr Horan the blacksmith that allowed him to buy riding boots and a new rug for Doctor, a little spending money as well as putting regular deposits in the bank. Every now and then he would insist on shouting Dad, Doug and me to milkshakes at Eleni's. With having a full time job, and sometimes the need to work some weekends, his weekends away in the bush became an irregular affair. When he did disappear even for one day, he was always back and ready for work come Monday morning.

Johnny's apprenticeship didn't mean our lawns and gardens were neglected. Every week or two we'd have a new man or woman, black or white, insisting on attending to it in lieu of Dad's waiving his fee. Some even chopped wood or painted the fence or dunny. One Aboriginal woman called Aunty Maisy and her husband Jacky used to bring along their two kids. While she tended the garden and he raked up the leaves and burnt them off or whatever, Nan would have their children sitting on the verandah drinking Milo and eating scones or fresh sandwiches. Inevitably, they went home with a dozen eggs and vegies from the garden as well.

Every other week, Johnny would hang out overnight with the mob that'd moved into the refurbished Hudson house. There was only an old man called Miro, his two adult sons, their wives and three children, two boys and a young girl, Binda. She was around Johnny's age. The two adult sons worked as itinerant farm labourers around the district. Others who had lived there before it being taken over by the Aboriginal Welfare Board, concerned for their safety, had heeded the directions of the white gangs that taunted and derided them, and moved on.

The gunshots I had heard on our first night in town became more frequent. It seemed every few weeks there was always some car chase, or shots fired into the air near the Hudson or the other Aboriginal houses late at night. Even neighbours living nearby them began to feel unsafe.

No one was ever hurt. It was just an ongoing campaign of intimidation to force them on their way and to let their neighbours know that any friendship displayed or assistance given to the Aboriginal families might see them getting some of the same treatment. It always occurred once Sergeant Farrar and the town had gone to bed for the night.

Johnny still stopped by for the occasional evening meal, after which he and I would go out onto the back verandah and sit on the cane lounge. While moths bashed away at the bulb overhead, I'd read to him. Dad had bought an illustrated children's collection of novels by Dickens. We both liked *David Copperfield* and *A Tale of Two Cities* the best. Each week we'd take up where we left off the week before. Johnny was able to read alongside me, my finger skipping from word to word. He'd mouth the words as I spoke. "'It was the best of times, it was the worst of

times, it was the age of wisdom, it was the age of foolishness ..."'
and more. Not being able to speak the words, did not mean he
couldn't hear, read and understand them for himself. Sometimes
he'd borrow one of the books and take it with him to reread by
himself.

❖

It was only a month after Doug had his cast removed, that the
next disaster struck. I was parking my bike under the house after
riding home from school. Doug was still out with some mates.

"Nan, I'm home," I called out. No response. I remember not
thinking much of it at the time, until I had run up the front steps
and on reaching the screen door, called out again.

"Nan, I'm home." There was still no response. As I entered
through the screen door, "Doug's off riding with ..." I stopped at
the kitchen door. Nan was on her back on the floor. I threw my
satchel on the floor and knelt by her side. In my panic, all I could
think of to do was to shake her.

"Nan, Nan, wake up!" Putting my ear to her mouth I felt a faint
laboured breath against my skin. She was alive. I ran out the front
door, down the steps and through the palings to Miss Kitty. My
heart pounded in my chest. She quickly telephoned Dad then came
back with me to our place, gently assuring me that Nan would be
alright, before sending me off to the bathroom to get a cool washer.
When I returned, she had her sitting upright against the kitchen
cupboard. Nan'd wet herself and Miss Kitty was mopping up the
urine around her with old newspapers. Nan's eyes were swimming
in her head. She slowly began to focus on the two of us.

"Wha haffen?" Her speech was slurred and the left side of her face had dropped ever so slightly. Miss Kitty folded the washer and pressed it gently on Nan's forehead.

"You've had a fall, love," soothed Miss Kitty. Nan made an awkward attempt to get up.

"Now now, you just rest there. Harry's on his way." Nan slumped a bit. Miss Kitty sat her back up. "Pat love, get us a glass of water will you."

Miss Kitty held the water to Nan's lips and helped her take a few sips. Most of it she dribbled down her front. We could hear Dad's Holden pull up then his running up the front steps and pushing through the screen door.

"How is she?" he asked as he knelt down beside her and Miss Kitty. I stood and moved away to give him room.

"She's had some sort of turn I think, Harry."

"Mum, I want you to try and smile for me." Her mouth twisted a bit but couldn't form a complete smile. "I want you to raise your right arm, good, now your left." The right arm was easy, but the left resting in her lap, just shook a bit. "Who's the Prime Minister?"

"Thath Menthies bath-ted. Not a pat-th on Cur-thin."

"Well, your mind's working okay." Dad looked into her mouth. Her tongue was curled a bit lengthways. He got out his stethoscope and checked her heart then her pulse, then re-examined her eyes this time with his torch. "I'm pretty sure you've had a slight stroke." Nan looked scared. "I'll take you to the hospital for some tests to be certain."

"Gonna die?" she forced out. My heart sank at the thought.

"No, not at all. It does mean though, you'll be on medication for the rest of your life. But there's no reason you can't make a full recovery." The relief showed on all our faces.

"However, for that to happen there has to be some changes." We all waited, especially Nan. "I'm talking diet and exercise. No more butter or dripping on your bread and only half a teaspoon of sugar in your tea for starters. Not to mention no more fatty chops or lambs fry, kidney and bacon."

"Bugger," cried Nan. "Why don't ya justh slith me throath and be done wiff it." Dad smiled and tapped her hand reassuringly.

"Now now, it's not as bad as that. You can have chops, but with the fat cut off. Same with steaks. But more fruit and vegetables and less salt on everything."

"Like bein' back on rathionth."

"The important thing is you have to move more. Walk up town once every day or so. There are exercises I'll show you that will get the strength back in that arm and some facial exercises as well. The speech should correct itself in time. But for now, it's rest. Mate, can you turn Nan's bed right down and Miss Kitty, could you give us a hand getting her to her feet?"

By the time I came back out of the bedroom the two of them had edged a wobbly Nan up the hall. They then led her into her room. Miss Kitty emerged first and closed the door behind her. It was a good half an hour before Dad came out with his medical bag, closing the door quietly behind him.

"She's sleeping. Thank you both for your quick thinking. It could have been worse."

When Doug got home a half an hour later, Dad was preparing a salad for tea. Doug was quickly filled in on what had happened by Dad, with my interjections rounding out the drama. He was allowed to tiptoe into Nan's room to see for himself, with Dad's specific instructions not to wake her. I had never seen Nan in such a vulnerable state before. It was the moment I first became aware that she was getting old.

The next day's tests confirmed Dad's original diagnosis. Things did change around the house after that. Doug and I now had cereal or toast and vegemite for breakfast with orange juice, which we got for ourselves. Dad would bring Nan a tray of cut fruit, toast with marmalade and a pot of tea in bed. Every other day we'd have a boiled egg with toast soldiers. Susan would come over and bathe Nan and prepare her for the day while Dad had his breakfast and a shave at the kitchen sink. He'd give Susan a peck on the cheek on seeing her, and Susan would return his kiss with a little smile, but there seemed a distancing in their relationship.

Susan would also take Nan through a series of exercises which she had to repeat by herself throughout the day. When we left for school, we'd stop at the Walshe house where Miss Kitty had packed our school lunch. Dad made tea most nights, picking up meat on the way home. Sometimes he'd make a big omelette or bring home takeaway. Once a week in turns, Miss Kitty and Mrs Symonds would deliver a casserole. Miss Bridget came through the day as well and cleaned and attended to Nan, while Miss Kitty got her lunch, with strict instructions from Dad about what she could and couldn't eat. He told her that under no circumstances was she to give into Nan's pleas for food he hadn't approved.

It was a good three weeks before Nan was up and about. Dad's change to the meals went on and Nan reluctantly fell into line by modifying her cooking. Rabbit or underground mutton as Nan called it, was still on the menu as a stew, casserole or pie and occurred at least once a fortnight – all dependent on Dad receiving one in lieu of payment at the surgery. Since the release of the myxomatosis virus into the rabbit population, it was now seen as almost a delicacy to have a clear-eyed, non-infected one and was highly prized by most. The actual virus wasn't harmful to humans once the rabbit was cooked. Even so, Nan wouldn't chance cooking a sick one.

By and large Nan stuck to the new exercise regime as well, at least in the beginning. After four months her face no longer drooped on the left side, but her left arm still maintained a residual weakness. Within her period of convalescence she had lost over three stone.

Boiled bacon was okay, but occasionally she'd sneak a piece of fried bacon that we were having. Keeping her back to us she'd scoff it down at the kitchen sink like a starving cat. If she thought she'd been seen, before Dad could reproach her, she'd jump to her own defence.

"Cook's treat. Oh, one little piece won't hurt."

This rationalising could also on occasion stretch to pieces of plain cake and even an extra spoonful of custard or gravy as well. However bread and dripping or any cake or dessert with cream was never prepared or eaten in the house ever again. Tea cakes, rock cakes, slab cakes and date scones took their place. Also, Dad didn't want her doing any more laundry. He advertised in *The Echo* and got a woman in town who would pick up, wash and return within a day or two, including ironing. No amount of persuasion could convince Nan not to do her own house cleaning though.

"I don't want no stranger running a gloved hand over my sideboard and passing judgement," was her definitive response.

After she'd fully recovered and back to her normal self, Nan, grateful to everyone who had helped out during her illness, invited them all to a new and revised CWA afternoon tea. That included Gwen Grady. She'd taken over Nan's monthly CWA afternoon teas while she was laid up. Susan couldn't come as she was working with Dad, but both Miss Kitty and Miss Bridget did. Johnny, Doug and I acted as waiters. All up, there were about thirty people present. We had to bring in chairs from the kitchen and verandah, and even borrowed some from neighbours, just to sit everyone.

Gwen Grady was the last to arrive, always making a grand entrance. When Nan saw her coming up the front steps, she had a quick aside to the gathering.

"Here comes 'old horse face'. Mutton dressed up as lamb," she said with only the slightest impediment from the stroke. She then had to shoosh everyone's laughter as she greeted Gwen at the door, taking her ten shillings donation to the day and depositing it in an old biscuit tin.

"Hello love, nice to see you," Nan gushed. Gwen swanned in. She was done up like a clown, all frills and ropes of imitation pearls, with her white powdered face and heavily rouged cheeks. Next Nan hit her for another pound's worth of tickets for the day's other fund raiser, the meat tray raffle, supplied by Kells' Butchery.

"Gee, that stroke's aged you, love," Gwen observed in a throw away line. You could see Nan's displeasure by the set of her jaw.

"Right," Nan muttered under her breath. We knew it was on.

Without any further 'hellos' to the rest of the group, Mrs Grady began telling everyone her tale of woe of how a 'bout of the trots' had swept through her whole family, as she waited anxiously for the food to be served.

She spied me in the kitchen doorway and all I could see were her pendulous breasts as she continued holding court while heading toward me. I felt another one of her examinations was imminent. At only feet from me she froze on the spot. I thought her eyes were going to pop out of their sockets as Johnny entered from the kitchen carrying the first plate, quartered corned beef and pickle sandwiches. They were one of Gwen's favourites. She hesitated at first, as he offered them to her. She looked at Johnny then back to the sandwiches, then Johnny and back again, before finally grabbing one.

"You know Johnny?" Nan asked over-pleasantly. The room came to a silent halt, waiting on Gwen's reply.

"Yes. How d'ya do," was her curt response as she paused, looking at him then the sandwich in her hand before devouring it in one mouthful.

"He made those sandwiches," Nan enthused. He hadn't, Nan did it all. Gwen nearly brought it straight back up. "Like another?" Nan cooed as I winked at Johnny. He looked back with a confused expression before the penny dropped. His eyes sparkled with conspiratorial acknowledgement of the game before giving 'old horse face' a beaming smile and offering her another. Funnily enough, Gwen declined.

"Oh, he had a hand in getting most of the food, didn't you love? Pity he can't join us at the CWA, we could use a bloke like him." Johnny, now going along fully with Nan's charade, continued serving the room. Gwen fell silent for the rest of the afternoon. Normally she'd make sure she got more than her ten shilling's worth of food. Able to eat practically her own weight in food at any one sitting, or at least give it a good try, she now had a face on her as long as a yard of tripe as us boys ferried in platters of food that were heartily eaten by all – 'cept her. Nan took secret delight.

"I hope that's not yer tummy still playing up. Never mind love, Johnny's just ripped up some fresh newspaper in the loo if you need to dash out at any time."

When Mrs Grady won the meat raffle there was a leadened silence in the room. The other women's expressions hardened towards her as she collected her prize from Nan. As soon as she turned around they smiled and congratulated her, even though it pained them to do so, for they needed Gwen at such functions. She always gave generously. And she'd be the first to let you know she did, as well. Nan's gift to all who helped out while she was sick was a box each of Winning Post chocolates, brought in on cue by the three of us boys on the large silver tray Poppie gave her on one of their wedding anniversaries. She even gave a box to Mrs Grady. As I handed her the chocolates she looked up at me but directed her comments to Nan.

"You're still giving him the fish emulsion Maureen? He's very pasty."

"Yes Gwen. He'll be right once he's filled out, don't ya think?"

"Mmm, s'pose. That's what happens when you give birth to a litter. There's bound to be a runt," she sniffed. I rolled my eyes at Nan and she hers back at me, then headed for the safety of the kitchen before Mrs Grady could get her hands on me for one of her examinations. I returned with the tray of pre-poured glasses of sherry that finished each meeting and led them into the ritual sherry nap. As per Nan's instruction, we waited the customary three quarters of an hour before waking them by turning on the wireless. They raised over forty quid all up for the CWA on the day.

❖

It was near the end of Nan's convalescence that I could see Susan and Dad slowly rekindling their relationship. Every evening they would go for a walk. One evening, I was just swinging gently back and forth on the swing while watching Johnny lead Doctor into his stable, when I saw Dad and Susan returning from up the street hand-in-hand. They didn't see me. I jumped down from the swing and crouched in the garden behind the plants along the picket fence. Dad walked her up the steps to her front door before giving her a brief kiss on the mouth. He began to move away, but she pulled him back and they kissed again but for even longer.

As he started down the steps, I scuttled around the side of the house and in the back door so he wouldn't see me. That night in bed I thought of telling Doug, but didn't. I wondered once again whether Susan might become our new mother and decided I liked the idea more and more.

❖

At the end of another uneventful Sunday, I was lazing on my stomach on the wooden platform under the yellowing leaves of the jacaranda canopy, reading about the pharaohs. Doug had asked me if I wanted to go with Barry and some other of our mates to the creek, but I couldn't put the book down once I started it. After a while in the distance, I could hear Johnny riding Doctor down the street from the old Hudson house. When he came into view I could see that Binda was sitting behind him, her arms tight around his waist. She was barefoot and wore an orange checked dress with a green ribbon in her hair.

"Hi Johnny. Hi Binda," I called from high in the tree as they got closer. They looked up and waved, before getting off the horse and leading him into his stall. A few minutes later Johnny and Binda went up the front steps and inside. After a half hour or so they came back out with Mr and Mrs Symonds behind them. Binda shook their hands then Johnny walked her hand-in-hand back up the street to her place. It seemed now that Johnny also had a girlfriend. Penny Farrar was still keen on me but I preferred to hang out with my mates. I didn't mind talking to her, but the thought of kissing her at ten years of age, yuk.

CHAPTER TWENTY-TWO

That same night, we were only in bed a couple of hours when we were woken by the loud clanging of the fire truck bell and the cries of "Fire!", "Fire!" coming from various houses in the distance towards town. All of us shot up and onto the front verandah. Other households in the street were out as well. There was a blaze coming from around the corner at the far end of Railway Street that was so intense, it lit up the dark sky brighter than any bonfire.

People began to run in its direction, not caring that they were half dressed or in their sleepwear, all carrying whatever buckets they owned. Dad grabbed his medical bag and a shovel while Nan told us to get our buckets from under the house. All three of us ran barefoot out the gate and up the street.

"Don't get too close. Stay with yer father," huffed and puffed an equally shoeless Nan following behind. Just then the town electricity was turned off as a precaution. All the houses and street lights went out simultaneously.

Johnny, Mr and Mrs Symonds and Susan were ahead of us. By the time we rounded the corner into Railway Street we'd been joined by the other neighbours along the way, all running in the direction of the fire. It was clear that it was coming from the Hudson house. The growing flames swirled in and around its weatherboard sides. Smoke was billowing out the windows as if fanned by bellows.

Seeing the house all ablaze was both a terrifying yet strangely mesmerising experience. I thought at the time of Nan's old movie magazine that had the black and white pictures from *Gone With The Wind*. It was just like we were watching Atlanta burn. Ned Spooner was already busy snapping off pictures for *The Echo* when we arrived.

This was not the time to stop and gawk though. Everybody quickly set about trying to control the fire. Some helped the Richardsons and the Palmers on either side of the Hudson house empty their similar weatherboard homes just in case the fire took off in their direction.

The fire truck was already on hand pumping water onto the house. The heat coming off it was like a furnace, blistering the paint on the houses on either side. Weatherboards began to crack and curl. It soon became apparent that there was little that could be done to save the Hudson place as the roof was on the verge of collapse. A check with Miro by Sergeant Farrar earlier revealed all the occupants were safe. There was only himself, one of his sons, Pindari, and his granddaughter, Binda. The others were visiting relatives working on a nearby property. Johnny put his arm around a trembling Binda.

"How did it start?" the Sergeant asked as Ned Spooner wrote

down every word.

"We asleep then boom, fire everywhere," explained Pindari. "We just got out." They were comforted by Miss Bridget and Miss Kitty, her face mostly hidden by a scarf.

Dad checked over all the family for burns and the effects of smoke inhalation. Some men brought out a trestle table from a house across the street and in no time they'd set up a mini canteen manned by a number of women including Nan, Mrs Grady and Mrs Wood. Father Prittenden in his dressing gown along with Sister Mary Placid, Mr and Mrs Carroll and two other nuns arrived on the scene and instantly set about mucking in with everybody else. Ned Spooner quickly packed away his camera equipment and joined in.

In a desperate attempt to contain little spot fires in the dry grass surrounding the houses, caused by spitting and floating embers, some men used shovels and rakes while others took off coats and shawls and began beating the grass with them as each spark took hold. Some even stomped on small sparks with their bare feet, for they knew the financial ruin that could follow if the blaze caught hold of the region's wheat crop across the creek.

All of us, men, women and children had by now formed a human chain, filling buckets from the creek and passing them hand to hand along to the firemen to throw on the flames. Ganan and his mob as well as all the other Aborigines about town joined the line. Black and white working side by side didn't matter when everyone had the same goal.

"Pat love, there's a bottle of cordial and some plastic cups in the top cupboard next to the fridge. Get 'em for us will ya love," Nan called to me. I left the bucket brigade and ran, taking a short cut through the back paddocks behind the houses in Main Street. The urgency of my task weighed on my mind as the waist-high grass flattened under my running feet.

I was halfway home, just behind the Wood's house when thump; I tripped over something solid in the long grass. I hit my head hard on the ground. Dazed, I got to my feet and wobbled about, trying to shake off the effects of the knock. Without any warning I was jerked roughly by the arm with the directive,

"Don't move a bloody muscle." It was Mr Wood. I felt I was done for, just him and me in the dark and no witnesses.

"Please don't hurt me," I begged.

"Shut the fuck up," he growled through clenched teeth. I closed my eyes, bracing for the first blow. Nothing. I slowly opened one eye to find him looking past me.

Without turning my head I flicked my eyes to the side to see what his gaze was fixed on in the grass where I'd tripped. Then there, right in front of me, from out of the long grass, a huge Big Red kangaroo raised itself slowly from a lying position to its full height.

"Don't let him smell yer fear."

It towered over me. It seemed nearly as tall as Dad with the build of an athlete. I froze. Its eyes were lit by the glow of the distant fire as it stared us down. I sensed a rustle in the grass around us. I turned my head to the right then the left, just a fraction each way. We were surrounded by a mob of them; three females and several immature males, now standing tall in the grass. I couldn't breathe from fear. My palms went all sweaty as the Big Red in one effortless bound moved forward, as close as a couple of feet from us – close enough for me to see its flaring nostrils. It gave a dominant snort. Whether he could smell my fear or not, he would have smelt the urine running down my leg.

In a flash, a shovel swung past my head and with one almighty whack of its broadside, Mr Wood hit the kangaroo hard on its shoulder, unbalancing it. It immediately bounded off into the darkness, followed quickly by the others in the mob. I breathed long and loud with relief.

"Never used ta get this close to town them 'roos. Y've gotta start pickin' yer fights within yer division."

"Thank you Mr Wood," I panted. I could see by his slight unsteadiness that he'd been drinking. You could smell it on his breath.

"The name's Bob."

"Thanks Bob."

"No worries. What are ya doin' out here anyways?"

"I took a short cut to get some cordial for Nan."

"Well go an' get it. I'll come with ya ta see ya don't get in any more blues. And I'd change me pants if I was you. No need to let the whole world know." He waited outside while I got changed and got the cordial and cups, then we headed up Main Street lit only by the moon and stars and the distant blaze in the sky.

"Y'alright?"

"Yeah."

"Ya sure? That's one hell of a shock."

"I'm sure." He gave my shoulder a reassuring pat like Dad might do. He seemed so different to the man shouting abuse and picking a fight with Dad.

"Why'd ya punch my dad? Is it because he helped Johnny?" He seemed a little taken aback.

"It's more than that. Ya dad wants ta change things, and

there's lots that are happy leavin' things just the way they are now. His helpin' the Abos –"

"Aborigines." I interjected. "Dad says ya gotta call people by their right names."

"Does he now. Well he can take a flyin' leap 'cause I ain't – Y've gotta keep 'em in their place. If ya don't they'll –"

"Dad says they've got no place. The white people took it."

"It's our bloody farms, our houses. Our bloody land. And no black bastard –"

"You don't like people much, do you?"

"Who says?"

"You're always angry."

"I s'pose yer dad's told ya that as well."

"No. It's what I reckon."

"Listen here ya little pipsqueak, I can say and do what I please 'cause –"

"Dad says you can act like a bit of a goose sometimes."

"A goose!"

"See what I mean, you're gettin' angry." He snorted at my observation. "And I reckon ya drink too much."

"I – I shoulda let that 'roo finish ya off. You're worse than the bloody missus, ya bloody little –"

"And Nan says ya shouldn't swear in front of kids either." He lifted his arm as if he was about to give me a backhander. I didn't know if he was pretending or not this time.

"I'm not Steve," I dared to say. We looked at each other, both aware of the meaning behind my words. He lowered his arm.

"Just shut up and keep walkin' will ya. Bloody little smartarse. All of ten an' thinks he's full of the wisdom of bloody Solomon," he added under his breath. I looked up at him. He caught me looking and broke into a little grin before giving me a playful flick on the ear. "Just keep 'effin' walkin'". Trees and power polls cast menacing shadows in the darkness but I felt safe beside him as we turned the corner into Railway Street and crossed the train tracks.

CHAPTER TWENTY-THREE

Telling others about my near-death experience had to wait. I handed over the cordial and cups to Nan and rejoined the bucket line. In my absence two old bathtubs were found and being used as reservoirs for the bucket loads of water. Just as quickly as one line filled them up, another was scooping out the water to douse on the fire.

Nearby gum trees began to burst into flame. The fierce heat ignited the eucalyptus oil in their leaves, making little 'pfft, pfft, pfft' sounds as they exploded then sailed upward on the breeze into the night sky like a galaxy of Queensland fireflies.

Mr Wood stood next to his mates, leaning on his shovel and watching the Hudson house burn. All of them had smirks on their faces. He looked straight at Johnny and imitated a person struggling to speak, then laughed. Johnny didn't bite, just got on with the job at hand but Pindari standing next to him witnessed it and his fuse was lit.

"You lot just gonna stand there or what?" Sergeant Farrar

shouted at Mr Wood and his mates. Before they could do anything, Pindari had flung his bucket to the ground and was storming up to Mr Wood.

"Pindari!" Miro called out as he went after him.

"You started this!" Pindari roared moving closer to Mr Wood. "We could have all died!"

"No mate, I didn't start it. But I'd like ta thank the man who did." Mr Wood let his shovel drop to the ground as he moved to meet Pindari head on. Johnny started running toward them both.

"Don't," Miro pleaded in Pindari's ear. "He wants you to start a fight so's —"

"You liar," Pindari hurled at Mr Wood, ignoring Miro's pleas.

"Liar, liar house on fire," Mr Wood taunted, then within a split second grabbed Pindari by the collar of his shirt, more out of drunk bravado than anything else, for drunk or not, it was an uneven match. Pindari was of solid build and pushed Mr Wood's hands away before taking a swing, landing a glancing blow to his jaw. He retaliated by lunging at Pindari's throat with both hands, in a tight choking hold.

Before it could escalate any further, Johnny charged up to them like a wild man. He grunted in Pindari's face his disapproval while at the same time taking Bob Wood's wrists with both his hands in a strong paralysing grip. I'd never seen such depth of emotion from Johnny before. He appeared to have a strength beyond his teenage years and a look so intense it could melt steel. Unable to hold Johnny's gaze, an under-the-weather Mr Wood conceded and dropped his hands from around Pindari's throat.

"Hey you lot! Save yer fightin' for the ring. There's a fire to put out and a crop to save!" yelled the Sergeant, observing the altercation. Johnny pushed his hand on Pindari's shoulder, to urge him away and back to work. Mr Wood gave Pindari and Johnny a contemptuous glare before beginning to beat the grass flare-ups with his shovel.

"This isn't the end of this. Not all of us afraid of your mob. We fight back. You'll see," Pindari threw back at Bob Wood as he returned to the bucket line.

"You two and who's army, ya pair of black cunts," Mr Wood joked to his mates as they banged away at the grass. He looked up and saw me glaring at him from the line.

"They're my friends," I called out over all the noise.

He stopped his efforts for a moment as we looked back at one another. I was certain he could read my thoughts. My eyes didn't waver from his. I felt relieved the confrontation was over, but confused. How could the man who just saved my life, be the same sort of man to deliberately start the fire as Pindari asserted? I turned away. My disappointment with him had registered.

"Come on fellas, the fire won't put itself out!" he bellowed to his mates, returning to the work at hand with a gusto.

The wind sprang up almost supernaturally from nowhere and suddenly we had a very serious problem on our hands. The fingers of flames reached out to the Richardson house next door on the right and soon were spreading up its walls. The firemen redirected their efforts to save it instead. Windows began popping from the heat as it too was engulfed by the ferocity of the fire. The Palmer's house on the left hand side of the Hudson's was luckier; the wind was in its favour. It was decided by the fire crew to try and save it as the other two houses were beyond rescue. They trained their hose on it, wetting down its roof and walls.

A small team of volunteers still kept trying in vain to contain the fire at the Richardson house though. The wind did indeed shift back in the direction of the Hudson house and ultimately beyond it, to the fire's new target, the Palmer house. Containment was paramount, for beyond the Palmer house, was the small bushy corridor leading to the creek and the wooden rail bridge that spanned it. If the sparks from the fire carried on the wind jumped the creek, ruin could be at hand for the town, for a relatively short distance away was the edge of the town's largest wheat field holding. If the bridge went, it would be almost impossible to get to the crop to save it. Not to mention the loss of the train tracks themselves.

Mrs Wood and Nan had started going up the bucket line with trays, handing out drinks and biscuits and scones, all cobbled from everyone's kitchens. Small enough to eat and give strength to those whose strength was waning but not so large as to interfere with the main activity.

From the trestle table Gwen Grady let out a scream that sliced through the night as she pointed to the Hudson house.

"Look! There!" she yelled. All eyes darted to where she was pointing. Inside the house, through the smokey haze, a figure was crawling along the hallway towards the front door. At the same time, a sheet of corrugated iron from the roof picked up by the wind, speared into the main part of the house, shearing through the disintegrating inner walls before falling flat over the person.

"Stand back everyone. There's nothing we can do. It's too

dangerous," shouted Sergeant Farrar.

Johnny didn't hesitate. Ignoring the order, he bolted toward the front steps.

"Johnny come back!" I called out as I instinctively ran after him.

"Pat, no!" screamed Doug. The heat drove me back, but not Johnny. He wrapped his shirt around his arm then shielded his face with it as he went through the flaming front door jamb and into the inferno, ducking out of the way of collapsing plaster ceilings as he went. I lost sight of him in the dense smoke.

"What were you trying to do, you stupid – ?" Dad began to chastise as he ran to my side and pulled me back roughly. He paused when I looked up at him.

"What about Johnny?" I cried.

Our eyes returned to the doorway engulfed in flames. Everyone held their breath, fearing the worst but hoping for the best. Binda stood motionless, tears forming in her eyes but with a look of desperate hope on her face.

"There he is!" screamed Miss Kitty and others. She ran forward like a distressed parent toward the house as did Binda, both only to be forced back by the heat as well. "Help him. Please someone help him," pleaded Miss Kitty.

Johnny had managed to get to the person inside and was leading them through the fire and smoke, pushing aside bits of burning debris that were falling all around them. Their dark forms were silhouetted against the flames. The victim collapsed near the front door. Johnny, with no regard for his own safety and with his shirt now catching on fire, picked the limp figure up in his arms and carried it as best he could, through the wall of flames now swamping the front verandah and staggered down the wooden steps.

One of the firemen ripped off his coat and smothered the flames on Johnny's arm as he fell to the ground with the rescued person still in his arms. Just as Miss Kitty dropped to her knees near Johnny, Dad raced to the side of the other blackened figure and gently turned it over. Whoever it was, they were barely hanging on to life. The face was black and the hair burnt back to the skin on the scalp. The smell of the burnt flesh was sweetly repugnant.

"It's young Steve Wood," a voice called out and soon his name was repeated over and over in whispers that rippled along the line. Mrs Wood screamed and pushed forward, joined by her husband, kneeling on one side of their son opposite Dad. Mr Wood sobered up in an instant.

"Save my boy, doctor," Mr Wood pleaded. There was little Dad could do. While his wife cradled Steve in her arms, he smiled up at his dad.

"Proud of me now, Dad? Got rid of them Abos for ya," he managed to get out before going limp. Mrs Wood hugged him hard.

"No, no, no ..." she wailed over and over. Horrified, Mr Wood attempted to stroke Steve's cheek.

"Don't you touch him, *ever* again." Mrs Wood spat out. She held Steve's lifeless body tightly to her chest as she rocked back and forth and wept. A distraught Mr Wood stumbled to his feet then looked into Dad's face. His eyes were moving pools of deep despair.

"I'm so sorry, Bob," Dad said softly, placing his hand on Mr Wood's shoulder. He looked at Dad's hand then into his face again. The aggression he had always shown had gone. It was the look of someone lost, someone searching for answers. He stayed looking at Dad like that for a few moments before fleeing into the night. Father Prittenden, who had at first stood back to give them some space, knelt down to comfort Mrs Wood. He began to say some prayers over Steve as people moved discreetly away to give them their privacy.

"Why my Stephen? Why Father? Why?" Mrs Wood asked in a desolate voice, before bursting into unrestrained tears.

While Dad was over with Steve, Doug and I looked at Johnny. He appeared not to be breathing. As tears began to fill my eyes, the same fireman who'd ripped off his coat for Johnny was already putting his fingers in Johnny's mouth to clear the airway. He started to give him mouth-to-mouth. There was no response. I was howling by this stage and making all sorts of promises to God if only he would bring Johnny back to us.

He was quickly turned on to his side and given a few sharp whacks on the back – still no response. He whacked him again, only harder. Johnny coughed and spluttered. He was alive. Binda was crying and smiling all at the same time. Her father Pindari comforted her. Miss Kitty, relieved as all of us cradled Johnny's head in her lap while Mrs Chang gave him some sips of water from a metal cup. Not thinking of his own injuries though in a lot of obvious pain, Johnny had to be gently restrained by Miss Kitty from craning his neck upwards to see how Steve was.

"Rest, rest. You just lie there and rest, Kevin," soothed Miss Kitty as she stroked his head. She looked up to see if her mistake was overheard by anyone. Only me, and I didn't let on.

Dad was now with Johnny who was going into shock. He

trembled as Dad gave him a shot of adrenaline and something for the pain. We could see his right arm and chest were badly burnt, all melted like candle wax.

The injection seemed to calm him. Mrs Symonds handed Susan a blanket and she placed it as gently as she could around Johnny to help keep his body temperature stable due to the hyperthermia. Miss Kitty graciously albeit reluctantly withdrew, allowing his 'mother' Mrs Symonds, to take her place cradling him in her lap.

"He'll be alright, won't he Harry?" worried Mrs Symonds.

"He's alive, let's start with that." But the concerned look Dad gave Susan, told a different story. Pindari left Binda and went over to Mrs Wood and Father Prittenden. He extended his hand to her. She looked up at him, bewildered.

"My name is Pindari. Come. We put your boy to bed," he said gently as he bent down on his haunches. She loosened her grip on Steve and let him pick his lifeless body up in his bear-like arms. The Sergeant began to make some objection but was silenced by Dad.

"Let them be. There's nothing can be done, except a mother to say farewell to her son in private. I'll drop in on her on the way home." The crowd parted to let them pass. I watched as they made their way slowly up the street as if in a solemn procession.

"And Sergeant, can you radio the Flying Doctor, please? Johnny needs urgent hospital attention to those burns." Dad then turned back to a more stabilised Johnny.

"You did well, son. Foolhardy perhaps, but heroic nonetheless."

❖

The fire was relentless, now spreading past the Palmer house and heading for the bushland beyond and nearby creek. Those volunteers who had taken a breather during Johnny and Steve's rescue had to quickly pick up where they had left off. A team of men armed with two-man saws, furiously carved a barrier between the creek and the encroaching flames, so that the fire could be held tightly on our side of the creek even though it meant the bushland leading down to it might all be lost. Within minutes large sawn eucalypts crashed to the ground. The force of the impact hurled cinders high into the night sky like glowing confetti.

The cry went up – "The bridge!"

There was a rush of people in its direction. The fire had taken off in the undergrowth as the men were sawing away further up the creek bank. We stayed with Johnny, but you could see in the distance how bad it was. Flames were starting to twist themselves around the bridge timber supports on the creek bank. Several men took off their pyjama tops, drenched them in the creek then wrapped them and then themselves around the supports in a desperate attempt to smother the flames. Others with full buckets just hurled the water in their direction. The men gripping the supports were soaked, but no one cared for it quenched the fire, stopping it from going any further up the bridge and onto the railway tracks themselves. A collective 'yahoo' was let out by those at the bridge, pleased with their efforts.

The fire had spread right to the very edges of the creek, but luckily did not jump it as feared. More trees leading to the bridge continued to be sawn, just in case, but in the end the wheat crop was saved.

Work on the remains of the three houses stretched into the

early hours of the morning. By the end the fire was tamed and extinguished. One by one, singed and exhausted people started to pack up and go home while the fire crew stayed on in case of any flare-ups. Some of the able bodied men in the town pledged to help them with the mopping up after a full inspection by Sergeant Farrar in the morning. A few others like Mr Renshaw and his wife, and the Greens, made the effort to thank Johnny.

"That was a selfless act young man. You are welcome in my store at anytime," offered a sheepish Mr Green. Johnny attempted a smile but had to close his eyes. Dad encouraged him to rest and take it easy as the hum of the Flying Doctor's plane could be heard in the distance.

The death of Steve ended the night with a sickening pall over everyone, for everybody knew everybody and to all townsfolk, Steve was, well, just like family. Binda was still crying as she sat down next to a sleeping Johnny and gave him a kiss on the cheek. I introduced her to everyone as Johnny's girlfriend. She blushed as she wiped her tears.

The Flying Doctor landed in the paddock nearby and Johnny was loaded carefully onto a stretcher then lifted into the plane. Mrs Symonds accompanied him. A concerned Miss Kitty waited with Mr Symonds until the plane took off and was out of sight.

In the meantime, the white neighbours who lived across the street from the three burnt out houses, set up their large holiday tent and canvas camp beds in their front yard for Miro and his relatives until the rest of his family returned. Others delivered blankets and assorted clothing to them as they only got out with what they had on their backs. The Richardsons and the Palmers, now both homeless, were to stay with friends and relatives in town. They were inconsolable but at least they had time to get out with most of their furniture, clothes, papers and irreplaceable photographs before losing their homes.

We all started back to our various houses with our buckets and shovels.

"Will he live, Dad?" asked Doug.

"The burns are very bad but I think he'll make a full recovery."

"Mr Wood saved my life tonight," I said, looking up at Dad.

"Bob Wood?" queried Nan, somewhat incredulous.

"How, son?" Dad asked.

"When I was getting the cordial. I was taking a short cut and tripped over a Big Red lying in the long grass behind Mr Wood's place. It stood up, this far away from me," I emphasised with my hands. "There was a whole mob of 'em."

"Was not," Doug interjected.

"Was so. You weren't there."

"Pipe down and let him tell the story," Nan demanded.

"He whacked it with his shovel and it took off. The others followed. Mr Wood made sure I was alright and walked me home then back to the fire. I can't work him out Dad. I told him you said sometimes he acts like a bit of a goose. But he's not that bad once you get to know him." Dad placed his hand on my shoulder as we continued on home in silence. He stopped at the gate of the Wood's house.

"I'll just check how they're going. You two go straight to bed. I'll follow shortly."

"Say 'hello' to Mr Wood for me. And tell him I'm sorry about Steve. And that I said 'thanks'. And that after what he did for me tonight, I don't think he's a goose."

"I will. Now home to bed, the pair of you."

❖

Doug fell quickly asleep, but I was curious to find out what was happening in the Wood house. I quietly pushed open the bedroom window so as not to wake Doug then stepped out onto the jacaranda's branch before treading onto the platform. Quickly I shimmied down the rope ladder and off across the road.

By now the electricity had been restored. Most of the lights in the Wood's house were on. I couldn't risk sneaking up the steps and have a creaking floorboard give me away. Looking around I spotted an old ladder lying at the side of the house. It was heavy but I managed to place it under the lounge room window. I could hear only Dad's and Bob Wood's voices. Careful to keep my head low, I peered through the lace curtains at a distressed Mr Wood standing with a drink in his hand.

"I'm not much of a fuckin' father, I know. But he's all I have. We couldn't have no more," he sobbed. Dad just stood there beside him and let him talk it all out. "He only did it to please me. Dear God what have I fuckin' done?" He fell to his knees, the glass and its contents spilling from his hand. I'd never seen him like this before, broken and unguarded. Dad reached out to him and gently rested his hand on his shoulder.

"Bob, say your 'goodbyes' together, with your wife. She needs you. Then both of you try and get some rest. I'll handle any arrangements for you, if you like."

"No. He's my son. I can look after it," he stated as he stood and stiffened.

"You sure? It's no –"

"We'll be okay." As Dad turned to leave, Mr Wood reached out and shook his hand.

"Thanks. Thanks for everything. And say a 'hello' to Pat from me. He's a good kid."

"He asked me to thank you again for saving his life tonight. My deepest thanks as well, Bob. And also, he says he doesn't think you're a goose." Mr Wood nearly lost it then, but held on as he wiped his eyes with his hand.

"How's the black boy?"

"Johnny. Badly burnt, but he'll be fine – in time. I'll drop back in the morning," Dad reassured softly.

"I can't go in there. I can't," Bob sobbed. Dad gently touched his arm.

"Go to her. You need each other more than ever." Dad moved to leave.

I raced to put the ladder back but waited until Dad was safely mounting our front steps before I scurried across the road, up the jacaranda and quickly to bed.

Chapter twenty-four

BANG!

A loud resonating sound louder than any bunger shattered the stillness of the night and lingered in the air. Honey and two other neighbouring dogs started barking. Doug and I both sat straight up in bed.

"Did you hear something?" Doug whispered in the darkness.

"I thought I dreamt –"

"It wasn't a dream. I heard it too – close by." Shortly after that the telephone rang and Dad answered it. We heard him leave quickly through the front door.

"Come on. Quick. Let's see what's happened," Doug directed. We were out the window, down the tree and crouched behind our front fence in seconds.

Lights had come on in some of the neighbouring houses by now as well. At the front gate we looked in both directions. Dad was just outside the Wood's front fence, talking to their neighbour Mrs Grady and some others who had gathered.

Sergeant Farrar's car was coming to a stop outside their gate. Dad and he went inside the house and emerged a few moments later holding tightly by the shoulders a distraught Mrs Wood. At the same time, Miss Kitty and Miss Bridget hurried across the road and joined them. Dad and Sergeant Farrar whispered to each other while the sisters and Mrs Grady tried to comfort Mrs Wood. Her arms were flailing about, trying to resist their attempts to calm her. Dad, with the Walshes' agreement, took Mrs Wood back to their place. Sergeant Farrar went back inside the house after thanking Mrs Grady and urging her and everyone milling around to go home.

While Doug and I waited until everyone was inside and the others had dispersed, Raymond came up beside us from over his side fence and put his hand on my shoulder, scaring the shit out of me.

"What's doin'?" he whispered. Doug's quick hand over my mouth stifled my scream.

Once the coast was clear we all crouched down so as not to be seen and slunk through the swinging palings. We kept ourselves as low as we could and scampered across the lawn and under the Walshe house. Their voices were muffled by the lino and barely audible. Mrs Wood was one minute wailing then the next sobbing loudly. This went on for what seemed like minutes before all went quiet. There were footsteps and a door closing, then Dad's voice.

"That'll calm Pam down and help her get some sleep. I'll call back tomorrow." Dad's slippered feet and dressing gown could be seen between the open risers of the wooden front steps as he quickly went down them heading back to the Wood's house.

The three of us shot across the road then down the side of the house once Dad and Sergeant Farrar were both safely inside. Lights were still on in the lounge room and one of the back bedrooms. I pointed out the ladder. Our three pairs of hands lifted it up and placed it silently against the wall near the back bedroom. Doug started to go up it and we pulled him back down.

"We'll toss," I demanded in a whisper, pulling out from my pyjama pocket my lucky halfpenny.

"You two first," Raymond suggested and I seconded. Doug won in our toss then again against Raymond. Up he went. We held the ladder steady after Raymond and I tossed for second. We spoke in whispers.

"What can you see?" Raymond asked after winning our toss.

"There's curtains ... hang on ..." Doug went quiet.

"What?" I quizzed, while trying to keep my voice down.

"It's Steve's body on the bed, all covered up with a sheet."

"Let me have a look," demanded Raymond, pushing Doug aside for his turn before he'd even reached the bottom rung.

"All the action must be in the lounge room," Raymond indicated as he moved quickly down the ladder. We grabbed it and edged it up to the next window. I pushed my way up between them for my go.

Nothing could have prepared me for what I saw. I felt my guts churn. I thought I was going to vomit. I wanted to scream but no sound would come out. No amount of questions from the others could elicit a single syllable out of me. I was rigid, transfixed with terror. My breath became laboured. Through the lace curtains I could see Mr Wood's body on the floor; the very man who only hours earlier had saved my life. Beside him was a single-barrelled shotgun. Dad was up near his head blocking my view a bit until he moved. He and Sergeant Farrar were talking over the body.

"Oh my God," I finally managed to get out, only to be greeted by Doug and Raymond's strained whispers.

"What, what?" they both pestered. I came back down shaking my head, trying to erase what I had just seen, trembling and unable to speak. Raymond pushed me aside as he scrambled up the ladder.

"Struth! There's blood and guts everywhere – up the walls, over the lounge, even on the ceiling. There's this big pool of blood coming out from under Wood's head," he relayed as he descended.

"Come on, let me see!" demanded Doug a little too loudly as he pushed Raymond aside. "Shit. The back of his head's blown off!" Doug started coming down the ladder at speed. "Sergeant Farrar's comin' over ta the window."

Doug in his haste, slipped on one of the rungs and fell with a thud. Getting to his feet, he vomited in the hydrangeas while Raymond and I quickly grabbed the ladder and placed it on the ground. The three of us then raced and hid behind the dunny.

We could hear Sergeant Farrar walk out onto the back verandah. My heart that had minutes ago been in my throat, now felt as if it would burst through my chest as we crouched like statues, too scared to even breathe.

The Sergeant removed a small torch he wore on his belt and shone it around the yard and up the side before going back inside. We waited until we heard him lock the back door. A few minutes later we peered out from behind the dunny and saw him drive off in his car. I was willing to take the risk of being caught, just to see what Dad was still doing inside.

"Help us with the ladder and hold it steady," I instructed.

Once at the top I peered in. Dad was kneeling, eyes closed in prayer, as he held the hand of the now sheet-shrouded body of Bob Wood. He placed the hand down by the side of the body then crossed himself. He held that position for a few moments before getting to his feet. Turning off the main light he slumped exhausted into a lounge chair next to the blood spattered lampshade of the standard lamp. His face and form were lit by its glow in the otherwise now darkened room. His hands were smeared with blood. I watched as he burst into tears then rested his head on the back of the chair. He stayed like that, staring up at the ceiling as he kept vigil.

The enormous tragedy of the scene hit me hard as well. Not only the death of Steve and his father, but the impact of seeing my dad so upset – and me being helpless to do anything about it. It was only Doug's pulling on my pyjama leg that brought my thoughts back to getting out of there and back home before we were missed.

"What's happenin'?" pestered Raymond, shielding his mouth with his hand to muffle his voice.

"What's Dad up to?" followed Doug.

"Oh nothing'," I lied. "Must've gone in to see Steve." Before we left the three of us made a vow that none of us would ever mention our being here to anyone – ever.

"Cross my heart and hope to die," we all repeated before dispersing quickly.

After creeping up the jacaranda and back into bed, Doug whispered to me in the darkness.

"I reckon she shot him after a row," Doug pronounced.

"Or after he'd hit her maybe. That's how poor Steve got all

his cuts and bruises, I reckon." But I wasn't fully convinced he had hit her, not after the incident with the Big Red. "I'm goin' to sleep." But I couldn't, at least not straight away. The enormity of the evening's events weighed heavily on me. There was the fire, my heart-stopping encounter with the Big Red, Steve's tragic death and the terrible burns sustained by Johnny, ending in the violent death of Mr Wood and Dad's heart-wrenching reaction to it. They were still all swimming around in my brain. Hours passed as I tossed and turned on restless sheets.

Breakfast was late but over by the time Dad came home. Standing in the kitchen doorway he looked like he'd never slept. His hands were cleansed of any blood but there were traces on his clothes. Nan turned from the sink. She pulled her chenille dressing gown closed over her nightie as she sat down in a chair across from Dad.

"Gwen phoned shortly after that shot. Is what she said true?" Nan asked. He hesitated, as if unsure whether our young ears should hear what he was about to say. He cleared his throat.

"Bob Wood shot himself." Doug and I were speechless.

"Dear God," Nan wailed, crossing herself. Doug and I copied her actions, not knowing what else to do. Dad motioned us over to him before giving both of us a long rib-crushing squeeze and a kiss each on the top of our heads.

"What about Pam? She must be devastated," Nan worried.

"The Walshes have taken her in. She's heavily sedated. I'm going to bed. Let Susan know will you. I'll drop by the surgery 'round lunchtime after I call in on Pam."

Once he'd left for bed, Nan pulled us aside.

"If yer father knew what you were up to last night, oh yes, I know you weren't in ya beds. You wouldn't be able to sit down for days," she whispered.

We were busting to tell our story at school, but kept quiet. We'd all made our pact. Mrs Grady had relayed the shooting around to all her team of gossips by now so the whole town knew already, anyhow. Nan was right as well. If Dad ever found out where we were, he might actually give us the belting he threatened from time to time. If not, there would be one helluva lecture and loss of pocket money – maybe for good we reasoned. Miss Kitty told me later while I practised the piano, that sometime early that morning, the Sergeant relieved Dad at the Wood house. He was joined by Mr Edwards from the funeral parlour, Father Prittenden and later on, some out of town official carrying a briefcase.

Nothing was the same after that. Our world had changed. We'd never witnessed death before. For weeks after I'd wake in a jolting cold sweat, the sound of a shotgun going off in my head. The nightmares were so vivid and in colour. I could see in my mind's eye the blood and tissue splattered interior of that lounge room and the growing pool of blood seeping out from under his head onto the rug. The most disturbing aspect of the dream was that the body I saw wasn't that of Bob Wood – it was Doug's. I felt I couldn't mention it to anyone, for telling might make it come true. I waited and in time the nightmares went away.

CHAPTER TWENTY-FIVE

Kerosene was the accelerant. A can was found in the burnt out remains of the Hudson house. Dad told us matches were found in Steve's pocket. All three houses were destroyed. Everything was either melted and twisted or reduced to black and grey powder. All bar the three metal milk pails converted to letterboxes that stood like scarecrows in ashen fields. In the ensuing months, top priority was given to the restoration of the bridge before anything else.

The temporary accommodation provided for Miro and his family wasn't used. While everyone tried to get some sort of sleep that night the owners of the tent told us that Miro, Pindari and Binda had left. The sound of Wood's shotgun going off they said had convinced them they were not going to stay around. Thanking them for their generosity, Miro told them he was leaving because he feared that if there was a next time, one or more of his family might be killed.

We found out later that they eventually got some work and

accommodation at several nearby farms with living quarters for workers. The two elder sons already had jobs there. They were split up, but not too far from each other and Johnny could still visit Binda when he returned.

Work started on the clean up, but almost in silence for the whole town was in mourning. Covered by insurance, the Richardsons and the Palmers began to rebuild almost immediately. Various local tradesmen suspended their other work to get it done so that they could all move back in as soon as possible. A new fibro house built by the Aboriginal Welfare Board on the old Hudson property was let out to a new group of black tenants.

The double funeral took some time to be held due to a Coronial Inquiry, but on the day it was scheduled, most of the town shut up shop. Mrs Wood, dressed from head to toe in black, was helped down the steps of the Walshe house by her brother and the funeral parlour director Mr Edwards into the front seat of his only hearse. Steve's coffin was in the back of the vehicle while his father's had to be put onto the back of a ute. Both were covered with large floral wreaths.

Unlike Poppie's, this funeral we were allowed to attend. School was cancelled and all pupils were there in full uniform as a mark of respect. To avoid any problems Pindari, Miro and other Aborigines who assisted at the fire and who wanted to pay their respects, stood outside the Sacred Heart Church. The eulogy was read by Mrs Wood's brother. Mrs Wood was understandably upset throughout the service. At the graveside she stiffened as Mr

Wood's coffin was lowered first. When Steve's was lowered she lost all control.

"My baby … my baby!" she screamed as she scratched up to the mound of dug out soil surrounding the grave, trying to get to Steve's coffin. She had to be restrained before collapsing to the ground weeping. Father Prittenden held her tightly as family members came and led her away.

Doug and I had never witnessed a coffin being lowered into the ground and shovel loads of dirt thrown over it. At this stage I began to feel my legs start to shake from all the emotion of the day, just as Dad steered us away. Looking over at Nan crying, I realised how upsetting it must have been for her to bury Poppie.

The wake is usually held at the family's house, but there was no way Mrs Wood would enter her own yard, let alone her house. Instead Miss Kitty and Miss Bridget put it on in their backyard. They'd stayed away from the funeral, being busy getting everything ready with the help of Nan and the ladies of the CWA. Even Gwen Grady assisted. She remained unusually in the background, taking and accepting directions from Miss Kitty without a challenge. We'd ferried over extra chairs for the women and older people, as did Mr Symonds. A tarpaulin was tied from the back of the house to some trees to protect all the food and drink from the elements and birds. A crowd of seventy odd was there to farewell two of their own. Doug and I were instructed by Nan to wait on those seated.

As the afternoon progressed, Mrs Wood regained some of her composure, though tears were never far away and at one stage she had to be helped to a seat by her brother's wife. She never re-entered her home, choosing to join her brother and other relatives living in Bathurst. Family packed up her belongings. Rugs and other furnishings soiled from the suicide were burnt. Steve's guinea pig was given to Mrs Wood's neighbour Gwen Grady, for her grandkids. The house was then cleaned from top to bottom and repainted before new tenants moved in.

Dad and Mr and Mrs Symonds kept us up to date with Johnny's progress. In time, we were able to visit him in the hospital, taking comics and lollies we'd purchased from our pocket money. Eventually allowed to come home, he would still have to go back to the hospital many times for skin grafts. This time, after the fire and funerals, there was reason for the town to celebrate. Our hero was coming home, and it was unanimous amongst the community that he deserved full recognition for his efforts.

Bunting was looped along the awnings of the shops down Main Street and a banner reading 'Welcome Home Johnny' stretched across the intersection of Main and Railway. As part of the school choir I joined them on stage for the preliminaries. Under the guidance of Sister Mary Placid and her baton, we sang Gounod's *Ave Maria*, followed by *Greensleeves* and *A Nightingale Sang In Berkeley Square* as people began to line the street waving homemade flags.

Our recital over, Mr Carroll played a scratchy recording of John Philip Sousa's *Stars and Stripes Forever* over a makeshift sound system. We kids knew the tune by the substituted lyrics 'Be Kind to Your Web-Footed Friends', and sang it over and over again, under our breath.

Johnny had no idea of the reception that was to greet him as they drove down Main Street. The crowd cheered as he past, then joined in behind the car before it came to a halt at Railway and Main where a small stage with seating was erected just in front of the railway tracks.

Seated on the stage were the mayor of the Shire in all his mayoral paraphernalia, his wife, Father Prittenden and Dad. The mayor was a little put out by the fact that the town was adamant that Dad and not he would be the MC for the day. All the mayor had to do was sit there and say nothing.

Choir duties completed, Doug and I were allowed to sit cross-legged to the side of the stage at Dad's feet. There were spare seats for Johnny and the Symonds. Miss Kitty in sunglasses, a new blue dress with a matching broad-brimmed hat and proudly wearing no concealing makeup, sat with other older people in the small number of seats provided in front of the stage. Barry, Shen, Snotty, Raymond, with his glasses glinting like two small torches in the sunlight, and a few of our other school mates stood at the side, their elbows resting on the stage itself.

Johnny was overwhelmed by it all as he got out of the car. Encouraged by Mr Symonds, he mounted the steps. Those seated rose to their feet. Once on the stage we could all see that his arm under his short sleeved shirt was wrapped in a bandage supported by a sling around his neck. 'Cept for that, he looked just like our old Johnny.

The crowd broke out with a round of applause. Without the aid of any notes, Dad stepped forward to the lectern microphone to say a few words. After welcoming everyone, he began.

"Let me introduce you to a young man – Johnny August. Most

would know him by sight, around town or doing chores in someone's yard, or as 'Johnno', Eric Horan's hardworking apprentice. Regrettably, there are some others present who have called him other names, turned their backs or deliberately ignored him. All I see is a fine young man who deserves our respect and gratitude.

"On that terrible night some months back, we all banded together as a community to fight the fire. This lad did likewise, but went further by risking his own life to save someone else's. It takes extraordinary courage to do what Johnny did. I wonder who among us would have done the same under the circumstances. Sadly the young boy, Steve Wood, died and we all know the tragic event that unfolded later that night." He paused, looking around the crowd.

"It would be a fitting beginning and by way of honouring and thanking young Johnny, that we as a community take a deep look inside ourselves and the way we treat each other. The colour of your skin does not reveal the goodness that lies innately within us all. Whether we choose to exercise that goodness, is up to each and every one of us."

I, like most of the people hung on Dad's every word. Looking out at the people as he spoke, I could see the various expressions that travelled over the faces. Most people were moved by his speech – some thoughtful, a few downcast eyes of shame and guilt, but mainly looks of love and compassion for Johnny. His words even had a sobering effect on one or two of Bob Wood's old drinking mates, standing on the sidelines in a group.

"Mr Mayor, Lady Mayoress, Father Prittenden, ladies and gentlemen, boys and girls, would you please put your hands together for Johnny."

"Bravo, bravo," Miss Kitty called out as she jumped to her feet and led the applause. The rest of the crowd quickly followed suit, clapping and cheering, as much for Dad's rousing speech as for Johnny. I never felt as proud of Dad as on that day. The crowd hushed as he raised his hand to continue.

"This is Johnny's day. And to mark it, Kells' Butchery and Green's Mixed Business have got together and put on a sausage barbecue, which as I speak is just about ready to start. There are drinks as well. All monies raised will go towards Johnny's ongoing medical bills. But before we do that, how about three cheers for our hero, Johnny August." After some urging by Mr Symonds, Johnny got to his feet.

With that, Dad led us into the 'hip hip hoorays'. Johnny stood there a little shy at first, looking at the ground, then raised his head proudly as the cheers were followed by even more applause. At the end of it, he smiled broadly at the crowd, waving in response to their show of affection toward him. Moving around the stage he shook all our hands. Mrs Symonds got a kiss on the cheek as well. When he got to Dad the handshake grew into a hug that even caught Dad a little off guard. As Johnny was leaving the stage Mrs Wood made her way through the crowd and headed straight towards him. Nobody knew she was coming. Still dressed in black, she'd made the trip from Bathurst especially for the day. She took Johnny's good left hand in both of hers.

"I wanted to thank you personally for what you did. You are truly a very, very remarkable young man. Thank you." She kissed his cheek. From her handbag she produced a small rectangular red velvet box and handed it to him, before disappearing back into the crowd that soon engulfed Johnny. She didn't join the rest of the festivities, leaving town with her brother as discreetly as she'd arrived.

Johnny was carefully hoisted on shoulders and carried aloft to the school playground where Mr Kells and Mr Green in butcher's aprons, had the metal barbecue plates loaded with sizzling sausages and onions. The CWA had various sauces and lots of buttered slices of bread on trestle tables. Another table had cups of cordial and wedges of frosted chocolate and walnut slab cake that Mrs Symonds donated.

Nan made both the peppermint and strawberry versions of coconut ice and along with Miss Bridget, Mrs Symonds and two other ladies looked after the food and drink. Gwen Grady, with her third place ribbon from the Sydney Royal Easter Show pinned prominently to her chest, supplied fruit cake 'from my award winning recipe' and helped out the others serving. It seemed her community spirit and her having witnessed first hand at the fire Johnny's true character, won out over her prejudices. She wholeheartedly embraced the event. Sister Mary Placid and Father Prittenden collected the money.

People not only bought the sausage sandwiches, but usually refused change. Some even gave extra as a donation. But the good thing about it was, the other Aborigines in the area, who had customarily stood at the back of the crowd during the ceremony, were ushered forward by Sergeant Farrar through the people and fed first and for free. Among them were Binda, Pindari, Ganan and Miro. They unobtrusively made their way to the front and stood at Johnny's side. They would later insist on contributing one pound collectively as their donation. Binda looked coyly at

Johnny, her missing him there for all to see. Johnny touched the small of her back briefly. Dad allowed us two sausage sandwiches each and Nan made sure we stuck to it. Placing the first sausage of what would be three sausage sandwiches that afternoon on Johnny's bread, Mr Green commented to Mr Kells as Johnny left.

"I'm the first to admit I made a mistake with that one. He's one of the gooduns."

Johnny spent the whole afternoon proudly wearing the contents of the velvet box – a solid gold Certina wristwatch bearing the inscription: 'Always in my thoughts – Lillian Wood'. Binda never left his side.

Money raised, including donations from town businesses was put into a special account at the bank. It met most of the costs of Johnny's multiple skin grafts and other medical bills. Dad would quietly top up the account when it was exhausted.

It took many months before our community could put Steve and his dad's death behind us and get on with everyday life. To some, Johnny's presence would always be a constant reminder of that night's tragic events. Sadly, the goodwill shown toward the rest of the town's Aboriginal population at the barbecue was brief.

They were banished to the edges of town, with restrictions on their movements. Most shopkeepers still only admitted them if they could produce money before entering.

It didn't take long for the conscience of Mr Green and a few other shopkeepers to revert to their old ways of treating them either, still only serving them at the doors to their shops.

Doug and I were there one day standing beside Johnny and a few other Aborigines outside Mr Green's. They waited patiently to be attended to – not in turn mind, but only after every white customer was served, whether they were there first or not. Johnny, though still welcomed to enter his store whenever he wanted, chose to stand and wait with his black brothers and sisters. It took over an hour and a half.

The last white customer left Mr Green's store a good fifteen minutes before he made any effort to serve the patient group outside. He checked they had money first, because unlike others of the community, he refused Aborigines credit. Johnny let everyone else go before him. Mr Green only showed any trace of embarrassment when it was Johnny's turn. A number of white households in the town had already joined the Walshes, Nan and the Symonds in boycotting Mr Green's store, but he remained steadfast in his beliefs.

More importantly, the badgering and violence toward the Aborigines and even the piercing almost nightly gunshots ended after Mr Wood's death. This season, this season of hate, had passed. Others would follow, bringing their own issues and violence. For as Pindari foreshadowed at the Hudson fire, not all the blacks were prepared to put up with the treatment they were receiving at the hands of some white aggressors. Some fought back, with varying success and the ensuing consequences.

Of great concern to our household was Dad. I can only ascertain that whatever atrocities he had witnessed or perhaps was even forced to perform to survive in World War II, must have resurfaced even stronger with his attending to Bob Wood's suicide.

Doug and I only saw the splatter of blood and human tissue from a distance. Dad saw the waste of human life close up. I wondered as well, had the shooting caused Dad to revisit the events surrounding the loss of his best mate Girra on the battlefield.

For Doug and me he was our dad and loved and cared for us, but from time to time there was the return of the darkness to his eyes that told us the 'Black Dog' had come to visit again. Seeking help for depression was not common in the 1950's, even if one were a doctor as in Dad's case, and should have known better.

People just got on with life as best they could. Anyway, out where we lived there were no specialist doctors you could pop in to for a session once or twice a week. Mostly, he continued to cope by going off into the shed by himself for a few hours until it passed.

One weekend well after the fire and the funerals, Nan had gone to a CWA fund raiser at Mrs Grady's place and Doug had shot off somewhere on his bike with Barry. It was around midday and I'd been in my room finishing a Social Studies project for school. I came out to the kitchen with the white shoe polish I'd used to paint the snow on my drawing of Mount Fujiyama. Dad was sitting with his back to me at the kitchen table reading his newspaper.

"Finished the drawing. Looks great. I'll just have an apple for lunch and a glass of Milo. Would you like a cheese and tomato sandwich? Dad?" He just sat there. I went around to the other side of the table and stood in front of him. His head was slumped forward as he stared blankly at the page. His hands gripped the edges of the newspaper tightly. I felt both worried and useless at the same time, not knowing what to do. I moved to his side and rested my hand on his shoulder. He turned his head and looked at me with haunted glazed eyes, as if trying to find his way back through the fog. Gently I released his hands from the paper and led him to his room, sitting him down on the bed while I took off his shoes.

With a gentle pressure to his shoulder I managed to get him to lie down. I closed the curtains and the door before getting up on the bed myself. By then, Dad had shut his eyes and I slid my hand into his. I just laid there next to him listening to him breathing. It was at least an hour before Dad emerged from that terrible place he inhabited. It was like a veil had been lifted from over his face. 'Dad' had returned. He sat up and looked at me as he got his bearings.

"Fancy some lunch, Dad?"

"That'd be great." He slipped his shoes back on as I headed for the door.

"And son …" I turned as I opened the door. "Thanks." followed by a warm smile. My heart soared. I had been of use.

❖

Doug and I prayed that Dad's 'turns' as we called them, would end and we'd have our old dad back again forever. We found out then, that not everyone's prayers are answered. He never wanted to talk about it or explain the cause of these bouts of depression and we respected his need to deal with it himself, in his own way. Whenever Nan asked us in a soft, concerned rather than her exasperated directive to "go outside and play", it was our signal that all was not well with Dad.

His changing moods however, eventually ended whatever relationship he had with Susan. Her plea to him that night to let her in, to open up to her about these dark episodes, must have eventually failed despite the best efforts on both their parts. Within six months, she'd moved to Brisbane for good.

On the Saturday afternoon she left, Doug and I felt empty and sad. Dad drove her to the station before coming back an hour later with four bottles of beer. He headed straight to the shed and locked himself inside away from us. His seclusion we understood, but this was the first time he'd taken in any grog or locked the door before. Through the window we could see the back of his head as he sat slumped in an old chair. He had the radio on and occasionally he'd sing along to a song being played. Nan sought us out and called from the verandah for us to come away and let him be. By the time we went to bed that night he was still in the shed, now with the light on. Next morning Nan came into our room and whispered to us to get dressed, not to wake Dad sleeping in his room and have our breakfast in silence.

"Ya dad's feelin' a bit off-colour. We'll walk to Mass and let him sleep it off."

We'd never seen Dad drink more than a glass or two of beer at any one time and certainly never seen him drunk in front of us. This behaviour would prove to be a one off. Susan's leaving had hit him hard. To the widows, divorcees and single women in town, Dad was again a good catch back on the market. They used every social opportunity to try and snare him, but he remained acceptingly single, sober and free of nagging from Nan to find a partner.

CHAPTER TWENTY-SIX

Our time revisiting the town was almost over. Penny and I had cleared out Kilkenny completely. Every surface was cleaned and painted readied for sale. The paling fence, although reasonably new was deliberately left with three swinging palings by Dad – as Poppie had done for him and he for us. Now it would be used as a short cut by the next generation of kids and their adventures.

With Johnny's and Pindari's help the three of us loaded into the rented van only what we wanted to take back to Sydney. Working shirtless, the raised welts on Johnny's back from the whipping all those years ago were now just faint shiny strips. The skin grafts to his arm and chest though were still plainly evident.

Johnny already had a truck of his own so we gave Dad's old Holden to Pindari and his family as we had two cars of our own back in Bondi. The rest of the furniture and belongings we put out on the street for the taking, were quickly snapped up.

Over the twenty years since I'd left town, Johnny and I had stayed in touch through letters and caught up with each other every time I'd visit. In those years I returned not only for our wedding but also those of Johnny, Barry, Shen, Raymond and Snotty Norris. Johnny was my best man. There were also the funerals of Doug, Nan and Miss Bridget, and to visit Dad, now with my own kids, during Christmas holidays.

During those stays Johnny and I became even closer. One weekend every visit, he and I and a couple of his Aboriginal mates, including Pindari would go bush while Penny and Binda looked after the kids. Barefoot, but now conscious of the sun's effects on my skin, I wore a hat and long sleeves. We'd take off armed with only a machete, spears, skinning knife and a woomera, along with basic supplies.

We'd sleep under a cloudless starry sky, just like when I was a kid, either with Dad and Doug camping in the bush, or on the front verandah sleep-out. We lived off the land the way Johnny's ancestors had done for thousands of years. He and Pindari and the others taught me how to hunt and forage, and more importantly, how we are all connected to the land through our ancestors; all of us, black and white. Of most importance, they believed that no one owns the land; the land owns us. We are mere custodians – carers only. And during our time on this land, we must all honour and protect it.

I became an expert at detecting the witchetty tree with its prized grubs buried in its roots. Johnny could eat them raw but I still cooked mine in the ashes. Honey ants were often on the menu as well as fish. Rabbit, bush pork or wombat, and kangaroo I could now skin and cook properly. There was never any wanton killing of animals for sport though, only what we needed to eat. Everything was precious and shared.

There were also those memorable holidays when Johnny, Binda and their kids visited our house at Bondi beach. It gave Penny and me great pleasure to see the stares of excitement mixed with terror on all their faces, as they gawked at the crashing waves, followed by squeals of delight playing in the surf. All our kids got on so well with each other.

Johnny and I struggled to make eye contact this visit. Neither of us wanted to be the one to broach the subject that this could be a long, if not possibly our last goodbye. With our life firmly established in Sydney – school, work and friends all there, there seemed little need to return, certainly not every year for Christmas as we had done previously when Dad was still with us. It was a wrenching decision, but Kilkenny was now on the market.

I watched as the real estate agent finish hammering the 'For Sale' sign in the purple petal-strewn front yard before driving off. It occurred to me that soon it would be time for the slow transport of the grain train along Railway Street, taking the season's harvest to the main line and on to market. I stood for one last time on the verandah as the warm memories of my childhood wrapped themselves around me.

It was a time of innocence and wonder, as the mysteries of life revealed themselves to us at a much slower pace. Those airless summer days, so hot that the whole wheat landscape was one hazy golden shimmer. Days when we'd spend all day catching frogs and swimming naked in cool water. That delicious squelch of mud between your toes as you searched for worms along the creek bank to skewer onto fish hooks. Times when we'd ride for miles on our bikes or run through the long dry grass playing hide and seek.

Those carefree days of street cricket, or others where you pretended you were a pirate or a cowboy, a Red Indian or an Aborigine as you acted out your fantasies. The time we first became aware of the changes in our bodies as we went from children to teenagers. Many seasons had past and yet it all seemed as real and remembered as if it were yesterday.

My children would never experience the joy we took sitting around at night listening to the serials on the wireless, the euphoria of dancing around in a drought-breaking rainstorm or going bush for a couple of days. There are no witchetty grubs or native berries in Bondi shops. They'll never know the bonds that bound us as a community either; all looking out for each other and lending support and comfort when needed.

Our kids, ten year old twins Harry and Charlotte, or Charlie as she prefers, are good kids, but city kids – exposed daily in subtle ways to all the bad influences city life can have on growing minds. No, they'll never know the anticipation we felt coming home and smelling the kitchen air, heavy with the aroma of a homemade mulberry pie baking in the oven from fruit we'd picked. The delirious taste of a slice smothered in custard and oozing warm fruit – mmm, magic.

Sitting on the rope swing, with the old shoebox we'd found at the back of Dad's wardrobe on my lap, I realised my life had been so rich and full. I'm so fortunate to have had that happy carefree childhood, a good education, a loving wife and children, and a rewarding profession. More really than a man could hope for, so much so that as Nan would say, "I wouldn't say 'bum' for sixpence".

Funny, you break your neck to leave home, to see other towns, cities, the world, yet something always draws you back to your little town. *My* town, not so different to most small towns I suspect – but special to me. It's like putting on that old comfortable cardigan you just can't throw away, or sitting out of the wind in the sun on a winter's day – mmm, magic.

I opened the lid of the box and sorted through its contents. There were Dad's WWII medals, unworn all these years, a stack of old photographs of himself as a child with Nan and Poppie as young parents and another of himself and his war mate Girra in army shorts having an arm wrestle over a wooden barrel in the jungle. Several letters were inside as well. I took them out and opened one up.

My darling, I cannot wait to see you tonight. You are my life, my knight in shining armour. I love you so much I feel I'll explode. They say there is one man for every woman and you are mine, now and forever. I'll have a beer on the bar waiting for you. All my love always, Claire.

I put the love letter back into its envelope, feeling a little grubby, like I had violated an intimate moment between them. I chose not to read any of the others. There was a larger photograph at the bottom of the box. I turned it over. It was a wedding photograph of Dad and Claire. She was as beautiful as Dad had said, in a flowing wedding dress and veil. He looked strong and handsome as he stood beside her in his dark suit. By their gaze into each other's eyes, you could tell they were so much in love.

I spotted Dad's gold wedding band and held it between my fingers. The inscription read, *Harry & Claire forever*. I sat there staring at it. My eyes moistened. Dad had lived the inscription. I remembered that meeting with our mother on the verandah and thinking how different her words to Dad were then, to the love letter I had just read. I felt so sad for Dad. He did love her so much, all his life. I slipped the wedding band on my middle right hand finger and set the box on the ground.

Swinging back and forth I looked up and could see suspended on the fat branches of the jacaranda, the wooden platform and the rope ladder Dad had maintained for my kids. Suddenly come to life in my mind's eye was a young Doug and me acting out our fantasies. All around the she-oak trees, more now then all those years ago, still whistled in the afternoon spring breeze, while two kookaburras laughed in a distant gum tree. What was that song we sang as a round in the school choir? Something about a kookaburra.

I pictured Honey wandering across the road and begging for a rub on her stomach, while Poppie shovelled chook poo around all the plants in the garden. And over next door, Miss Bridget hacked away at the lantana while the kind and lonely Miss Kitty sat on the verandah with a glass of her homemade ginger beer and biscuits ready for me. She was one of the first I visited this trip and the last I'll say goodbye to before we leave. Now in her nineties, she still lived at home with a live-in nurse. Her hearing was intact but cataracts had almost completely spread their milky film across her eyes. Yet she still knew my voice and who I was.

"I've still got all me marbles. Not bad for an old chook," she restated as she did on most visits. Only this time there was the early onset of a Parkinson's tremor to her voice. "You pair of little scallywags. Remember the time you fell off the lattice?"

She retold the story to the nurse for the umpteenth time as we shared afternoon tea on the verandah. This time there was a difference to our time together. She wanted to hear me play *Heart and Soul* on the piano and we all moved inside to the lounge. The piano was just in tune and I managed after a few attempts to get it right and repeated it several times at her insistence. When I finished it she started to sing/talk the lyrics as if transported to another time.

"Heart and soul, I fell in love with you, heart and soul, the way a fool would do, madly ..." her voice trailed off as tears formed in her eyes.

"There, there Miss Walshe. Don't go upsetting yourself," soothed the nurse. Then returning from the past, Miss Kitty sobbed.

"He told me I was beautiful. And with him, I was."

"You are. And always will be," I whispered before kissing her cheek.

"Some days she doesn't know what she did five seconds ago. The past seems clearer than the present," the nurse conveyed as I was leaving. But it didn't matter, for she was Miss Kitty and I loved her. It would be hard to say goodbye this time for I was conscious of the fact that it could be the last time I see her alive.

Ahead, there was Doug and I as eight year olds, necks craned as we hung over the front fence, watching our first wheat train roll through town and counting the number of boxcars that passed into view at the intersection of Railway and Main.

❖

Opening our picket fence gate I decided to take a last walk down Main Street. I was still greeted by cordial cheerios from well known faces from my school days, now parents themselves. I called out to Barry as he played with his youngest baby daughter in a tiny swimming pool in his front yard.

"G'day Barry."

"Oh hi Pat. Settled yer dad's affairs?"

"Yeah. Leave tomorrow."

"Pity, it woulda been good to catch up and have a good old chinwag over a coupla beers."

Though there had been several other families living there over the years, passing the old Wood house still disturbed me. It was like I was moving in slow motion. Closing my eyes I could still see vividly Steve's young body stretched out on the bed. I swallowed deeply to keep my stomach down at the memory of seeing Bob Wood's brain splattered violently around the lounge room and Dad distraught over the waste of human life. A chill ran through me.

Further on was Snotty's, or rather *Carl* Norris' place. He and his wife and son lived at home with his mother. I waved at him as he did the mowing. He waved back before miming a big nose wipe up his arm and finishing with a huge laugh. The only one missing from our group really was Raymond from next door. He'd moved his family to Melbourne in search of work over ten years ago.

I was sickened to see small groups of Aborigines gathered under the clump of gum trees in the distance. Malnourished fringe dwellers, humiliated and degraded and some, not all, drinking from flagons and falling about – their wages from what little work they could get and welfare payments often blown this way. It seemed like their spirit was disconnected from the land and their very being, vulnerable to abuse from unscrupulous white landlords, shopkeepers and publicans eager to exploit the situation. The amount of government housing had increased over the years but was still inadequate for the size of the town's black population.

The irony of this scene was that some of the white drinkers at the Exchange Hotel, some on welfare assistance as well, were doing the same thing to their bodies on a regular basis and it was accepted. Yet only the Aborigines were subjected to public condemnation and ridicule.

In 1965 Charlie Perkins and the other students of the University of Sydney's Freedom Ride had drawn the attention of the Australian public to the discrimination and segregation of the indigenous population from the whites. We all thought it would galvanize Australians into affirmative action like the American Civil Rights Movement, and for a while it seemed it might, but over the years Perkins' efforts lost their impetus with the Australian public at large.

1965 was also the same year I finished High School and the year we got our first television – one of only the first half a dozen in town at the time.

On the Friday and Saturday nights when there weren't any pictures showing in town, Dad would get an extension cord and with assistance, mount the television on a box out on the front verandah. All the neighbours including the local Aborigines and their children would sit on the verandah or on the lawn or scattered throughout the jacaranda tree and watch it for hours, eating sweets and potato chips and chatting between shows. Along with all our teenage mates, including Johnny, Binda, Penny and some other girls, Doug and I would take up position on our platform, lying flat out with our heads resting in our hands on pillows as we watched the flickering images.

The 1967 Referendum had provided the Federal Government with a clear mandate to implement policies to benefit Aborigines. The setting up of the Council for Aboriginal Affairs later was to gain full ministerial recognition as the Department of Aboriginal Affairs. Prime Minister Whitlam in 1975 handed over the title deeds to part of their traditional Northern Territory lands to the Gurindji people and later Acts would pave the way for traditional ownership of land to be judged in Court. For us and Dad especially it seemed we were at last moving in the right direction. Something had to change.

Many blackfellas and a lot of whitefellas are watching closely the progress of Eddie Mabo's case before the High Court over native title to their land. He began proceedings in 1982 but now in 1985 there is still no decision coming from the High Court. I won't contemplate it, but with this length of time in the proceedings, some feel it may never be resolved.

It angered and frustrated me that even with all the small advances, there was little tangible difference to their lives. There appeared to be a more alarming number of these lost souls, young and old, just drifting through life than in my childhood, but more importantly, their conditions seemed to have worsened.

Reduced to such conditions it is hard to hold on to any sense of dignity, but like a small flame that refuses to be extinguished, the greater majority did and still do.

Why as a nation do we seem unable or unwilling to redress this situation? Widespread changes to white people's attitudes in small towns like ours appear to be a long way off. Johnny, Pindari and their families, and a few other lucky Aborigines' begrudged acceptance by the town's white population, was an exception few others experienced. As I moved on through town this welling of emotion would not subside. I felt sorrow for what I saw and anger at my own uselessness to make a difference.

❖

There were more cars on the road now as the town had grown, but driven slower than those in Sydney, for here there was still no real rush even after all these years. Shop facades and names had changed. Mr Green and his wife had both passed away and there were new more tolerant owners of his store. Kells' Butchery was still family operated. Likewise, Shen Chang and his wife were now running his father's Golden Sea restaurant, and Eleni's children now operated The Parthenon milk bar.

A new coat of paint and contrasting lettering spelling out 'School of Arts' was the only change to the building that for a few pence on a Saturday afternoon transported us to other worlds. Though now, blacks were long ago allowed to watch the pictures side by side with the whites in comfort.

The shopping area had expanded along with the growth of housing in town. There were now two motels and a library as well. Traffic lights had been installed at the intersection of the Main and Railway streets rail crossing.

With the help of the Symonds, but using his own money saved over all those years, Johnny had bought the blacksmith shop from a retiring Mr Horan ten years ago. JOHNNY AUGUST BLACKSMITH, with Pindari as his assistant was doing good business, but with the ratio of the number of horses to cars dropping, not as well as it had done in Mr Horan's day. But country people still needed a farrier and a blacksmith to forge bits and pieces of metal for any number of farm applications.

'Kookaburra sits in the old gum tree-ee ...' That was it, the round we sang in the choir. It came floating back as I peered through the old classroom windows and recalled the smell of overripe banana forgotten at the bottom of school satchels hanging on pegs before me. The school, 'cept for a couple of new demountable classrooms had remained the same. There's where I mixed up ink and there I'm hiding a sandwich in the school bin for Johnny.

They say we look back on our childhoods and remember only the happy times. I find that not always to be true. The sad and serious events also have a place in determining who we are, who we've become – all part of becoming an adult. Love, happiness, rejection, pain, forgiveness, acceptance and death; all part of life's cycle.

And so the gut wrenching loss of Doug at twenty five behind the wheel of a speeding car in the early hours of the morning had lessened also. It was outweighed by the happy memories of

SEASON OF HATE

growing up together and the times I spent with him as an adult on holidays from Sydney on the wheat farm he managed.

We were more than brothers and confidants. As twins we shared that unique telepathic bond that only someone who has a twin could understand. It's funny, but the thing I miss the most about the loss of Doug, even after all these years, is that there is no one beside me to finish off my thoughts, or me, their's. Those times when our minds were working as one and each completed or repeated part of the other's sentences. At times, we intuitively knew exactly what the other was thinking and feeling, even when miles apart. His loss was like being cleaved in two. There were times I wished I was more like him, more spontaneous and reckless. Yet when I look at Harry and Charlie, I'm grateful I wasn't.

At Doug's funeral Johnny stood side by side with Dad and me. At the graveside Johnny put his arm around my shoulder and gripped me tightly. It helped me through the sadness of the day. It was at that moment our deep friendship changed into more of a brotherly love – my big black brother, Johnny.

Now the pain of losing Dad to cancer, I know will recede in time as well. There will be the memories of his black depression of course, but I'll cherish the good times and the love that flowed so freely from him. Love, that emotion that sustains all life. For a world without love, is like a farm without rain. His influence on my life and the town's will always remain. His voice is in my head echoing through time as clear as the day we visited the old Reserve.

"I made a promise when I became a doctor, to help anyone in need of medical help, be they black, white or brindle."

277

The day of Dad's funeral was a still summer's day with not even a flutter in the jacaranda's canopy. People came from miles around; rich, poor, black, white and brindle. So many people in attendance, it was standing room only in the church. The rest spilt out into the car park. Even those so old or sick that they should have stayed at home, made the effort to pay their respects. The white townspeople sat in the pews and the Aboriginal community stood around the side walls and the back of the church. I met no opposition from the new Father Tomas, when I asked that Johnny, Binda and Pindari be allowed to sit with Penny and me. Johnny and Pindari had already assisted the funeral parlour director and me as the pallbearers for Dad's coffin.

Though only some were Catholic, all the Aboriginal women wore scarves or hats or bits of material on their heads as a mark of respect. They were all there to see their 'white father' off.

It was stifling inside the church even with the stained glass windows pushed right out. Only one of the three ceiling fans was working. The hot air was churned by its limp wobble. You could feel the perspiration running down your back and underarms. Everyone was using the Order of Service with Dad's photo on the front to fan themselves.

As the service progressed, the emotion that poured from the Aboriginal women through their soft wailing was extremely moving yet comforting. So heartfelt was their sorrow it was as if they had lost a close relative, not just their doctor.

Penny's dad in his eulogy spoke of Dad as, "A man with more kindness and conscience than any man I have ever known". We decided on an open coffin at the urging of a delegation of elders from the wider Aboriginal community. They wanted to see Dad for one last time. After the white people had quietly viewed the body, the Aborigines in an orderly procession filed pass the coffin; men, women and children, some visibly distressed.

The wording of the epitaph on his headstone I worked out with Johnny. We both felt it summed Dad up. It simply read: 'He cared'.

At the wake many strangers came up to me, shook my hand and usually relayed an anecdote about Dad.

"Balls bigger than a mallee bull's, the way he kept on at the Mayor an' the Shire Council – wearin' 'em down 'til we got us our own proper sports field, not some rough field carved out of the scrub, an' the community swimmin' pool for *all* of us to use. Not ta mention the school bus, so's even blackfellas like us livin' outta town, could get our kids ta school," one Aboriginal farm worker had to say as he pumped my hand vigorously in a handshake.

"I just wanted to say that your dad was an exceptional human being," another old patient needed to convey. Dad would have winced at receiving those sorts of compliments. He just truly believed that all men were equal in the sight of God and deserved to be treated as such. Those patients who came to see him and could afford it, paid. Those who couldn't didn't, but they all got the same attention and care.

He had one exception. He would not accept any monetary payment from the Aboriginal community. If offered, he would graciously decline. A hug or a handshake was a sufficient substitute for his fee. For those who insisted, like Aunty Maisy, Dad would make up some chore or other around the house for them to do in lieu of payment. Consequently, we had the best kept lawns and gardens in town, and more rabbit stews, casseroles and pies then I could count.

Up until a few months before his death he continued to visit the various camps around the district dispensing medicine and handing out food and water, blankets, clothing or whatever else was needed.

Needless to say, Dad didn't die a rich man, but a happy, respected and much loved member of the community. One who made a difference to so many people's lives. How many of us will be able to say the same of ourselves when our time comes?

On what was supposed to be our last afternoon in town before leaving early the next morning, Penny and I were invited to Johnny and Binda's for their weekly barbecue. We were joined by their three teenage kids, now enrolled in High School, Mr and Mrs Symonds, Pindari and his family and another large black family. Johnny had a job, a business and was living in a house. He therefore saw it as his duty to share his good fortune with his extended family and those less fortunate – at least his food. In Aboriginal communities, if someone has food, everyone eats.

The Symonds had moved into Johnny's old flat, happily turning the upstairs over to Johnny, Binda and the kids for the lesser upkeep of downstairs. They still had the tearooms and spent a couple of hours a day there, but someone else ran it. Unused cakes would still find their way home for other outstretched kids' hands to take – more often than not those of Johnny's and other Aboriginal kids nearby.

Sometime late in the afternoon, while sitting on their back verandah watching Mr Symonds holding the hose for all the kids to run about under, Binda made a comment.

"Doctor Crabbe's leavin' town end of the month. We're back ta havin' no doctor again. Apart from your dad, Crabbe was the fifth new doctor we've had in as many years."

"No one wants to stay," lamented Mrs Symonds.

The end to the evening we couldn't postpone any longer. Johnny and I stood awkwardly to shake each other's hand.

"We'll come and visit. And you must come and stay with us again sometime, ya hear?" I struggled to get the words out. We couldn't look each other in the eye. Johnny reached into his pocket and produced one of the old marbles we had given to him years ago and handed it to me as a parting gift. I held it up to the light, as memories of our playing with them flashed inside my head. We both mustered up strained smiles, realising its significance in both our journeys. Without warning he pulled me towards him in a bone-crushing hug followed by mutual rubbing pats to each other's back that lasted minutes.

"See ya soon then, eh brother?" I managed to get out as we loosened our grip to arm's-length. Johnny with his head down gave a weak nod. I felt the emotion welling inside me. We were both seconds from tears but still held on to each other's wrists. One last hug then we shuffled apart.

❖

That night, lying in the darkness of our motel room, Penny spoke straight out,

"So when are we moving back?"

I turned the bedside light on and she was smiling.

"As soon as Binda said 'no doctor again', I could see it in your eyes."

"You know me too well. It'd be a big upheaval. It'd mean taking the kids out of school before end of term. New school, new friends."

"They'll cope."

"My partners at the practice, I can't leave them in the lurch."

"They'll have a dozen doctors breaking their necks to join that practice. Not that you won't be missed, but –"

"What about the big drop in income?"

"Since when has money been the driving force?"

"Of course there's all the moving … Selling our place. What about the beach? You think the kids'll be happy swapping waves for wheat fields?"

"There's the creek or the community pool."

"I guess."

"Patrick McNally, you're as keen as me to come back. The kids'll adjust believe me – you and Doug did. This place is in both our blood. So stop throwing up obstacles and start planning how we can make it work. I'll check with the school here tomorrow. I can pack our things back home and have them freighted up while you get yourself established here with the kids. Doesn't matter how long our place is on the market. It's not like we need the proceeds before we can move. It's exciting, don't you think?

I kissed her and we spent the next hour cuddled together, excitedly discussing the details of the move.

"Wait 'til I tell Mum and Dad we're moving back. They'll be over the moon to have Harry and Charlie up here," she gushed. I jumped out of the bed grabbing at clothes thrown over a chair as I went.

"I'm off to Johnny's. Can't wait to see his face when I tell him the good news."

❖

Everything had become clear. I had the answers to my questions at last.

'Who am I?' Well I am not just defined as one half of twins, or husband, or father of twins. I am my own entity. I am me. I am a doctor. But I am also my father's son, brought up on his principles and beliefs. I had found my purpose for being as well. I chose to return and continue his work and also help those most needy in the community. But doctoring is one thing. With Johnny and Pindari's guidance I'm prepared to help in any way, against the discrimination of my black brothers and sisters – help make their voices heard.

❖

The 'For Sale' sign came down next morning.

THE END

Michael Costello is an AWGIE winning playwright, television and screenwriter. His plays have been produced around Australia and New Zealand.

Of his award winning play *Royal Affair*, Chris Mead, the Curator of the Australian National Playwrights' Conference, stated "... rich, intelligent and seductive, (Michael Costello) writes with sagacity and wit".

Michael was commissioned by Sue Smith to write an original episode for her *Close Ups* series for the ABC and has received funding from the NSWFTO for a feature film.

He is currently working on a new play and has two other novels in the works.

Order Form

☑ Please send me ___ copies of
Season of Hate
Price $29.99 plus $7.00 postage and handling

Name: _____

Address: _____

Town: _____

State: _____

Postcode: _____ Country: _____

Tel no. _____

Fax _____

E-mail _____

Method of Payment

☐   VISA   Cardholder's name _____

☐   Mastercard   Card Number _____

☐   Cheque   / _____

                      Signature _____

Please make cheques payable to:
A&A Book Publishing Pty Ltd
PO Box 449 Leichhardt NSW 2040 Australia
E-mail: admin@aampersanda.com
Books may also be ordered at our online store at
www.shortstoppress.com